THE NIGHT OF

A BURKE AND BLADE MYSTERY THRILLER, BOOK 1

MICHAEL LISTER

ALSO BY MICHAEL LISTER

Books by Michael Lister

(John Jordan Novels)

Power in the Blood

Blood of the Lamb

Flesh and Blood

(Special Introduction by Margaret Coel)

The Body and the Blood

Double Exposure

Blood Sacrifice

Rivers to Blood

Burnt Offerings

Innocent Blood

(Special Introduction by Michael Connelly)

Separation Anxiety

Blood Money

Blood Moon

Thunder Beach

Blood Cries

A Certain Retribution

Blood Oath

Blood Work

Cold Blood

Blood Betrayal

Blood Shot

Blood Ties

Blood Stone

Blood Trail

Bloodshed

Blue Blood

And the Sea Became Blood

The Blood-Dimmed Tide

Blood and Sand

A John Jordan Christmas

Blood Lure

Blood Pathogen

Beneath a Blood-Red Sky

Out for Blood

What Child is This?

(Jimmy Riley Novels)

The Big Goodbye

The Big Beyond

The Big Hello

The Big Bout

The Big Blast

(Merrick McKnight / Reggie Summers Novels)

Thunder Beach

A Certain Retribution

Blood Oath

Blood Shot

(Remington James Novels)

Double Exposure

(includes intro by Michael Connelly)

Separation Anxiety

Blood Shot

(Sam Michaels / Daniel Davis Novels)

Burnt Offerings

Blood Oath

Cold Blood

Blood Shot

(Love Stories)

Carrie's Gift

(Short Story Collections)

North Florida Noir

Florida Heat Wave

Delta Blues

Another Quiet Night in Desperation

(The Meaning Series)

Meaning Every Moment

The Meaning of Life in Movies

MORE: Do More of What Matters Most and Discover the Life of
Your Dreams

For Sophie
A new series
for a new girl
with hope for a new world

ONE

"My daughter and granddaughter are missing," she says.

I attempt to stifle a yawn into my fist. We usually don't take meetings this early, but Blade said our empty bank account left us little choice. Well, what she actually said was, "You know what they say, broke-ass bitches can't be choosers."

Most of the work we do is at night—often late at night, which is fine by me. I love the night.

The matronly middle-aged lady sitting across the desk from me in our posh office has the unfortunate name of Candace Landis. She and her husband Harold, the used car lot king of Alabama, have fostered and adopted countless kids over the years—including Nora Henri, the missing young mother.

"What brought you to us?" I ask.

She looks confused. "Haven't I just said? I'd like to hire you to find them."

I wonder if her use of the word *you* is intentional. She has yet to even acknowledge Blade, who is leaning against a filing cabinet on the far wall behind her.

Depending on the client, Blade and I take turns sitting

behind the desk and being the face of the agency. We had assumed that with a white woman of a certain age from Alabama it'd be best if I played the part today, and maybe we had been right.

Subtle sexism and mostly unconscious racism dictate that I as the white man sit in the chair the most, though it's far more Blade's agency than mine—as in it's all hers. Sure, as far as we're concerned we're equal partners—always have been, always will be—but she's the one with the private ticket and it's her name on the lease, and that part isn't up to us.

"Sorry," I say to Candace, "I meant how'd you hear about us?"

Hearing how a client found us is usually a pretty good indication of what kind of client they're going to be.

Most of the work we get, which isn't often all that much, happens by referral—somebody who has used our services before and wasn't too dissatisfied with our work, or some of our remaining friends around town still willing to toss a little chicken scratch into our particular pen.

More recently we've been getting potential clients sniffing around because of some free publicity the press had splashed across the front page when we found little Amy Littleton and returned her home to her mother—something the police had been unable to do.

"Oh, just did a Google search," she says. "Y'all weren't the first listing, but . . ."

Baker and Burke Investigations and Security Services wouldn't be—not when there's an A+, an AA, and an AAA Investigations in town.

". . . Y'all had the most—" she waves her hands searching for the right word "—recent coverage of your cases. Just brought that little girl back home to her mama. Figured maybe you could do the same for my little Emma."

I know what Blade's thinking. Same thing I am. It's a good thing the paper hasn't done any stories on all our failures.

"And," she adds, "y'all have the nicest office. My Harold says you should always judge a book by its cover."

"Your Harold's a big reader, is he?" I say.

From what I knew of the used car lot king of Alabama, I'd be willing to bet he hadn't cracked the spine of a book since school—and maybe not even then.

"He's more of a doer than a reader," she says.

Like our reputation at the moment, our office is better than it should be. It's located inside the posh law firm of Lewinsky, Clemons, Bradley, and Sykes on 15th Street near St. Andrews. One of the non-partner attorneys, Ben Simmons, is a fellow survivor and friend of ours who arranged it so we could barter skip traces and defense investigator work for the use of the digs.

The luxurious office we occupy had been decorated by a young, indulged female attorney from a family with money before she moved on to bigger and better things. Fortunately for us she left everything behind, including her new furniture.

"I know y'all know what it's like to lose someone," she says. "That's got to count for something."

She has no idea what it counts for. If it weren't for that, we wouldn't be sitting here right now.

For a while, Blade and I had it pretty good. We had been taken in by the Walsh family—genuinely generous and decent people—and we thought our days of crappy children's homes and the Russian roulette of foster care situations were over for good. But that was not to be our fate.

Kaylee, the Walsh's twenty-one-year-old daughter, who Blade and I had come to love as our own cool older sister, vanished off the face of the earth in inexplicable circumstances, and that was when good went bad again.

Kaylee was a junior at the University of Florida in

Gainesville when, for reasons no one has ever discovered, she lied to her professors about a family emergency and left campus without telling anyone. Later that night, on a flat stretch of rural road in Georgia, she ran off the highway into a ditch. Then, even with witnesses watching from a nearby farmhouse, in the span of some six minutes, she disappeared without a trace. Now, after massive manhunts and multiple official and unofficial investigations, over a decade has come and gone and she's still missing. Blade and I have dedicated our lives to looking for her. It's why we do the work we do, but we haven't come any closer than anyone else to finding her.

"The police have given up . . ." Candace continues. "Stopped looking—not that they ever were doing much. Oh, they say it's an open and active investigation, but . . . they have their theories and . . . well, a girl like Nora was never gonna get the kind of treatment a fair-haired girl from a good family was, now was she? We're a good family, I don't mean that. I mean . . . money and the rest. Y'all get it."

Not sure I get it, but if I do, she means that Nora is a poor, mixed-race, troubled twenty-something instead of the blond-haired, blue-eyed, innocent child the media prefers. And though Nora's daughter and Candace's granddaughter Emma is young enough, she's not quite white enough to be a true-crime media darling. And the reason Blade and I should get it is that, like Nora, we grew up in foster care. Of course, she could just mean we get how the police are or how unfair life is or how money makes the world go round. I can't know for sure without asking her, and I'm not about to do that.

Blade clears her throat.

"Mrs. Landis, our agency would be more than happy to help you get your daughter and granddaughter back, but an operation such as this isn't inexpensive."

It's odd to hear Blade speak like this. She only does so on

certain occasions—usually with a particular type of client or witness. Most of the time her speech is a playful type of Ebonics-laced street poetry.

"Harold and I have emptied out our savings account," she says. "And our church took up a collection for us. I hope it's enough. We'll go back and borrow against our home if we have to."

"Hopefully that won't be necessary," I say.

"But it might be," Blade says. "It's good to know your priority is finding your family."

Ignoring Blade, Candace opens her purse, withdraws an envelope full of cash, places it on the desk, and says, "Just find them as fast as you can."

She has just placed several thousand solutions to our problems on the desk in front of me, and I can feel an inaudible sigh beginning to rise from deep within me like a water bubble from an unseen sea creature near the ocean's floor traveling to the surface. I resist the urge to grab the envelope and laugh maniacally while making it rain on the desktop.

"Look," Blade says, walking over to join me behind the desk.

Candace's eyes widen and her breath catches as she gets a good look at Blade.

Resembling a slightly undersized collegiate linebacker, she is wearing a version of what I think of as her uniform—a pair of black ninja webbing drop-crotch multi-strap cargo pants, matte black greasy leather boots, a black retro leather biker jacket with lots of silver-toned zippers and a buckle belt at the bottom, a plain black tee fitted to her powerful frame, and small, round dark shades beneath a black snapback hat worn backwards. Every shade of black she's wearing either matches or compliments her smooth dark skin.

I stand because even though it means we're both now

staring down at Candace, I can't stay seated with Blade standing there beside me.

I can't imagine what the two of us must look like to Candace. Perhaps the unlikeliest of partners, probably the most improbable of investigators—a twenty-five-year-old straight white man who looks a bit like a struggling musician and a twenty-six-year-old gay black woman who looks a bit like a comic book badass. My light brown hair is still growing back out and my casual clothes look like an unmade bed, while everything about her is precise and pristine. I've been told I look a bit like a young Paul McCartney, while Blade has been told she looks like a mashup of Black Panther, Blade, and Storm.

"Before we agree to this, there're some things you need to know," Blade says.

Candace looks from me to Blade and then back to me, then finally back to Blade as she continues to speak.

"We're good at what we do," Blade says. "Maybe the best around, but . . . the police have far more resources than we do. They have an entire department and access to other agencies. Truth is . . . if the police don't find a missing person during the initial investigation . . . they usually don't get found."

"But you found Amy Littleton," Candace says.

Blade nods. "We did, but . . . case like that . . . it's the exception that proves the rule. You said we know what it's like to lose someone. Well, think about how long ago that's been, and we still haven't found her. We've looked for her more than anyone —ever. And with more—"

"I'm confused," Candace says. "Do you not want the job?"

"What I *want* is for you to have realistic expectations and know what you're signing up for. We found Amy. And we'll do everything we can to find Nora and Emma too. If I were you I'd hire us. We're relentless. We won't quit. We'll chase down every lead. We'll track down every witness. The cops have hundreds of cases. We'll have one. We'll give your case the attention and time the cops can't or won't. But even with all that . . . there are no guarantees."

"I'm not asking for guarantees," Candace says.

"Good, 'cause what I'm tellin' you is we can't give you any."

"Just promise me you'll do all you can to find them."

Blade nods very slowly. "You have my word on that."

TWO

After a trip to the bank to proudly deposit most of the used car lot king's ill-gotten gain, we meet Pistol Pete at Bayou Joe's for breakfast.

Situated at the end of an old wooden dock some twenty-five yards out onto Massalina Bayou in downtown Panama City, Bayou Joe's is a waterfront grill that's actually on the water.

Blade is having the catfish and eggs, Pete, the Cajun shrimp and grits, and I'm doing damage to a big plate of garbage potatoes.

"I can always tell when y'all've got a payin' client," Pete says.

Pistol Pete Anderson is an investigator with the Bay County Sheriff's Office. He's a lean, clean-cut late-twenties white man with pale skin and short reddish-blond hair. And though his nickname has its origins in adolescence, he has become a world-class marksman winning regional, state, and national competitions—all in an attempt to change the narrative of his name. Like Ben Simmons, he's part of our network of fellow survivors and friends. One of our primary law enforcement resources, we pump him for information every time we get a new case. And on the rare occasions we have a paying client and are bucks up for the moment, we buy his breakfast.

"Client on this one came across with a big-ass wad of cash," Blade says. "We bucks up as fuck this morning, so have seconds."

I say, "Compliments of the used car lot king of Alabama."

"I wondered how long it'd be before they hired someone," Pete says, a fork full of Cajun shrimp and grits hovering near his mouth. "Glad they went with y'all."

It's mid-September and the first hints of fall can be felt— slightly cooler temperatures, a drop in humidity, and a decrease in tourists.

The sliding glass panels that make up the walls of Bayou Joe's are open, the briny smell of Massalina Bayou blowing in on the breeze, as the morning sunlight causes the rippled surface of the water to sparkle. The moored boats in the marina bob like corks whose unseen bait is being nibbled below, the lapping of the water against their hulls joining the clanging of their rigging and the *thu-dump* of vehicles passing over the seams of tarpon dock to create a serene soundtrack to eat our breakfast by.

"Strange case," Pete says. "Never seen anything like it."

"Tell us about it," Blade says.

Pete nods as if she's merely agreeing with him.

"No," she says, "*tell us about it*. Act like we just know what's been reported by the press."

"Oh," he says, "well . . . young single mom from Dothan, Alabama, comes to the beach with her baby daughter. She's broke so she barters for a room at Footprints—"

"Barters with what?" Blade asks.

"Officially . . . cleaning rooms."

Footprints in the Sand is a religious retreat center on the west end of Panama City Beach that Blade, Pete, and I have a history with.

"No one saw her leave, but apparently one night she packs up her baby and goes out. She left most of her things behind in the room, so . . . we think she was planning on coming back. Evidently, she left her kid in the car while she went in certain places and did certain things. We got eyewitnesses who say they saw her out and about at various places that night—mostly bars. At some point she hooks up with someone because she goes out with him. Later that night something goes wrong because she calls 911. Her car is found abandoned but she nor her baby are ever seen again."

He pauses and takes another bite of food and washes it down with a big gulp of his coffee.

"The 911 call is the strangest one you'll ever hear," he says. "Truly bizarre. And though it came into Bay County dispatch, her car was found abandoned in Palm County, so they took the lead on the case. Happens a lot—caller is near the county line and because of the tower the phone pings off of, the call is routed to the wrong county. A lot of times a tri-county area will have a system in place so that if the lines are busy in one county, the calls are sent to another county. Her 911 call didn't make any sense, she couldn't tell the operator where she was, and even with enhanced 911 her location didn't show up. So dispatch wasn't sure where she was. But a trucker called in to Palm County and reported that an abandoned car was blocking part of the highway, so a Palm County deputy was dispatched and arrived on the scene within minutes of her 911 call. 'Course he didn't know she had called 911 because her call went to Bay County. He was just responding to an abandoned vehicle blocking part of the highway. Keys were in it but it was out of gas. He put it in neutral and pushes it off the road onto the shoulder. Meanwhile, Bay County is calling her number back over and over and not getting an answer. Dispatch gets an investigator involved who because of exigent circumstances is able to work with her cellular provider to triangulate her location. Eventually, a worker from Footprints, new guy named Willie Cooper, shows up with a gas can and says she had called him for help, so he and the Palm County deputy start searching. Not long after that a Bay County deputy arrives and tells them about her 911 call. All three search the area but found no sign of her. Palm County had her vehicle towed the next morning and a more extensive search was conducted. But so far there's not a single trace of the mother or the child."

He pauses as the waitress comes back, refills our drinks, and asks if we'd like anything else.

"I'll do that again," Blade says, nodding toward her plate.

"There're a lot of theories," Pete continues when the waitress is gone, "but mostly because not much is known. I think it's safe to say, based on the 911 call, that she was trippin' her balls off. Makes a lot of people believe she was hallucinating and whatever happened to her and her kid must've been self-inflicted—like maybe she ran into the woods and got snake bit or bear attacked or drowned, but you'd think we'd've found 'em by now if that was the case. Some say she was paranoid about the police and just wouldn't come out as long as the cops were there, but it's not like she came out and got into her vehicle and left after the cops left. She could have, because ol' Willie put gas in her car and insisted they leave the keys in it overnight in case she came back to it. And just because she was trippin' . . . doesn't mean someone wasn't really after her. Others think she staged all of this and ran away, but . . . no way she had the resources for something like that. Some people believe she must have hooked up with a guy and he did something to her, but why were they in her car with her child and why was there no sign of anyone else having been out there? Anyway . . . whatever happened . . . it was . . . I mean, they just vanished off the face of the earth. It's all just . . . so bizarre."

THREE

After breakfast we walk over to McKenzie Park to listen to the 911 call.

Beneath the enormous oak trees the public park is quiet and empty, its fountains off, its homeless inhabitants absent—most likely the result of Hurricane Michael shutting down the 6th Street shelter and the coordinated efforts of certain downtown businesses to drive them out.

We find an empty bench and take a seat, Pete between us with his phone out.

"First time through, I'll just let you listen to it," he says. "See what you hear, then we can talk about it."

Holding up his phone, he brings up the audio clip, presses Play, and turns up the volume.

911 Operator: "911. What's your emergency?"

Nora: "Yes, I'm in the middle of a field."

The connection is bad and Nora is speaking fast and breathlessly. It sounds like she is moving—walking or running—and that her head is turning, as if looking around, moving her mouth closer to and farther away from the phone.

Nora: "... Escaped. May ... My ... baby. Runnin' from ... [garbled] and he ... shot ... somebody. We're out here goin' toward Jefferson ... outskirts on both sides. No ... cell serv— My car ran ... gas. Stolen. There's two ... cars ... truck ... out here. Guy ... [garbled] chasin' ... me ... out ... hiding ... tigers ... like ... frond ... Empty ... through the woods. Please help ... Please ... come out here ... Hurry."

911 Operator: "Okay, now run that by me once more. I didn't—"

Nora: "They ... to be ... not ... talkin' to him. I ran ... into ... like me, but ... the hole."

911 Operator: "Oh, okay. Someone ran into someone? Is that—"

Noises in the background are loud and distorted—maybe someone saying or shouting something, maybe gunshots.

Nora: "... [garbled] ... of the only ... or some ... know. Guy is ..."

More loud noises—maybe the backfire of a vehicle, maybe a gunshot, or maybe someone yelling in background.

Nora: "Not ... way ... but ... over ... tricked ..."

911 Operator: "Where are you? Do you need an ambulance?"

More background sounds—maybe someone yelling something, maybe the phone being dropped or moved around quickly or bumped into something.

Nora: "... for ... to ... me ... so ..."

911 Operator: "Ma'am, what is your location? Do you need an ambulance or—"

More garbled sounds—maybe from Nora, maybe from someone else farther away from the phone.

Nora: "Uh huh."

911 Operator: "Can you tell me where you are? Do you need an ambulance or the police?"

Nora: "Yeah . . . no . . . I need the police."

911 Operator: "Okay, can you tell me where you are? Is anybody hurt?"

More garbled noises and loud sounds.

And then it sounds like Nora drops the phone, picks it up, moves it around, then disconnects the call.

911 Operator: "Ma'am? Ma'am? Ma'am?"

No response.

911 Operator: "Ma'am? Ma'am? Ma'am? Are you there? Ma'am?"

A few more noises like maybe the call hasn't been disconnected, and then nothing.

911 Operator: "Ma'am? Ma'am? Ma'am?"

We are all silent a moment as the call comes to a close, the haunting exchange echoing through us.

As if muted before, the desultory sounds of downtown begin to slowly register in my awareness again, the slow-moving morning traffic on Harrison, the unloading of delivery trucks, the breeze blowing in off the bay, random disembodied voices and the snatches of conversation that don't sound dissimilar to Nora's broken 911 call.

"She sounds terrified," Blade says. "And high as hell."

Pete nods, "Yeah."

"There's more that can't be made out on it than can," she adds.

"Has led to a lot of speculation," he says.

"And those noises in the background . . ." she says. "Was someone else talkin'? And did I hear gunshots?"

"Opinions vary," Pete says. "Some people are convinced that there's at least one other person with her, maybe two, and that those are gunshots being fired, but others don't think either of those things are true."

"Can you imagine if we had a call like this from Kaylee?" I say.

When our sister vanished, she did so without calling 911 or any of us.

"Might would've helped us find her," Blade says, "but probably just driven us mad."

"-er," I say.

"True," she says. "Not like it ain't driven us mad as it is."

Kaylee is the reason we do what we do—and finding her or figuring out what happened to her is what we spend nearly all our extra time and money on.

We are all quiet for another moment until Pete says, "I need to be gettin' to my actual job while I still have one. Want to hear it again?"

We nod and he plays the call again.

As I listen this time, it sounds different, and words I thought I understood the first time I'm not as certain about this time.

"Like I said, there's a lot of speculation," Pete says. "Different people hear different things, but there seems to be a few things most everyone agrees on. Nora is scared and upset and is asking for help. She ran out of gas. She's in a field. She needs the police but not an ambulance. It sounds like she's moving—either walking or running and looking around a lot. She's out of breath. She's not making sense. She feels threatened by other people that may or may not be there with her. What we don't know is what was actually going on, if she's hallucinating all of it or some of it or none of it—though that's hard to believe. We don't know what the background sounds are and if some of them are gunshots."

"I'm not sure this call's going to help us find her," I say.

"Hasn't helped *us* so far," Pete says. "She made other calls that might help more, but . . . only if the people she called are tellin' the truth about what she said. We don't have recordings, just their witness statements. They're in the file I gave you. There are so many contradictions in this case . . . so many conflicting . . . It's going to—"

"Like what?" I ask.

"I've got to go, so I'll just give you one, okay?"

"Okay."

"The guy from Footprints that she called, Willie Cooper, the one who took the gas out to her vehicle . . . When he pulls up and finds the Palm County deputy there . . . he claims he's on the phone with her and she tells him she can see him. She tells him to stay away from the cop. According to him, she says a few other things that convinces him she really can see him, but . . . In the 911 call from a few minutes before, she says she's in a field. It's one of the clearest statements from her we have and one that most everyone agrees on."

He pauses and Blade and I both lean in toward him.

"Okay," I say. "Yeah?"

"There are no fields anywhere around that area," he says. "Not only is it not possible that she was in a field watching Willie when he pulled up . . . she also couldn't have been in a field when she called 911 and gotten back to a place where she could've seen Willie when he pulled up. Both statements can't be true. And it's possible that neither one of them are."

FOUR

"You're workin' for the devil," a twenty-something woman with caramel skin and a shortish afro says as we walk up to our office building.

Her denim jumper, light, white cotton shirt, and leather sandals show off her long, muscular legs and taut body—something the baby girl on her hip argues against her having.

"If we are," Blade says, "won't be the first time."

I say, "You want to bring her in out of the heat and tell us about it?"

She's a little taken aback, but after a moment says, "Sure. Thank you."

"What's her name?" I ask. "She is so cute."

"Imani," she says, more of the aggressive tone draining from her voice.

"She's beautiful like her mother."

As I'm talking to the young woman, Blade unlocks the door and leads us into the huge, open marble-tiled foyer, past the swanky reception area with the attractive young blond receptionist, and down the long corridor to our office.

Blade takes the seat behind the desk and I join the young woman and her baby in the client chairs across from it.

"I'm Alix Baker," Blade says, "and this is my associate Lucas Burke. Neither of us were aware we were knights in Satan's service."

"I'm Shanice Wright," she says. "Nora Henri's foster sister, best friend, and roommate."

"It's nice to meet you."

"Would you like something to drink?" I ask.

"I'm okay," she says.

She carefully and tenderly rocks Imani on her shoulder as she speaks.

"We want you to tell us what you came here to tell us," Blade says, "but we'd also like for you to tell us all you can about Nora too."

She nods. "She's a good person. Truly good—to the bone. Her life ain't been easy—like any of the rest of us, but she's . . . She never let it make her mean or bitter. She's a good mom too. Bein' a single mom is the hardest job on this planet, 'specially when you broke and got no family. I mean, she had me. We had each other. We helped each other—a lot. But we both broke and . . . I mean when you got no parents who can help in all the ways—with money and skills and babysitting and all the things."

It sounds like Shanice and Nora had formed an alliance not unlike the one Blade and I had—something probably not all that uncommon for orphans.

"She's smart," she says. "Real smart. She was studying to be a reporter when she got pregnant and had to drop out. But she still writes—always got a journal and notebook going, working on story ideas and investigatin' this and that. She's had some stuff published too. Most of it under a different name, I think."

"Any idea what name or where it was published?" I ask.

She shakes her head. "She loves her little Emma as much as any mother in this wide world loves her baby," she says. "She'd never put her in danger. Not ever. No way. I don't know what happened, but I know it wasn't that. I want that known."

Blade nods and seems to think about it. "People can act different once they get down here on vacation," she says. "Not sayin' she intentionally put her little girl in danger, just that . . . people get away from home, don't have the same structures and obligations, they loosen up, got time on their hands—along with thousands of other people in the exact same position."

Shanice shakes her head. "Not Nora. I'm tellin' you. We spoke and texted every day. She was detoxin'—I mean emotionally, spiritually, she didn't drink or do drugs—she was hittin' the reset button, regrouping. It was like she was on some sort of spiritual retreat or somethin'."

"What did she need to detox from?" Blade asks.

"Evil, manipulative, controlling people. The Landises —'specially Candace—and her ex Tyler Reece. She had been tryin' to break up with him for a while. He'd been stalkin' and harrassin' her."

Blade begins making notes on the pad on the desk.

"Did Tyler know she was here?" I ask.

"No. She didn't tell anyone but me and I didn't tell anyone."

"Just 'cause y'all didn't tell him, doesn't mean he didn't find out she was here," Blade says. "Stalkers stalk."

"Tell us about the Landises," I say.

"He's a crooked used car salesman and she's a twisted, controlling religious wingnut. She doesn't care anything about Nora. She just wants that baby. She's been tryin' to get her since the moment Nora had her. She's the most rigid, controlling, cruel person you'll ever meet. And she's payin' you with fuckin' blood money. And not just from the corrupt car dealerships. She has a newsletter to get donations for all the kids she takes in. She doesn't know I get it 'cause I signed up under a fake name. She's been using Nora and Emma's disappearance to fundraise. It's how I knew about her hiring y'all."

"You and Nora grew up in the Landis home?"

"Not grew up, but we both wound up there eventually. Last option sort of thing. We were both teenagers by the time we got there. It's private, so they can do what they want. They don't take any state or federal funds, just private donations. Not that they need those—they're loaded from all the car lots and crooked deals they do. It's like *Flowers in the Attic* meets *The Handmaid's Tale* or something. I don't know what Candace told you about Nora, but it isn't true."

Blade says, "Actually, she didn't say much about her."

"Good. It's not like she knows her that well anyway. I'm tellin' you, she wants Emma. That's who she really hired you to find."

"You and Nora stay in contact while she was down here?" I ask.

"Every day," she says. "She even called me right before she went missing."

"Can you tell us everything she told you while she was here and what she said the night she went missing?"

"Like I said, she was spending her days reading and meditating, spending time with Emma. 'Beach therapy,' she called it. They went to the beach every day. Spent time by the pool. Went to the park. Just the two of them. She was healing, getting her mind right. She cleaned rooms at the retreat center where she was staying and did some odd jobs, but mostly she was just taking it easy."

"She have any run-ins with anybody?" Blade asks.

Shanice shakes her head. "Everything was going great. She said everyone was nice and helpful and left her alone."

"What about the night she went missing?" I ask.

"The reception was shit. Kept breaking up, fading in and out. Her carrier—I think she has Sprint—works fine up in Dothan where we live, but get out in the country and you might as well have two cans and some string."

"It's that way for everyone out where she was," Blade says. "It's rural AF."

"But even when I could hear her, it didn't make any sense," she says. "Sounded like she was high as hell, trippin' her ass off, but I'm tellin' you she doesn't do drugs. Never has. Never will."

"Can you remember what she said?" Blade asks.

She nods. "It's burned into my brain. Plus I have a voice-mail message from her when I was on the other line."

"Can we listen to that too?" I ask.

She nods. "'Course. I just don't want it online or anything. Her call to me and her voicemail message sound like the 911 call. She's talkin' ninety to nothin', cuttin' in and out, not makin' any sense. What I made out of what she said was that she was out of gas, needed help, didn't know what to do or who to call, didn't know where she was, was scared. I told her I'd drive down from Dothan, but that it'd take me over two hours to get there and she'd have to figure out where she was so I'd know where to come. But she didn't seem to hear or understand me. She really didn't stop talkin' while I was talkin'. She's never acted or talked like that in all the years I've known her."

"I'm sorry," I say. "I know you had to feel so helpless."

She frowns, nods, then begins to shake her head slowly. "I've been through some bad shit in my life. But this is the worst. She was so scared. I could hear it in her voice. I've heard her scared before—plenty of times when Tyler was threatening her or trying to break in—but this was by far the worst."

She pulls out her phone, swipes and taps a few times, and sets it on the edge of the desk.

Both Blade and I pull out our phones and record the voice-mail as it plays.

"... call ... back. Need your ... Don't ... do ... Out ... gas. We're ... Jefferson ... sides. No ... cell ... two ... truck .. . out. Field. .. me ... out ... hiding ... Help me ... Take ... Emma ... wo— Please help ... Please ... call ... Hurry."

FIVE

That night I have Alana while Ashlynn works her shift at Cloud Nine.

Alana is a smart, sweet, fun, and funny four-year-old with dark hair and eyes and tan skin like polished sandalwood. Her young single mom is one of our sisters and survivors and we take turns keeping Alana while she works, though I keep her the most—and am happy to do so.

We are on the sidewalk on the west side of Beck Avenue in St. Andrews on our way to get ice cream, holding hands and walking slowly—the only pace her tiny strides will allow.

"Let's get *all* the sprinkles," she says with her usual enthusiasm.

"*All* of them?" I ask.

"*All* of them," she says.

"What flavor of ice cream do you want to put *all* the sprinkles on?"

"Hmm," she says, tapping her face with her little index finger from her free hand as she carefully considers my question before coming up with the obvious and inevitable answer. "*All* of them."

"Then we're gonna need a bigger boat," I say.

"*A boat?*" she says in humorous disbelief. "We don't need a boat, you nitwit."

Both highly intelligent and a master mimicker, Alana often uses gestures and expressions she hears on the many videos she watches or said by the many adults she's around—and nearly always uses them in the right way.

"Luc, is *nitwit* a bad word?" she asks.

Most people call me Burke. I love that she calls me Luc.

"It's not nice, but it's not bad. And for the record, I'm not a nitwit."

"Is *damnit* a bad word?"

"You'll probably get in trouble if you say it at school," I say.

"But is it bad?"

"Go by what your mommy says," I say. "Ask her."

"Is *oh my gosh* a bad word?"

"No."

"Is *oh my God* a bad word?"

"Did your mommy tell you not to say that?"

"No."

"Go by what your mommy says."

"Is *God* a bad word?"

"No, but a lot of people think you should only say it respectfully."

"Is *booty-butt* a bad word?"

"No."

Thankfully, we arrive at the ice cream shop and I get a reprieve from *what is a bad word* for the moment.

"What a pretty little girl," the slightly creepy-looking old man behind the counter says.

"Say *thank you*," I say.

"Thank you."

"What's your name?" he asks.

"Alana," she says. "But I'm shy."

I laugh out loud at that.

"Don't laugh at me, Luc," she says.

"I'm not, sweetie. I would never laugh at you. I just think you're cute and sweet and you make me happy."

"'Cause I'm shy?"

"Yes, because you're shy."

"What can I get y'all today?" the white-haired man asks.

"We're here for all the flavors and all the sprinkles," I say.

"Yeah," Alana says. "*All* of them."

"Okay," he says. "That'll be two million dollars."

"Pay him, Luc," she says.

A little while later, we are back out on Beck with large cardboard cups of rainbow ice cream and rainbow sprinkles.

We are moving slowly, doing more eating than walking. In between bites she says, "Is *butt* a bad word?"

"I don't think so," I say, "but go by what your mommy says."

"How about *chicken lickin' mickin'*?"

"Nope," I say. "Not bad."

"Is *fuck* a bad word?"

I actually do a spit take as if we had rehearsed it, rainbow ice cream and sprinkles streaming out of my mouth.

"You'll definitely get in trouble at school if you use that one," I say. "Where did you hear it?"

"Mommy says it sometimes."

"Yeah, best not to say that one."

"Okay."

"Mr. Burke?" a female voice from behind us says.

I turn to see a middle-aged blond-haired white woman with pale skin and lots of makeup in a blue pantsuit.

"Yes?"

"I'm Karen McKeithen. I'm a producer and I'd like to talk to you about being part of a special we're doing about Kaylee Walsh."

"What sort of special?" I ask.

"We're talkin' TV," she says. "I have a production deal with Investigation Discovery. We want it to air on the tenth anniversary and we'd love for you and Ms. Baker to be involved. I spoke to Ms. Baker briefly last week. She said she'd get back to me but she hasn't yet and time is ticking. If you two are to be involved, we've got to get moving."

"Give me your card and I'll call you tomorrow."

"I realize you're busy, but I've come all this way to see y'all in person. Could we at least have a face-to-face meeting tomorrow? Let me give you the full pitch."

"I'm sure we can," I say. "But I'll get back with you either way after I speak to Bla—Ms. Baker."

SIX

Alana is fast asleep—and has been for several hours—when Ashlynn comes in from Cloud Nine.

She smells as she always does—like fragrant body lotion, booze, and cigarette smoke.

Cloud Nine is a relatively new strip club where Ashlynn makes anywhere from five hundred to a few thousand bucks in a single six-hour shift. We keep Alana during that time, and Ashlynn, who's a caring and invested mom, is with her the rest of her waking hours, which means Ashlynn usually only sleeps from two or three until eight or so when Alana wakes up. But on certain nights, like this one, she's too keyed up when she comes in to fall asleep, so she gets far less sleep than the usual too-little she regularly gets.

"How many propositions did you get tonight?" I ask.

I speak softly, trying not to wake up Alana.

My unit at Beach View Bungalows, which does not include a view of the beach, is small and only has three rooms—the main room, a bathroom, and a bedroom, where through the open door Alana is sleeping in my bed. Occasionally, Ashlynn will take Alana back to their place, but most nights she joins her in my bed and I sack out on the couch.

"Four," she says.

Nearly every shift, Ashlynn gets asked out or offered money to perform at private parties, go on dates, or give the girl-friend experience.

"And one proposal," she adds. "Guy legit asked me to marry him tonight. In the champagne room. Had a ring and everything."

"Wow."

"I know."

"He a regular?" I ask.

"First time he's ever paid for a private dance. Says he's been watching me for a while."

"That's not creepy at all," I say. "Have y'all set a date yet?"

She laughs.

"Do I need to talk to him?"

"I think he's harmless, but I'll let you know. Well, I'll let Blade know. You can't afford another pop."

"I'll be okay," I say.

"Can't do anything for Alana or me or anyone else from inside."

"I know."

"How'd she do tonight?"

"Great. Didn't want to go to bed, of course, but . . . we had a good night. She's so smart and fun and funny."

"She's a great kid," she says. "She ask you about boys?"

"Tonight it was mostly about bad words," I say. "Evidently, sometimes Mommy says *fuck*."

"*Fuck*," she says. "I was hoping she didn't hear me."

"She hears all."

"I burned myself with my straightener and it came out before I realized what I was sayin'.""

"She realized it," I say. "She's so in-tune she can pick up on inflection and tone and—"

"Mimic it all back."

"Yep."

She glances over at my laptop and the file folders beside it. "What're y'all working on?" she says. "Kaylee?"

"Always, but also Nora and Emma Henri."

"That the young mother who went missing with the crazy 911 call?"

I nod.

"She came into Cloud Nine looking for work."

"Really?"

"I'm pretty sure," she says. "We get it all the time. Girls down here on vacation, run out of money or think they can make quick bank. I think she asked about just working a night or two to make enough money to get back home."

"Did she?"

She shakes her head. "Don't think so."

"Was she with anyone? Did anyone take special interest in her?"

"I'm just not sure. I can ask Miss Rachel. She'll know all the info."

Miss Rachel is the house mom at Cloud Nine.

"I can talk to her if you—"

"Either way," she says. "I'm happy to do it, but you might get more of what you need if you talk to her."

"Okay," I say. "Thanks."

"Hope you can find them," she says, shaking her head. "I mean alive and well, but . . . what are the chances of that?"

"Not great."

SEVEN

"Producer wants us to be involved in a show they're doing about Kaylee," I say. "It'll come out on the tenth anniversary of her disappearance."

It's the next morning and we are in our office planning our next move, neither of us wanting to go to see Willie Cooper. Blade is behind the desk. I'm in one of the client chairs. Each of us is sipping on our breakfast beverage of choice—for me a cold brew coffee, for her a Code Red Mountain Dew.

"Yeah, meant to mention it to you," Blade says. "You talkin' about the McKeithen chick?"

"Yeah."

"I's hopin' we'd find her before then," she says. "Disappearances shouldn't have anniversaries. 'Specially ten. I mean *fuck*. I can't believe that shit."

"I know. I think we should do it. Sounds like she wants to use us as resources for research and development and not just for onscreen interviews. Think we could make sure they're accurate and get the right info out there."

"Maybe," she says. "She's got a new production deal. It's a

bigger and better network than she's ever worked with before, so it could be five by five, but I looked at some of her earlier work and . . ."

"What was wrong with it?"

"It was . . . It lacked production quality and polish like you'd expect. It was pretty old. That won't be the case with this one—not with this network and the budget she has. The thing that . . . It was the tone and the angles she took that . . . It was pretty damn tabloid. Lots of theories, innuendo. Seemed like she just wanted to cast suspicion on everyone—'specially the family."

"You think she'll do that to us?"

"Maybe why she wants us involved. I don't know."

"Maybe if we're involved we could keep that from happening."

"You know no matter what you say they can cut it to fit their narrative."

"But if she's gonna do that anyway . . . we might be able to . . . I don't know . . . mitigate it some."

"*Mitigate it?*" she says, the amusement in her voice matching her expression. "You spendin' way too much time with convicts or lawyers. Or both."

"We find Kaylee between now and the show airing," I say, "give it an ending . . . keep them from—"

A quick knock at the door is followed by Lexi Miller stepping in.

"Morning," she says. "Sorry to interrupt. Luc, you got a minute?"

Blade and I both stand.

"Of course," I say.

"Holla when you done," Blade says to me, then nods to Lexi and leaves the room, closing the door behind her.

Lexi takes a seat in the other client chair, each of us turning and angling our chairs so they face each other.

She is a petite, athletic bottle blond with Gulf-green eyes and the body of a runner. This morning she looks and sounds a little sleepy, which only adds to her cute, sweet sexiness.

I'm excited and nervous to see her. There's an undeniable something—allure, attraction, curiosity, desire?—between us, and not just because nothing can ever come of it. She feels it too. She's made it clear without ever saying anything directly.

"How are things going?" she asks as she pulls out her pen and pad.

The ends of her blond hair, which touches the tips of her shoulders, are still damp, probably from an early morning run and shower.

"Pretty good," I say.

"Counseling?" she asks.

"Haven't missed," I say.

She makes a note on her pad and I notice the sweet hint of citrus on her wrists as it wafts over in my direction.

"Does it seem like it's helping?"

I nod. "I think it is. She has me doing mindfulness meditation and that seems to be helping as much as anything."

"That's good. I've found that practice to be very beneficial for me."

"She says not only will it calm me down and give me more peace, but it should help me not . . . It's supposed to help give me some space between my triggers and my responses, so . . ."

She nods. "It will."

"Hasn't been put to the test yet, but I'm hoping it will."

"How about the support group?" she asks.

"Not gettin' as much out of it as I was," I say, "but I'm still attending just like I'm supposed to."

"What changed?" she asks. "Why are you gettin' less out of it?"

"The people attending," I say. "Few new guys coming now. Court mandated like me, but they really don't want to be there. They dominate the discussions—and all they do is share war stories. Brag about the damage they've done."

"I think that's pretty typical," she says. "They're angry about being arrested instead of remorseful for what they've done. Resent being made to attend."

"Yeah."

"You're the very refreshing exception."

Our eyes lock for a moment and a certain forbidden something passes between us.

I clear my throat. "Thank you," I say, my voice hoarse.

She holds my gaze for a little longer, her green eyes seeming to shimmer.

The pull we feel is palpable, but we can never do anything about it.

When I got popped for aggravated battery, which is a felony, the judge looked at my rap sheet and saw a history of violence—a series of assaults and simple batteries, mostly fights, all of which carried misdemeanor charges. But because there were so many, because my sentencing score sheet was so high, he sentenced me to a year and a day of state prison time and two years of probation. The counseling and support group are just some of the conditions of my probation. Lexi is asking about them because she's my probation officer. It's her job to keep an eye on me, to make sure I'm meeting the conditions of my probation. In addition to everything else I have to do, I have to check in with her regularly and she can drop in on me at any time, at work or home or anywhere else I might be—something she does far more of than she has to, presumably because of her feelings for me and her commitment to seeing me succeed. If we ever acted on our attraction, she would lose her job and I could lose my freedom.

Eventually, she says, "Thought about tryin' another group?"

"Not many options," I say. "Would be if my issue was alcohol. Plenty of AA meetings around, but anger management meetings . . . not so much. Plus . . . I figure every group has narcissistic assholes who don't want to be there and want to make sure everyone knows it."

She nods. "Sadly, I think you're right. How about work?"

"It's going well," I say. "We just got a new case."

"Nora and Emma, I heard. I hope y'all can find them and bring them home like you did the Littleton girl."

I shrug and frown. "Chances of that aren't great, but . . ."

"I think you're really doing well," she says.

I shrug. "About as well as I can be, given the situation," I say. "It's hard for me not to be free. I really hate all the limitations put on me and the constant threat of going back to prison, but . . ."

"I've worked with a lot of people over the years," she says. "I'm cynical and wary and not easily impressed. Most offenders are criminals living a criminal lifestyle. They've usually committed far more crimes than they've been arrested for. Their mindset and mentality is fucked—they rationalize and justify everything they do, they always work the angles, they're morally weak, have no character, never take responsibility for anything, and everything is someone else's fault. With you . . . there's none of that. You're a great guy with anger management issues. And given your background . . . it's understandable, but it has the potential to fuck up your life, send you back to prison, or even get you killed. It's a deep, deep flaw. The question is . . . is it fatal?"

"That *is* the question," I say. "'Whether 'tis nobler in the mind to suffer the slings and arrows of outrageous fortune, or to take arms against a sea of troubles, and by opposing, end them.'"

"See?" she says. "Like that. That's a perfect example. You're the first offender to ever quote Shakespeare to me."

"I didn't just fight growing up," I say. "I read some too. And not just the kind of poetry made to woo women."

"I notice you stopped before you got to the *to die—to sleep* part. But, Burke, that's the thing—the sea of troubles never ends and only a fool takes up arms against them."

I nod as I think about it. "Probably so."

"As well as you're doing . . . that's why I'm worried about your work. It's a stressful, high-pressure job that brings you into contact with some dangerous, violent criminals. How long before there's a confrontation that becomes a physical altercation? That happens and . . . you'll be back inside—not only serving out your entire sentence, but getting additional time for the new charges."

If I get sent back to prison for violation of probation, I have to serve out the remainder of that probation sentence inside. If I get caught committing another crime, even so much as the simple battery of a bar fight, I'll get additional charges and time.

"Not a lot of options for a convicted felon," I say. "Got no desire to be a cook at Waffle House."

As a convicted felon, I'm extremely limited in what I can do. I can't vote or legally carry a weapon and I can't be a private investigator in the state of Florida—which is why, though Blade and I are equal partners, she's the only licensed PI and everything is in her name.

"This is what I'm good at," I add, "what I want to be doing. And it lets me work on finding Kaylee. Blade's already said she'll handle the fisticuffs if any come up."

"Oh, they're going to come up," she says.

"Yeah," I say. "They will."

"You've got so much going for you," she says. "Place like prison is such a waste for a man like you. And . . . I'd . . . miss you." As if realizing she's gone too far, she adds, "You're the best probationer I've got. I'm pinning all my hopes on you."

"*Uh oh*," I say.

Recidivism rates in the United States are astronomical. I've looked them up. Recidivism is the relapse of criminal behavior that results in rearrest, reconviction, and reimprisonment—all the things I'm trying to avoid. The recidivism rates of ex-offenders are 10% in 6 months, 17% in 1 year, 29% in 2 years, 36% in 3 years, 41% in 4 years, and 45% in 5 years. And all of those rates go way up when the offender is on probation like me.

"Two more years is a lot of time inside," she says.

"One day is a lot of time inside," I say. "I'm gonna do everything I can to make sure I never go back."

EIGHT

"What's the deal with your hot probation officer?" Blade asks.

We are on the Hathaway Bridge, above the moat-like divide between Panama City and Panama City Beach. We are on our way to Footprints, the religious retreat center Nora and Emma were staying in before they disappeared.

Panama City is a small, Deep South, blue-collar town of some 36,000 people—the largest town between Tallahassee and Pensacola. Panama City Beach is a resort town of just 12,000 permanent residents, but has 17 million visitors each year. Once known as the Redneck Riviera, PCB has undergone a transformation in the past few decades—old beach cottages and mom-and-pop motels torn down and replaced with high-rise condos and resorts, amusement parks and roadside attractions bulldozed down and replaced with national chains and premier shopping and dining destinations, Old Florida kitsch replaced with New Florida respectability.

I've heard it said that the universe was created out of chaos, and that sometimes through the order, the chaos shows through.

The current iteration of Panama City Beach was created out of tacky, touristy, redneck disreputableness, but sometimes through the resort respectability, the Floribama Shores shows through.

"Don't act like your ass didn't hear me," she says. "What's the deal with your hot probation officer?"

"Whatta you mean?" I ask.

"You *know* what I mean," she says. "Bitch shows up more often than the damn mailman. And I see the way y'all look at each other."

"She's a decent and caring person," I say. "Really trying to help me."

"Y'all playin' nug-a-nug?"

"*No.*"

"Good, 'cause let me tell you what'll happen . . . You'll do something she doesn't like—not text her back quick enough or not go down on her enough or break her heart or some shit—and she'll violate your ass back to the big house faster than you can say 'Jackie Robinson's your uncle.'"

"She's not like that, but—"

"You don't know what she's like."

"But I'm not going to—*we're* not doin' anything and we're not going to."

"Just make sure you don't," she says. "Hate to see you get sent back to the clink over a little raw doggin'—no matter how cute she is or how tight her little runner ass might be."

"*Dude*—"

"I mean it," she says. "Find some other sweet little honey to stick your little red rocket in. No piece of pussy on the planet is worth goin' to prison for."

"Give me some credit," I say. "I'm not capable of doin' something that stupid."

"Oh, you not, huh?"

"Not anymore," I say. "Can we change the subject? Let's talk about your love life."

"Don't have one," she says. "And you just told on your ass by calling it a *love life*. Been bad enough if you'd've said *sex life*."

"How're we gonna handle things at Footprints?" I ask. "Talk to Ted first or go straight to Willie?"

"Even if we try to find Willie and talk to him first, Ted'll know we there in a matter of minutes. Might as well start with him."

"You okay to talk to him?" I ask. "I can go in alone."

"Ain't a scared little homeless teenager anymore," she says. "I'm lookin' forward to havin' a little chat with Ted, adult to adult."

NINE

Footprints in the Sand Christian Retreat Center is located on the west end of the beach. It began as a single hotel giving Christian groups and families an alternative to the more secular and sinful party parts of the devil's playground. As youth groups and churches and families from all over the United States flocked to it, it expanded, buying up other hotels in the area and purchasing adjacent property and building additional cottages and pools and conference centers and gyms, until its campus became one of the largest religious retreat centers in the country.

The mammoth facility is owned and operated by Theodore Van-Allen, a real estate developer turned Fundamentalist preacher and podcaster.

THE FOOTPRINTS WEBSITE has this poem and message on its homepage:

One night I dreamed a dream. I was walking along the

beach with my Lord. Across the dark sky flashed scenes from my life. For each scene, I noticed two sets of footprints in the sand, one belonging to me and one to my Lord.

When the last scenes of my life shot before me, I looked back at the footprints in the sand—there was only one set of footprints. I realized that this was at the lowest and saddest times of my life. This always bothered me and I questioned the Lord about my dilemma.

"Lord, You told me when I decided to follow You, You would walk and talk with me all the way. But I'm aware that during the most troublesome times of my life there is only one set of footprints. I just don't understand why, when I need You most, You leave me."

He whispered, "My precious child, I love you and will never leave you, never, ever, during your trials and testings. When you saw only one set of footprints, it was then that I carried you."

Welcome to Footprints in the Sand, a spiritual retreat center located on the sugar white sands of the Gulf of Mexico on the west end of Panama City Beach, a sacred place built on holy ground. Our facility is a consecrated place, quiet, uncrowded, set apart. We provide a spiritual atmosphere for restoration, regeneration, and revival, serving the needs of churches, families, and individuals who desire a deeper walk with Christ and the power to change the world.

WE PARK out front and walk past the welcome center toward Ted's office, which is located upstairs in the back of the main chapel and broadcast studio in the heart of the enormous site.

As we walk past the various resort-appointed buildings, we glance back at the dorms on the far edge of the property where we had briefly resided as teenagers.

I notice Blade shake her head, an expression of disgust on her face.

The dorms are for orphans, runaways, and the homeless. In exchange for room and board, those with few other options work each day to maintain the facilities up front for the paying guests. If not slave labor, it's company store labor—the vulnerable, helpless, weak, and poor kept out of sight, cleaning up after the monied guests.

Blade and I stayed here for nearly a year until she was caught having sex with another girl in her room and was kicked out. I packed my few things and left with her that night and we have been each other's person ever since.

"Never forget what you did that night," she says.

"Well, I wish you would, 'cause gettin' away from this place and partnering with you are two of the best things I did."

"I'm serious," she says. "I was so fuckin' scared and alone and felt like a . . . freak . . . until you put your hand on my shoulder and I saw you had your backpack."

"I'm tellin' you, you did me a favor."

I glance around at the many cameras covering the compound. Ted has a security and protection force second to none in the area—mercenaries who enjoy threatening, intimidating, and beating people up.

"We went through some shit comin' up," she says, "but the year we spent here was one of the worse."

I nod. "I know and I'm sorry."

Part of the price of admission for Blade was undergoing conversion therapy and certain exorcism rituals, attempts to pray her gay away that involved an all-out assault on her self-esteem, identity, sanity, and sexuality.

She shakes her head and shivers. "The physical abuse of some of the other places—even the sexual shit, can't compare with the psychological warfare I was subjected to here."

Sexual battery is the reason Blade is never without a blade —and hides so many in her clothing and on her body. There are predators everywhere, but the highest percentage of them can be found among the vulnerable, and who's more vulnerable than orphaned, at-risk kids? I only know some of what Blade endured, but even the little she has shared with me was hard to hear. I think the abused and victimized like her live under a constant feeling of threat, believe nearly everyone they encounter has the potential to harm them. It's something I really didn't understand until I went to prison.

I shake my head. "Wish we'd've left sooner."

"Thought I could handle it—"

"And you did."

"And I did, but it was doin' a number on me that I didn't even realize."

Inside the inner sanctum, we are greeted by a young Barbie Doll blonde with impossibly long, thick hair provided by high-quality extensions and enormous fake tits provided by a high-quality plastic surgeon—all paid for by Ted no doubt. Around her doll-dead eyes, her Botox-taut face is expressionless.

"How can I help?" she asks without meaning it.

"We're here to see Ted," Blade says.

She looks mortified that Blade would dare to use his first name.

"Do you have an appointment with Revered Van-Allen?"

"No, but he'll see us," she says.

"It's about the young mother and child who went missing from here," I add.

"All inquiries about that should be submitted in writing to our director of media and communications—"

The phone on her desk buzzes and Ted says, "It's okay, Katie. Send them in. Thank you."

If she were capable of an expression, she'd be showing that this displeases her greatly.

Shrugging and shaking her head, she gestures toward the imposing doubles doors behind her with her tiny hand.

TEN

When we enter the large, ornate office, we find Ted sitting behind his massive dark wood desk.

We walk past the leather couch and loveseat seating area on the left and the long solid-wood conference table on the right on thick, plush white carpet. Behind him on the wall is a large 3-D composite etching of his family-crest-looking logo. It's surrounded by his many civic and social awards and framed photographs of him posing with various B-list celebrities known for sharing certain of his religious and cultural views. Most of the other walls of the enormous office are filled with the mounted, trophy-like heads of big game.

"Burke, Alix," he says, nodding toward us but not getting up. "Take a seat, please." He gestures to the two leather chairs across from his desk.

It's rare to hear Blade referred to as Alix. Very few people know it, but Alix Baker, her legal name, is a name she gave herself, partially in an attempt to free herself from any connection to her abusers and abandoners and partially to conceal her true identity.

THE NIGHT OF   47

As usual, he's in an expensive navy blue suit and a ridiculous matching silk shirt and tie combo—today it's burgundy—his longish, bottle-black hair slicked back like a pyramid scheme promoter or a televangelist.

"I heard you all had been hired by the young woman's family to find her," he says. "I wondered how long it'd be before you came calling. How are you? Seems like I saw something in the paper about some recent success you had. Good for you."

He speaks slowly and deliberately with no discernible accent. His tone is cordial but cold. He saves his warmth for cameras, microphones, and true believers. Like many sociopaths, he can be extremely charming. What he can't be is genuine or sincere. And since we've seen through him, he doesn't waste any of his considerable manipulation skills on us.

I say, "Things are going well. Thank you."

Beside me, Blade is statue-still and quiet, and if she can remain that way we might just get what we need and get out of here in one piece.

Though the three of us are the only ones in the room, I guarantee you there is now a member of the security staff right outside the door.

"I was sorry to hear about your incarceration," he says. "Glad it was brief."

There was nothing *brief* about it. Prison time is slow time—the slowest time that exists.

"I remember warning you about your temper back when you were a kid," he says.

"Yeah," I say. "You were right. And I'm workin' on it—harder than ever before."

"I would think you would be," he says. "I understand the consequences of that kind of behavior would land you back in prison for a lot longer this time."

I take it that he knows and lets me know he knows that as a not-so-veiled threat. I'd expect nothing less from him.

"It certainly would," I say, "yes, sir. I'm going to do my very best to make sure that doesn't happen."

"Good," he says. "I'll be prayin' for you and if I can ever do anything for you, you don't hesitate to let me know."

"Thank you," I say. "I really appreciate that."

It's not a genuine offer, but even if it were it would come with conditions that include swearing allegiance to serving him and his little kingdom and renouncing Blade as an unrepentant sexual pervert bound for hell.

"We're here today because we wanted to ask your permission to speak with anyone who may have interacted with Nora Henri. We want to find her and bring her home."

In addition to all the other things Ted is, he's controlling—likes to be the alpha in charge. By being polite and asking his permission, I'm giving him the illusion of power and control that is mother's milk to an ego like his.

"Poor thing," he says. "And her precious little baby. We did all we could for her and it breaks my heart she went off and got into trouble like that. But . . . as you well know . . . no matter how hard you try, there's just some people you can't help—" he shoots a quick glance over at Blade "—can't keep them from self-destruction."

Blade tenses beside me. *Please don't respond. Keep your cool. Just a little longer.*

"If we can find them and bring them home safely," I say, "that would be . . . But just finding out what happened to them . . . would remove any suspicion on anyone here. We understand a man named Willie Cooper tried to help her. Could we speak with him?"

"I know how the mainstream media can be," he says, "but I can't imagine anyone here is under suspicion. Still, I want to do all I can to help you find her. You're welcome to speak with Willie, a truly guileless soul, and I'd be more than happy for you to avail yourself of my security staff. They can be of great help in your investigation. I'll have Fred take you over to talk to Willie and you can tell him how his team can help on the way."

At the exact moment he finishes what he is saying, Fred Stone, Ted's head of security, opens the door and walks in.

I stand and say, "Thank you. We appreciate your time and assistance."

Blade remains seated for a moment longer then gets up slowly.

"Happy to help," Ted says. "Just find her and bring her home."

"How well did you know her?" Blade asks.

Ted turns toward Blade, looking at her as if surprised she's capable of speech.

"Pardon?" he says.

"How well did you know the victim?" she asks, holding his gaze with a calm and quiet intensity.

"I don't believe I even met her," he says. "I do a lot of traveling—more than ever. When I'm here I'm busy with the day-to-day operations, interviews, and our various media outreaches. She may have come to hear me speak one night, but I can't be sure."

He and Blade hold each other's gaze for a long moment, then he eventually smiles without warmth or humor and says, "You all have yourselves a good day now. And find that young woman and bring her home. I'll be praying for your success."

ELEVEN

"Guess you two landed on your feet," Fred says.

His walking us across the campus to see Willie is not unlike the night he escorted us off the premises.

He's older now, less hair, less muscle mass, but still just as quietly menacing—maybe more so.

"Not right away, no," Blade says. "But we got there eventually."

"Well, I guess that's good," he says. "Most don't."

"Most what?" she asks, her voice hard, her tone aggressive. "Orphans? Blacks? Lesbians?"

"People," he says. "I was talkin' about people. Simmer down. Quit lookin' for a fight."

Ex-military, Stone is calm and confident and quiet. I've never seen him lose his cool, never seen him get rattled.

"We weren't people. We were children," Blade says. "No parents. No place to go."

"You dealt the play," he says. "Knew the rules. Knew the consequences. You're not the victim here."

"Then who is?" she says.

"There wasn't one," he says. "And as I recall . . . you pulled a knife on me that night. I could've taken it away from you and force-fed it down your throat, but I didn't. I was more than fair with you two. Figured you'd be okay. And you are."

She doesn't respond right away.

Though the huge Footprints campus is actually comprised of several older hotels and motels being joined together, it's not evident because each and every structure now has the same beach-resort-style edifice. Instead of a random collection of older and smaller mostly mom-and-pop motels and hotels acquired over time as Footprints grew, the facility looks more like a self-contained resort like those found in the most popular and exotic vacation spots all over the world.

I try to change the subject.

"What can you tell us about Willie Cooper?" I ask.

"Good kid. Good heart. Hard worker. Not surprised he tried to help her."

"He been here long?" I ask.

He shakes his head. "Less than a year."

"Did you get to know Nora and Emma?" I ask.

He shakes his head. "Weren't here long. I was traveling with Mr. Van-Allen for part of that time. Heard she was a good girl. Did her work. Kept to herself."

Fred shows an adequate amount of respect for his boss, but never more than that. Always calls him Mr. but never Reverend. He's a professional, does his job well and is paid well to do it, but as far as I can tell he's never had even a sip of Ted's Kool-Aid.

"Got a theory on what happened to her?" I ask.

"It's obvious from the 911 call," he says. "She got on something that really messed her up. Started hallucinating. Got paranoid. Thought someone was after her. Broke down. Ran out into the woods and died. When I was an MP I had more than one case like this."

"So why wasn't she found?" Blade asks.

"No one has looked in the right place yet," he says. "Animals got her. She went into a river and got washed away. Or she made it farther than anyone thought and the remains are outside of the search area."

The phone on his belt begins to ring and he answers it and listens. "Understood."

He stops walking and returns the phone to the clip on his belt.

"Willie is unavailable right now," he says. "Leave me your card and I'll have him call you when he can talk."

"This is 'cause I asked Ted if he knew her, isn't it?" Blade says.

"I'm just passing along the message I just received," he says. "Wouldn't begin to waste time wondering why it came. Deal with what is, not what we want to be."

TWELVE

"You okay?" I ask.

Blade nods but doesn't say anything.

We are back in the car, pulling away from Footprints. I'm driving. She's seething in the passenger seat beside me.

"Since we're this far out anyway and we have extra time on our hands," I say, "want to ride up and take a look at where she went missing?"

She nods.

I take Highway 98 to 79 to 321 toward Palm County.

We ride in silence.

"Mind if I play the 911 call?" I ask.

She shakes her head.

I tap a few buttons on my phone, which is on the seat between my legs, and the call begins to play through the car sound system.

911 Operator: "911. What's your emergency?"

Nora: "Yes, I'm in the middle of a field . . . Escaped. May . . . . My . . . baby. Runnin' from . . . [garbled] and he . . . shot . . . somebody. We're out here goin' toward Jefferson . . . outskirts on both sides. No . . . cell serv— My car ran . . . gas. Stolen. There's two . . . cars . . . truck . . . out here. Guy . . . [garbled] chasin' . . . me . . . out . . . hiding . . . tigers . . . like . . . frond . . . Empty . . . through the woods. Please help . . . Please . . . come out here . . . Hurry."

911 Operator: "Okay, now run that by me once more. I didn't—"

Nora: "They . . . to be . . . not . . . talkin' to him. I ran . . . into . . . like me, but . . . the hole."

911 Operator: "Oh, okay. Someone ran into someone? Is that—"

Distorted background noises. Shouts? Shots?

Nora: ". . . [garbled] . . . of the only . . . or some . . . know. Guy is . . ."

More loud noise.

Nora: "Not . . . way . . . but . . . over . . . tricked . . ."

911 Operator: "Where are you? Do you need an ambulance?"

More background sounds.

Nora: ". . . for . . . to . . . me . . . so . . ."

911 Operator: "Ma'am, what is your location? Do you need an ambulance or—"

More garbled sounds.

Nora: "Uh huh."

911 Operator: "Can you tell me where you are? Do you need an ambulance or the police?"

Nora: "Yeah . . . no . . . I need the police."

911 Operator: "Okay, can you tell me where you are? Is anybody hurt?"

More garbled noises and loud sounds . . . then silence like the call has been disconnected.

911 Operator: "Ma'am? Ma'am? Ma'am?"

No response.

911 Operator: "Ma'am? Ma'am? Ma'am? Are you there? Ma'am?"

A few more noises like maybe the call hasn't been disconnected, and then nothing.

911 Operator: "Ma'am? Ma'am? Ma'am?"

I play it again, and again, listening to it as we speed down the rural pine-tree-lined highway toward where the call came from.

"You think Fred's right?" Blade says.

They are the first words she's uttered since we left Footprints.

"About?"

"Her just runnin' out into the woods and dyin'."

I shrug. "It's possible. Certainly more likely than a lot of other scenarios. She does sound delusional and paranoid."

"She does, but . . . I found Shanice Wright convincin'."

"Yeah?" I ask, not sure what she's getting at. "Me too."

"She said Nora didn't do drugs."

"She might not know everything her friend does," I say. "Or it could be something new she just started once she got down here. Or . . . maybe it's not drugs at all, but some sort of psychotic break."

She frowns and nods. "Don't know which is worse."

"Neither's good."

"Sorry I fucked up things with Ted," she says.

"You did great," I say. "We'll get to Willie another way."

"I tried so hard to hold it all in, even as he was purposefully provokin' me, but I just reached a point where I couldn't take any more without respondin'. And the response I wanted to give him was jumpin' over the desk and slicin' him up a little, maybe cutting out his tongue."

"You showed great restraint," I said. "You really did."

"But I let him get to me," she says. "I lost control, gave it to him. You're supposed to be the one who does that shit, not me. I fucked up and I'm sorry."

"You really did great," I say. "Give yourself some credit and let it go."

"If Nora did just lose her mind, for whatever reason, and ran off into the woods with her little girl and died . . . why hasn't she been found?"

"Good question."

"You'd think somethin' would've been found—some personal affects or phone or something."

"Yes, you would."

When we reach the spot where Nora's vehicle was found, we pull off the road near a white wooden cross with *Nora and Emma* written on it, surrounded by flowers, notes, stuffed animals, and other mementos.

Parking and turning off the car, we get out and look around.

The day is bright, the September sun high in a clear blue sky, and though it's subtle, there's something distinctly autumnal about the breeze.

The area is a random point on a rural highway with nothing but woods visible for miles in either direction.

Across the street is a tall metal-grate fence with rusted sheets of tin behind it and barbed wire on top of it, which according to the file Pete gave us, encloses a private hunting lease and the dilapidated remains of an old mom-and-pop zoo. The imposing fence appears impenetrable—particularly for a young mother and her baby—so if they went into the woods it was almost certainly on this side.

I pull out my phone and check the signal. There is very little.

"Call me and leave a voicemail," Blade says. "We'll listen to it later and compare it to hers."

I do.

The forest on both sides of the road is dense with mature pine and oak trees and thick understory that even without the fence of the other side of the highway looks nearly impossible to enter.

"Hard to see her running into there with a baby," I say.

Blade nods. "Wouldn't think she'd get very far if she did. Sort of shoots a big-ass hole in ol' Freddy's theory. No fields around here either."

Beyond the shoulder and the ditch and the makeshift memorial to Nora and Emma, the tree line of the forest is filled with *No Trespassing* signs and security cameras.

"Those are new," Blade says.

I nod and look across the highway to see the same things on the fence on the other side.

We had heard that some of the property owners in the vicinity of where Nora and Emma went missing didn't want reporters, citizen detectives, family members, interested parties, or anyone else searching their property. Evidently, we heard right.

"Makes you wonder what they're hiding," I say.

"Yes, it does," she says. "Look forward to findin' out."

"This is a lonely stretch of road in the middle of nowhere with nothing around," I say. "Wonder what brought her out here? And I assume the only thing that made her stop here was running out of gas. You can imagine how dark and desolate it was, how scary it would be with a baby and poor cell service."

She nods. "You can hear how terrified she is on the 911 call."

"So," I say, "she runs out of gas, then what? If someone was with her or following her, if she were running from someone, they could've taken her."

"But she had time to call 911, Shanice, and Willie."

"Which means either they weren't right with her when she

broke down, so she had time to make some calls, or no one was following her."

"Maybe she got away from them, but then broke down so they were able to catch up to her or find her again," she says. "She could've grabbed Emma and run into the woods, hidden there to make the calls, but been found eventually."

"Right," I say. "Or, no one was after her. She was paranoid and hallucinating and took her child into the woods, running from someone or something that wasn't there, and they died out there."

"What if . . ." she says. "Think about how hard these bitches don't want anyone on their land. What if she went into the woods and stumbled onto somethin' that got them killed?"

"Certainly a possibility," I say. "Another option is no one was chasing her and she never went into the woods. What if someone stopped to help her, offered a ride, took her away from here and either killed them or dropped them someplace, and whatever happened to them happened there."

"She wasn't here with her vehicle," Blade says, "so . . . seems like the only two possibilities are that she went into the woods or someone picked her up. She goes into the woods and somethin' bad happens to her or she gets in a vehicle with someone and somethin' bad happens to her."

"Lot of similarities to Kaylee's case," I say.

She nods. "To every case where someone goes missin' from a broken-down car on the side of the road."

Kaylee vanished off the face of the earth after she ran off the road into a ditch. Unlike Nora, there's no 911 call, no calls to family or friends. But like Nora, part of the mystery is why she was where she was. Of course, in the case of Kaylee, where she was and why she was there is far more mysterious than Nora and Emma. And what makes her case even more baffling is that there were witnesses and an extremely narrow time-frame and she still vanished without a trace.

"And like in all those other cases," she adds, "be a big-ass coincidence that a serial killer—or any kind of killer—just happened to be passin' by at the exact moment she broke down."

"Unless . . ." I say, "he sabotaged her vehicle in some way at her last stop."

"Sure," she says, "but that doesn't work with runnin' out of gas."

"Does if he siphoned some of the gas out of her car," I say.

"True," she says. "Makes much more sense and the timing fits if someone fucked with her vehicle and just followed her waitin' for it to break down."

"We've got to retrace her steps from that night," I say, "and find out what the deal is with these property owners and how we get on their land."

She starts to say something, but stops as a Palm County patrol car pulls up.

THIRTEEN

The Palm County deputy crawls out of his car, his large belly pressing against his green uniform adding to the awkwardness and difficulty, and ambles over to us. He's a white man in his forties with a flattop, glasses, and the ill-fitting uniform.

"Help you folks with something?" he asks.

We both shake our heads and shoot him expressions that convey our surprise and confusion that he's asking.

"Y'all break down?" he asks. "Run out of gas?"

We both shake our heads again and I say, "No."

"Well, what're you doing here?" he asks.

"Nothin'," Blade says.

"Just lookin' around," I say.

We all turn and look as a new tricked-out black Ford F-150 pulls up and a thickish, once athletic white man in his early sixties climbs down out of it.

"What seems to be the problem, Walt?" he says.

"That's what I was tryin' to ascertain, Mr. Holt."

"There's nothin' to *ascertain*," I say. "There's no problem here. At least we don't have one. Do y'all?"

"Y'all reporters?" the deputy, whose name is apparently Walt, asks.

"You don't recognize them?" Holt says. "These are the two private investigators who found that little girl who was stolen and brought her home. You should pick up a newspaper sometime."

"Yes, sir."

"I'm confused," Blade says. "What's goin' on here?"

Holt says, "This is posted private property and you two are trespassing."

"Actually, this is a public road right-of-way," Blade says.

"Looked to me like y'all were about to go onto the private property," he says, nodding toward the cameras.

"*Looked* like?" Blade says. "Y'all are out here because it looked like we might be about to go into that dense-ass forest right there?"

"Is this your property?" I ask.

Holt shakes his head. "I'm the caretaker."

"And doin' a hell of a job," Blade says. "Harassin' people who stand anywhere near it."

"Who owns it?" I ask. "We'd like to—"

"I'm not a liberty to say," he says, shaking his head.

"It's public record," Blade says.

"Then look it up," he says. "But don't even think about trespassing. Walt, make sure they don't."

"Yes, sir, Mr. Holt."

Holt turns and walks back to his truck. When he reaches it, he says, "I wish you luck finding that young woman and her little girl, but she's not on our property. It has been thoroughly searched."

He then climbs into his truck and drives away.

"Are all property owners in Palm County that paranoid?" I ask Walt.

"We're gettin' a lot of crazies obsessed with this case," he says. "Internet detectives or whatever. Think they can make a name for themselves by finding her. I don't know what happened to her and her baby, but they're not here and we're not about to let outsiders trash our little community."

FOURTEEN

Leaving the site where Nora's vehicle was abandoned, we drive toward the gas station where the trucker called 911 to report it.

We cross a bridge over a creek about a quarter of a mile from where Nora broke down, but otherwise the two miles or so to the gas station, apart from one curve, is like the rest of the highway in this area—flat, straight, desolate.

As we ride, we listen to the voicemail message I left for Blade.

It doesn't fade in and out quite as much as Nora's, but it's close, and even though I'm not running, moving my head side to side or frightened, it's a challenge to understand me.

"Just confirms what we already knew," Blade says. "Bad coverage out here."

I nod.

"Looks like the landowners and law enforcement are gonna be a bitch to deal with," she says.

"Yeah, even worse than I thought."

"Won't do any good, but we need to go meet with the sheriff."

"Agree," I say. "Sooner the better."

"Probably too late today," she says. "In the morning?"

"Okay."

The small mom-and-pop gas station on the right side of the road has two pumps out front and exterior restrooms on the right side of the building.

The front windows of the dingy little store that time forgot are plastered with old and fading advertisements for beer, tobacco, and lotto. They peek out from behind a rusted propane rack, a dirty ice cooler, and a row of once bright plastic newspaper-type boxes with free religious, political, and real estate publications.

Inside, we find a mid-thirties Pakistani man with dark skin nearly the identical shade as his lips. His coarse black hair is straight and closely cropped on the sides and back but longer and curly on top.

He gives me a quick glance, but his eyes widen and he does a double take when he sees Blade.

I hand him one of our cards and tell him who we are and why we're here.

From the moment he reads the card, he begins shaking his head.

"You go now," he says. "Nothing to say to you. No reporters. No podcasters. No—"

"But we're just—"

"No," he says. "Go. Now."

"Nora's family hired us to find her," I say. "We're not just—"

"I call police now," he says.

He lifts the grimy receiver of the old landline phone on the counter and we walk out of the shop, get in our car, and leave the unwelcoming Palm County.

As we cross back into Bay County, I say, "But we'll be back."

FIFTEEN

Miss Rachel, the Cloud Nine house mom, is a large white woman with a pretty, pale face, hair dyed a bright red, and an enormously ample bosom.

She's the girlfriend of one of the bouncers, which is how she initially got the job.

She's genuinely sweet and kind, and though she's not much older than the girls who work here, she has a mature maternal nature that makes her good at her job.

Strip club house moms, who work primarily behind the scenes in the dressing room, do a variety of things to take care of the dancers, minimizing drama and trauma, protecting the girls, and making everything run smoothly. They often cook dinner and have snacks available for the dancers, they collect the house fees from the girls, keep track of attendance, help with hair, makeup, wardrobe, and any feminine hygiene issues that arise, and they maintain order in the dressing room and in the ladies restroom. For these and other duties they are tipped out by the dancers and staff and can make between one hundred and a thousand dollars a night, depending on how busy the club is on a given night.

"Ashlynn said you wanted to ask me about the girl who went missing," she says.

I nod. "If you don't mind."

"Not at all. Happy to help. Hope y'all find her. She was a sweet girl. I felt bad for her. We get a lot of girls in her situation —come down to the beach with a guy who ditches them or with other girls or by themselves and just run out of money. Things are a lot more expensive on the beach than people realize. They need a way to make a quick buck to get out of a jam or just to get home. You can tell a lot of them are very troubled. Most of them are strung out and just trying to get their next fix, but this girl was different. She was clean and together. I work with a lot of girls—and have for a long time now. I can tell. She said she was out of money. Owed a few people. Wanted to earn enough money to pay her debts and get back home."

"She say who she owed or what kind of debts she had?" I ask.

She narrows her eyes and twists her lips as she thinks about it. Eventually, she shakes her head. "No, not really. What I gathered was she had borrowed a little money for food—mostly for her kid—gas for her car, and room and board, that kind of thing, but I don't think she said exactly."

"Did she work any shifts?"

"I thought about letting her do a few afternoon shifts," she says. "They're the least pressure, but she just wouldn't make enough money doing them to really help."

"Did she say how much she owed?"

She shakes her head. "No. I don't think so. It has been a while and I can't remember everything exactly. But I don't remember her saying an exact amount. Anyway, I just thought . . . this girl doesn't need to be dancing. She was pretty enough. Had a good body. But she was too . . . I don't know . . . naive, maybe. Not in general, but . . . I think she would've been—the learning curve for her here would've been steep. She wouldn't've made much money at first, so it'd take too long for her to make what she needed to and I figured she'd go deeper and deeper in debt while she was trying to figure things out. So . . . I just gave her some money."

"You did?"

"Yeah."

"That was such a decent thing to do," I say. "But I'm not surprised. You're such a good person. I appreciate all you do for Ashlynn. She says you're more of a mom to her than her mother ever was."

"Really?" she says, her eyes glistening. "That's so nice."

"Do you mind me asking how much you gave her?"

"Not much. Not enough, I'm sure. Two hundred bucks. It was all I had on me at the time. She insisted on calling it a loan and swore she would pay me back—got my address to mail it to me and everything—but I considered it a gift and didn't expect to see it again."

"Was anyone with her when she came?" I ask.

She shakes her head. "Not that I saw."

"Do you know if she left her baby in the car?"

"I don't think so. I hope not. She didn't act like she was in a hurry or anything."

"Did she interact with anyone else?" I ask. "Notice anyone checking her out or—"

"We met back here. I think she just came straight in here and went straight out, but I don't know for sure. I'll ask Declan."

"Anything else you can tell me about her that might help us find her?"

"I wish there was. I feel so bad. She really was a good girl."

I sense the presence of someone else behind us.

"Rach, what the hell?"

We turn to see her boyfriend, Declan, standing in the doorway.

He's a large, muscular black man nearly as wide as he is tall, in black slacks, a white button-down, and a black vest—the uniform for male Cloud Nice employees. He's so wide he has to stand at an angle to fit in the doorframe.

"You know you can't have people back here," he says. "'Specially men. You tryin' to get us fired? Hey, Burke, how are you? You understand, don't you?"

"Hey man," I say. "How's it going? Yeah. No problem."

"Walk him out," Rachel says. "He's got a question for you."

"Thank you again," I say to Rachel. "For everything."

I turn and follow Declan out into the club, past the tall, skinny dancer on the small stage and the thick, big-breasted dancer on the main stage, and the handful of old men who make up the regulars of the afternoon crowd.

When we step out of the double doors into the parking lot, he says, "Whatcha got?"

"Blade and I are lookin' for that young mom and daughter who went missin'," I say. "Rachel said she came here to talk to her about a job. Did she hang around, talk to anyone? Anyone follow her or—"

"Straight in and out I think," he says. "But I was working the champagne room. I'll ask Bubba to be sure and let you know if he says different."

"Thanks man. And thanks for all you and Rachel do for Ashlynn."

"Our pleasure, dog. She good people."

SIXTEEN

Before I went to prison, I played in a band and had a nice guitar collection going. Now, I play alone with a banged-up pawn-shop special that wasn't good to begin with.

The guitar in question is a black laminate wood dreadnaught cutaway acoustic, which I guarantee when new was touted as "highly affordable" and "perfect for beginners." When I first got it I had adjusted the truss rod and put a new set of strings on it—both of which helped with the playability and sound, but there's only so much that can be done for a POS model like this one.

I'm just getting back into gigging and I'm still not doing much, but since I live in St. Andrews within walking distance of nearly all the live music venues, I sometimes get last-minute calls when the scheduled musician doesn't show.

Tonight I'm playing in the back room of a literary-themed bar on Beck called the Lie'Brary.

A dark, quiet lounge with vintage and eclectic decor, the Lie'Brary has a wide variety of craft beer and wine, mismatched tables and chairs, a huge buffalo head mounted on the wall, and shelves and shelves of old books—mostly hard-covers without their dustjackets.

The area where I'm playing in the back has a small seating area with couches surrounded by chessboard tables and upright chairs. Through the windows behind me, the last of the setting sun over St. Andrews Bay streams in and gives everything a dusky glow and gloaming groove.

Most of the patrons are in the front at the bar, but there are a few back here listening to me.

I play an eclectic acoustic mix of classics and singer-song-writer tunes—Lennon and McCartney, Dylan, Young, the Stones, Eagles, Skynyrd, Van Morrison, Townes Van Zandt, Dan Fogelberg, John Mellencamp, Jason Isbell, Tom Petty, Gin Blossoms, REM, Green Day, and the like.

I enjoy being the background music for a venue like this where those present are talking and drinking, eating and wooing, and I'm just providing the soft soundtrack for them.

During most songs, I close my eyes and concentrate on the song, losing myself in the process of recreating my version of tunes I've spent most of my life loving.

I remember reading someone saying, though I can't remember who, that at the moment of climax our lovers disappear like the gates of paradise as they open. Or something sort of like that. That's how I feel about the songs I play—the best thing I can do is get out of the way, be the invisible gateway to the awaiting paradise of a great song.

I'm playing my version of Johnny Cash's version of the Nine Inch Nails' song "Hurt" when Lexi Miller appears with a glass of wine and takes a seat on the antique parlor chair most directly in front of me.

Dressed more casually than I've ever seen her, she is striking—even more alluring than usual—and I begin to feel self-conscious. My fingers stiffen and my voice tightens and the quality of my performance diminishes.

Closing my eyes, I refocus on the song, relaxing into it, the world around me, including Lexi, dimming.

When I finish, she claps the loudest and stands and places a generous tip in my tip jar.

"You sound so good," she says in a soft, breathy voice. "I had no idea you played."

"Thank you," I say. "That's so kind of you. Any requests?"

"I love 'Same Old Lang Syne,'" she says. "Do you know that one? Seems like most people only do it around Christmas and New Year's, but . . ."

"It's a favorite of mine too," I say. "Be happy to do it."

She sits back down, and I say, "I'm going to do one more then take a short break. This one is by request. One of the best songs ever written, by an incredible songwriter who left us too soon. Based on an actual experience he had . . . 'Same Old Lang Syne' by Dan Fogelberg."

My love for and appreciation of the song enables me to let go of everything else and play and sing it like I'm alone in my apartment, and I recall reading something Rumi said while I was in prison. *"I want to sing like the birds sing, not worrying about who hears or what they think."*

I'm pleased with how the cover turns out and the response is great, especially to me playing the notes of "Auld Lang Syne" that the sax does in the original song.

"Thank you," I say. "I'm gonna take a short break and be back for another set in a few minutes."

After placing my guitar on the stand and turning on a playlist I created to run during my breaks, I step over to Lexi.

She stands.

"Thank you for your generous—"

"You play and sing beautifully," she says. "I had no idea.

And the way you did 'Same Old Lang Syne.' Wow. By far the best cover of it I've ever heard."

"Thank you," I say. "That's—"

"I know you only have a short break and probably have people to see, but I'd like to talk to you for a minute if you have time before you start again."

"Of course," I say. "Let me just grab something to drink and—"

"Take your time," she says. "Do what you need to do. I'll be here."

"Be right back," I say.

I walk to the front and over to the bar. I had been looking forward to the great pineapple cider they have here, but not wanting to drink in front of Lexi, get a bottle of water instead.

"Sounding good, man," an older man with long gray hair says.

"Thanks."

The other patrons seated at the bar nod their agreement and add a few compliments and requests of their own.

I duck into the restroom and pee, and when I reach the back again, Lexi is at one of the small tables against the wall.

I take the seat across from her.

"I just wanted you to know that I'm not here officially," she says. "I had no idea you were playing here tonight."

I believe her.

"I didn't either until about fifteen minutes before I started," I say.

"So you know there's no way I could," she says.

I nod.

"I'm off-duty," she says. "I'm down here to meet some friends at the Slice House for dinner. I got here early and love this place so just came in for a drink while I waited. I just wanted you to know."

"I appreciate that," I say.

"But I have to say . . . I'm so glad I did. Running into you like this . . . It's . . . Well . . . I'm just really glad I got to see and hear you. You're really good."

"Used to be better," I say. "Just getting back into it. I'm out of practice and I have shit gear, but . . . Thank you."

"I . . . I really want to help you," she says. "I don't want you going back. I'll do everything I can to make sure you never do."

"I really appreciate that."

"I'm having a hard time . . . seeing how someone who plays and sings with such sensitivity is capable of violence."

"I'm usually not," I say, "but in certain situations . . . under certain circumstances . . . I . . . just . . . lose it."

She nods and seems to think about it. "I know you've got to start your second set, but . . . I just . . ."

Our eyes lock and she stops speaking for a moment.

"I feel . . ." she says. "Well, I can't say how I feel, but I wish I could. I want to stand up my friends and stay here and listen to you."

"Y'all could always bring the pizza over here."

"Honestly," she says, "I'd rather them not see the way I look at you. Sorry. I've said too much. It's the wine and the way you play. I'm gonna go now. Sorry for being inappropriate. Please don't use it against me."

"I would never—"

She stands, touching my hand on the table before making a quick exit.

SEVENTEEN

My next set goes fairly well. I'm less self-conscious and make fewer mistakes.

I'm tempted to step next door to the Slice House during my break between sets two and three, but resist the ill-advised urge.

Near the end of my last set, Lexi walks in the back door with a white triangle-shaped to-go box. After disappearing up front for a few moments, she returns with a bottle of water and takes a seat at the table we were at earlier.

After concluding the last song of my last set, I thank everyone for coming, though I know they didn't come to see me, speak to a few people who come forward to drop a tip in the jar and tell me how much they enjoyed it, and step over to the table where she is sitting.

"I brought you a slice and an apology," she says.

"Thank you," I say. "For the slice. I'm starving. But you don't have anything to—"

"I had too much wine on an empty stomach earlier," she says. "I crossed a line."

"If you did, you didn't go very far across it."

"No, but farther than I ever should have. I've never ever done anything like that before. I would never get involved with an . . ."

"What is the term y'all use these days?" I ask. "Ex-offender? Probationer? Inmate? Convict? Felon?"

"Obviously, I don't see you as any of those, but . . . the reality is . . ."

"I am."

"You are," she says. "You're unlike anyone I've ever had on my caseload, but that doesn't matter—not when it comes to . . . I can't get involved with . . ."

"I didn't think from what you said earlier that you had any intention of getting involved with me," I say. "I just thought you were being . . . honest and vulnerable and nice."

"That's the thing," she says, "I can't be . . . I'm not allowed to be vulnerable with you. It's . . . it puts me in a very compromising and dangerous position."

"If anything happened between us, and it's clear it won't, I would be the one who was by far the most vulnerable. You have all the power. You hold all the cards. If I did something you didn't like, you could . . ."

"I would never do anything like that," she says. "Never."

"Neither would I," I say. "I would never take advantage of . . . well, anything. And here's how you can know that for sure. You were kind and vulnerable earlier tonight. You say you crossed a line. Well, if you did, I will never use it against you. Not for any reason. Let's act like it never happened. I'll never mention it again. And you have my word that it will never come up—no matter what. Even if you ever decided to violate me back to prison. Okay? Thank you for the pizza. And if you want to get me reassigned to another officer's caseload, I'd appreciate it if you don't jam me up when you do."

"I won't," she says, shaking her head. "Again, I'm sorry. Look how messy this is already . . . and all I did was have a personal conversation with you and admit I wouldn't be able to fool my friends about how attracted to you I am."

My phone vibrates and I can see that Ashlynn is calling.

"I'm sorry," I say. "I have to take this. Could be about my niece."

She nods. "Of course."

"Hey," I say into the phone.

"Where are you?" she asks.

I can hear the muted house music of the strip club in the background.

"Lie'Brary on Beck," I say. "What's up?"

"Can Staci drop Alana off with you?"

"Of course."

Staci is Alana's dad's mother, and though he's not involved in Alana's life, she tries to be, but seems to only ever be able to keep her for an hour or two at a time before getting overwhelmed or something coming up that she'd rather do.

"She was supposed to keep her tonight, but . . . she's flakin'. I knew better than to let her even try, but she swore she was up for it."

"It's no problem," I say. "Happy to have her."

"You're the best. She's already in St. Andrews looking for you. She'll drop her off in just a few minutes."

"I'll be looking for her. See you later tonight."

"Okay," she says. "Oh, and Declan said to tell you that Winston, one of the new bouncers, saw someone talking to Nora when she came here. Said get up with him and he'll give you the info."

"Thanks. I really appreciate that."

When I end the call, Lexi says, "Sorry. I started to get up

and give you some privacy, but I didn't know . . . and then I thought you were done and—"

"It's all good," I say. "One of my foster sisters needs me to watch her daughter tonight."

"This late?" she asks. "How old is she?"

"Yeah. She's four. Her mom's a dancer at Cloud Nine."

"Oh."

I laugh. "That may be the most judgmental *oh* I've ever heard. She's a good mother, especially to not have had one and to be as young as she is. She makes good money doing what she's doing and she uses every dime of it to care for Alana. Spends every waking moment with Alana and we take good care of her when she's working."

"You're right," she says. "I'm sorry. It's just that environment. And so many of those girls are on drugs and get taken advantage of."

I nod. "I get it. And you're right. But Ashlynn is clean and sober and smart. She—"

"*Uncle Lucas,*" Alana yells as she runs in the back door.

"Hey, girl," I say, jumping up. "How are you?"

"You wanna play princesses and the bad sister?"

"You know it," I say.

"Well, come on, let's go to your house."

"We will in a few minutes," I say. "I need your help packing up my equipment first."

"Thanks, Burke," Staci says from the open door. "I appreciate it."

"Happy to have her," I say. "Always."

"He misses me when I'm not around," Alana says.

"Yes, I do," I say.

"I couldn't get her to eat much of anything," Staci says.

I nod. "We'll find her something good."

"Bye, baby," Staci says. "Grandma loves you."

Staci disappears into the night, the door closing behind her.

"I'm Alana," she says to Lexi. "What's your name?"

"Lexi."

"Do you wanna play princesses and the bad sister? You could be the mom."

"I'd love to, but I've got to go home."

"I can be the bad sister and the mom," I say.

"Okay. Let's go play."

"I have to pack up my stuff first," I say. "Are you hungry? Want some pizza?"

"*Pizza*," she squeals.

I lift her into the seat I had been in before she arrived and open the white cardboard box.

"I just got cheese since I didn't know what you liked," Lexi says.

"Perfect."

"Yum," Alana says when she sees the slice.

"Eat that while I pack up and then we'll go play," I say.

"I can sit here with her while you do that," Lexi says.

"You sure? You don't have to."

"I'm happy to."

"Okay. Thanks. I really appreciate it."

"Luc, I need chocee milk," she says.

"We'll have to get some when we get home," I say. "They don't have any here. They probably have juice. Do you want some juice?"

"Okay."

"Okay. Eat your pizza and I'll go grab you some juice."

I return a few moments later with some watered-down pineapple juice in a plastic to-go cup with a straw and a lid to find Alana and Lexi in an intense discussion about their favorite Disney princesses.

"Mine is Arial," Alana is saying. "I'm Luc's favorite princess."

"Yes you are," I say. "It's not even close."

"Belle is his second, isn't she?"

"She is," I say. "Smart, well-read, and beautiful. Just like you."

"I like Belle too," Lexi says.

"Rapunzel is my second favorite," Alana says.

"She's a great one," Lexi says.

"What the fuck?"

Every muscle in my body tenses at the sound of that voice.

I turn to see Logan Owens standing near the restroom door, staring at us. He is a young, thin, pale white man with freakishly light blue eyes and wild bleached-blond hair. Behind him is an enormous black man with both a big belly and plenty of muscles. No doubt his bodyguard.

Immediately my heart begins to race, adrenaline flooding my veins, anger humming along my nerves like current in an electrical line.

"You," Logan says. "You . . ."

Logan Owens is the reason I went to prison. As far as the legal system is concerned he is my victim—though he's never been anything but a victimizer—and one of the conditions of my probation is to have no contact with him.

Instinctively, I step over so that Alana and Lexi are behind me.

"You can't be here," he says. "They serve alcohol here. And what's the kid doing here? You can't be around kids. Haven't been out long, have you? But your ass is going right back in." He glances over his shoulder and yells, "Bartender."

In another moment, the young twenty-something white girl with pale skin, black hair, red, red lips, and black frame glasses appears.

"What is it?" she asks.

It's obvious she doesn't appreciate being called away from the bar—or the manner in which she was. It's equally obvious that Logan, who is from a wealthy family and accustomed to an indulged accountability-and-consequence-free life, doesn't care.

"This man is a convicted felon. He's not allowed to be in here. He's not allowed to be around alcohol, other criminals, or children."

The jagged edges of my anger threaten to turn into rage.

I take a breath and a moment, aiming myself before I respond.

"I'm sorry about this, Janey," I say. "I am a convicted felon —for beating him up—but everything else he said is false. I can be here or anywhere else I want to. And I can be around my niece or any other child."

"But you can't be around me, can you?" Logan says.

"That's true," I say to Janey. "I'm not allowed to go near the victim in my case."

"Toss him out, Clyde," Logan says.

The huge black man behind him steps around him, and as the first drops of gasoline being thrown onto the fire of anger in the basement of my being, I glance around the room for anything that might be used as a weapon.

"Wait," Janey says. "Mr. Burke was here first. And you can't just throw people out of our bar."

"Thank you, Janey," I say, "but I was leaving anyway. Just have to pack up my gear and—"

"Toss him and his shit out the back door," Logan says to Clyde. Then to me, "You know your psycho ass is the reason I even have a bodyguard. And just try to resist him. He'll beat the hell out of you and you'll go back to prison where you belong. That's called a win-win."

"Uncle Lucas, I'm scared," Alana says.

"It's okay, baby. Everything's fine."

I reach behind me and pat her on the head and shoulder.

Lexi stands and steps beside me.

Lifting her untucked shirt above her waist on her right side, she reveals the weapon holstered there. Pulling out her badge and displaying it, she says, "I'm Officer Miller. If you attempt to throw anyone or anything out of this establishment, you'll be arrested. Now, here's what's going to happen. You two are going to return to the front part of the building and Mr. Burke is going to remain back here. He'll pack up his things like he was already planning to do and he will exit from the back door. Understand?"

Clyde holds his huge hands up in a placating gesture and turns and begins walking toward the front of the bar.

"This isn't over, fucktard," Logan says.

"Make another threat against Mr. Burke and I'll arrest you for assault," Lexi says.

"Bitch, I'm the victim here. He nearly killed me. I'm still in rehab. Had to have plastic surgery."

"Looks like with all your money you could've afforded a better doctor," she says.

"What? What'd you say to me?"

"I'm familiar with your case," she says. "Well, cases. I know what you were doing when Mr. Burke kicked your ass. Turn and walk away. Now."

He starts to say something, then shakes his head and slowly turns and walks back up front.

"Janey," she says, "do you owe Mr. Burke anything for playing here tonight?"

She nods. "Yes, ma'am, we do."

"Would you bring it back here to him so he doesn't have to go up there near that asshole?"

"Sure," she says, nodding profusely. "Absolutely. Yes, ma'am."

As she turns and walks away, Alana says, "Luc, is *asshole* a bad word?"

EIGHTEEN

"You're gonna have to be even far more careful than I thought you were," Lexi says softly.

I nod and frown. "I know."

"What a little prick," she says.

It's later and we're in my apartment. She had insisted on seeing us home to make sure Logan and Clyde didn't take a run at us once we left the Lie'Brary. We are standing in my small kitchen area, speaking softly. Alana is asleep in my bed, the bedroom door open so I can hear her and so she won't be scared if she wakes up.

If Alana wasn't asleep she'd be asking if *prick* was a bad word about now.

"He's going to keep harassing you," she says. "Gonna try to set you up so you go back."

"I know."

Though my apartment is clean, it's old and small and sparsely furnished with second-, third-, and fourth-hand furniture that wasn't nice to begin with, and I'm self-conscious about having her here.

"I'm scared for you," she says.

"You have good reason to be," I say.

"He's got so much money," she says. "So many connections. He can just hire someone to attack you and . . ."

"Think we could talk about something else?" I say. "Thank you for helping us out tonight. I was worried what would happen to Alana if I got into it with Clyde."

"I was worried about all of us," she says. "And I really didn't want to have to shoot Clyde in his big fat head. I was impressed with how you kept your cool."

"Maybe all this shit I'm doin' with counseling and meditation and anger management is working."

She nods. "Or . . ." she says, "the balloon just hadn't gone up yet."

"There's that," I say. "Clyde would've killed me, but he'd've known he'd been in for a fight."

She smiles and we fall quiet a moment, our attraction and connection coming to the fore again.

"Why the fuck didn't we meet under different circumstances?" she says.

"Probably wouldn't be who we are if we had," I say. "Amor fati."

"Yeah, I guess that's true," she says. "Love what?"

"Fate," I say. "Embrace what is instead of wasting time wishing things were other than what they are."

She closes the distance between us and kisses me—a full, intense, passionate kiss that lingers and lasts.

"I had to kiss the mouth that that just came out of," she says. "So embrace that. And now I'm gonna go before you say something that makes me rip my own clothes off."

I nod and walk her to the door.

"Thank you," I say.

"For?"

"Everything. That extraordinary kiss, saving our asses tonight, the pizza, the tip, the—"

"My pleasure," she says.

"And Lexi," I say, using her first name for the first time ever. "You have nothing to worry about from me. No matter what. Don't waste a single second worrying about anything where I'm concerned."

"I actually don't think I will," she says. "Which if you knew me . . . you'd know what a miracle that is."

As she leaves, I step outside and leave the door open so I can still see and hear Alana while being able to watch Lexi walk to her car.

"Would you mind texting me when you're home safe and sound?" I ask.

"*Who even are you?*" she says.

She then disappears into her dark car, and a moment later her car disappears into the dark night.

NINETEEN

The next morning, with Ashlynn and Alana asleep in my bed, I sit on the floor in the living room, attempting to meditate.

Many times when I first wake up—especially in the middle-of-the-night darkness—I still feel like I'm in prison and it takes me a few moments to adjust to my new reality. This morning, probably because of unremembered nightmares, was especially bad.

I've never been particularly good at meditating, but this morning I'm even worse than usual.

I keep thinking of Lexi, of all the ways we connected last night, of her interest, kindness, concern, of how attractive I find her and how attracted she seems to be to me, of our kiss and the way she felt when I held her.

Focus on your breath. Let go of everything else. Let your thoughts drift by like clouds. Don't reach up and grab or cling to them. Just let them come and go. Observe them. You are the thinker, not the thought.

No amount of reminding myself what to do helps.

I may be imagining it, but I swear the sweet scent of her still lingers in the room.

Abandoning all attempts to meditate, I decide instead to recite the 12 Steps of Anger Anonymous.

Speaking softly, I say, "'We admitted we were powerless over rage—that our lives had become unmanageable. Came to believe that a power greater than ourselves could restore us to sanity. Made a decision to turn our will and our lives over to the care of God as we understood God. Made a searching and fearless moral inventory of ourselves. Admitted to God, to ourselves, and to another human being the exact nature of our wrongs.'"

That's as far as I get before my thoughts begin to wander again. And unlike most other times, this morning they are all wandering in the same direction.

You can't afford to be this distracted. You know how important it is to put in this morning practice. If you don't stay in a good headspace, you're going to lose it again and be right back in prison.

I walk about with so much rage. I can feel it in the tension in my neck and shoulders and in my general irritability. I'm trying to change, attempting to let go of the rage, better manage that which I've yet to release, but most of the time I feel like I'm drowning in it.

I open my phone to an article on anger management strategies and begin to read.

It has a list of obvious strategies like identifying triggers, recognizing warning signs, stepping away, changing the channel, creating a calm-down kit, and the like. Though they are patent and plain, they are good reminders, but it isn't long before I'm swiping away from the article to see if Lexi has texted.

She hasn't, so I reread the texts from last night.

Home safe and sound. Thank you for a lovely evening. You play and sing so beautifully. I'm trying so hard not to be, but I am one smitten kitten. What am I going to do?

Glad you're home safe. Thank you for all your kindness and care. Especially for Alana. And for saving my ass. As far as the other, I'm in the same place you are, but I have no idea what to do about it. Was hoping you would. :-) But no matter what, you are safe with me.

I know what you're saying but there's nothing safe about any of this.

I'm safe.

No you're not.

I just meant I will never do anything to hurt you or take advantage of you in any way.

Damn. I was hoping you'd take advantage of me.

Definitely want to. In that one way.

Just so you know, I'm going to tell my supervisor about randomly running into you last night and what happened with Logan Owens. I think that's the best way to protect us both.

I think that's wise. I trust you. Just do what you think is best.

You can, you know. Trust me. If we crash and burn or any other bad thing happens to either one of us it won't be because I betrayed you.

I know.

Good night. Thank you again. I'm going to sleep now and dream of you and all the things we can only do in dreams.

Plan to do the same thing myself. 'Night.

TWENTY

"Heard your ass had an excitin' night last night," Blade says.

We are in her vehicle headed back out to Palm County and the city of Jefferson. I'm driving.

"Your ass ain't supposed to have excitin' nights," she adds.

"You keepin' an eye on me?"

"'Course I'm keepin' an eye on your angry ass," she says. "Somebody got to. Can't have you goin' back to prison. Sort of been thinkin' maybe you shouldn't go out until you're off probation."

"Spend the next two years sequestered in my apartment?" I say. "Which I won't be able to afford since I can't go out and make money to pay for it."

"Ain't sayin' I've perfected this shit yet."

"You're talkin' about exchanging one prison for another."

"One without the threat of ass rape and hep B," she says.

"You may be onto something there."

"But seriously," she says. "You hangin' out with your probation bitch like you on some sort of fuckin' first date and you almost get into it with Logan Owens's bodyguard?"

"The former actually prevented the latter," I say.

"*Do what?*"

"If Lexi hadn't been there I'd probably be in the hospital *and* in custody right now, instead of enjoying this pleasant conversation with you."

"*Lexi?*" she says. "What? You on a first-name basis with her ass now? What the fuck, bruh?"

"Can we talk about something else?" I say. "Or enjoy the rest of the trip in silent reflection?"

"Your ass needs to do some silent reflection," she says. "Seriously, you break my fuckin' heart, man."

"I haven't done anything yet," I say.

"You sabotaging the shit out of yo-self," she says. "Again."

"You really think so?"

"In all seriousness . . . *hell* yes."

"Then I'll take a much harder look at everything I'm doin'," I say. "I wasn't aware I was, but I trust your judgement."

"That's all I can ask," she says. "Now, what the fuck we gonna do about Logan?"

"I'm gonna stay as far away from him as I can," I say. "Just like I'm supposed to."

"You know he's gonna keep seekin' you out," she says. "Tryin' to set you up. He won't quit."

"I know."

"So my question remains . . . What we gonna do about it? And by *we* I mean *me?*"

"You need to stay away from him too," I say. "Both of us going to prison isn't a solution either."

"How his evil ass stay out of prison this long?" she says, shaking her head.

"Same way all the little sociopaths like him do. Money. Power. Connections. Minions. But mostly money."

"Got to be a way to neutralize his ass as a threat," she says.

"Pistol's doin' what he can," I say. "Leave it to him."

"I can tell you, ain't nothin' inside the system gonna work," she says. "System is set up to protect people like Logan fuckin' Owens."

"Just promise me you'll steer clear of him," I say. "If you want me to . . . then you have to too. Deal? Take it. 'Cause it's the best one you're gonna get."

"I don't know . . ." she says as if thinking about it. "I'll probably just stick with my original plan."

"Which is?"

"Cut his creepy little ass open and see what his evil insides look like."

I shake my head. "How is it that out of the two of us, I'm the one who's done time?"

"You gotta learn to control your rage," she says, "keep it on lock. Channel that shit. Keep it ice-cold like me, *ba-bee.*"

TWENTY-ONE

"Ahmed's not a bad guy," Sharon Rolland is saying of the owner of the convenience store near where Nora and Emma vanished. "But you can't imagine how much harassment we've gotten since that woman and her baby went missing."

Sharon Rolland works part-time at Ahmed Farooqi's convenience store and was working the night that the trucker stopped in and mentioned seeing Nora's abandoned vehicle partially on the road.

Blade and I are at a little laundromat in Jefferson speaking to her over the noise of the commercial washers and dryers. Luckily, we are the only ones inside the establishment.

"I understand why he is the way he is," she says. "It's like all the time. Some people are just curious, but others are like obsessed. These web sleuths or whatever . . . they are . . . relentless. And they have all these crazy theories. Have actually accused me and Ahmed of being involved. It's nuts."

Sharon Rolland is a mid-forties white woman with strawberry-blond hair, too much makeup, and too much jewelry. She has a youthful energy and bearing that makes her seem younger than she is. She's dressed like it's laundry day in faded, holey jeans and a wife beater that reveals a small pink bra beneath. And though she's a single woman in her forties with a couple of low-wage jobs who cleans her clothes at a laundromat, she lacks the patina of poverty I expected her to have.

"Like I said, I don't mind talkin' to y'all," she says. "Y'all are like legit private cops hired by her family. But I'm not talkin' to anyone else."

She only has our word for it that we are in fact legit and were hired by Nora's family. Well, and our legit-looking business cards.

"Do y'all have any leads as to where they might be?" she asks.

"Not yet," I say, "but we're hoping you can help us."

She shakes her head. "Don't think I can be much help."

Though allegedly air-conditioned, the air inside the laundromat is thick and warm, its dry currents scented with lavender and lack, hibiscus and hardship.

"You got a theory?" Blade asks.

She shrugs. "Not really, no. I mean . . . Small town like this . . . there's a few bad people but not many. We got a few dealers. A few skin heads. A couple of brawlers. A few pervs. A handful of losers who batter their wives. But . . . kidnapping a mother and child . . . that's . . ."

"May not have started off as that," Blade says. "Could've just given them a ride and . . . maybe expected the kind of payment she wasn't willing to pay and things got out of hand or something like that."

"Could be someone who's never been in trouble before," I say. "If someone did abduct them or . . . worse . . . he'll probably be acting very differently since he did it. Notice anyone who has had a drastic change since it happened?"

"I'll have to think about that one," she says. "But I see what y'all are saying. I'll keep my eyes open. Small town. Hard to keep secrets. 'Course somehow some people do. I'd say there's more so-called white-collar crime than the other—least as much. Our so-called public servants don't serve the public. They serve themselves and those who also have power and money. Guess that's the same thing. And it's probably that way everywhere, but . . . It's a strange place. I don't know. It seems . . . . Sometimes it seems like fuckin' *Mayberry R.F.D.*, others like *Twin Peaks*. Maybe it's that way everywhere. I don't know. Anyway . . . maybe if I had any money and power I'd see it differently. Probably would. Changes everything, doesn't it. What does that mean anyway?"

She pauses. Evidently, the question isn't rhetorical.

"What does it mean that money and power change everything?" I ask.

"No," she says. "R.F.D. Why is it *Mayberry R.F.D.*?"

"Rural Free Delivery," I say. "It was the program that got the mail delivered to rural areas for free instead of the residents having to drive a far distance to get it or hire a private carrier to bring it to them."

"He reads a lot," Blade says.

"Interesting," Sharon says. "So many things we take for granted now that haven't even been around that long."

Blade says, "You mentioned the white-collar crime of those with power. That include the sheriff?"

Sharon shrugs. "Sometimes I think he's truly one of the good guys, like some kind of Buford Pusser. Others . . . I don't know like maybe some kind of . . . who did Denzel play in *Training Day?*"

"Alonzo Harris," Blade says.

"Yeah. Him. Crooked cops are the worst."

"What can you tell us about the trucker who stopped in that night?" Blade asks. "What's his name? Jerry . . . Melvin."

"Yeah. That's it. I know what it's like to be accused of something, so I'm not about to do that to anyone else, but . . . he was a little . . . off."

"How do you mean?" I ask.

"Hey, maybe it's just because it was late at night and I was alone in the store . . . But . . . he sort of like creeped me out. And he wasn't going to call in and report the car in the road. Wanted me to do it. I think that's the only reason he stopped in the store that night. I was like, you've got to do it. He didn't want to, but I kept after him until he did."

"So glad you did," I say.

"You know how some people are just like weird?" she says. "It's not any one thing they say or do . . . More like a vibe, you know?"

Blade nods. "We know a lot of people like that."

"You *do*?" she asks, surprised and a little disturbed.

"In our work," I say.

"Mostly in our work," Blade corrects.

"Oh," she says. "Makes sense. Mine too—'specially middle of the night."

"I bet," Blade says. "Freaks come out at night."

"You have no idea," she says. "Can't tell you how many times I catch people having sex in our bathroom—alone or with someone else. How many people use it to shoot up or get high or sleep. I'm like, dude do that shit in your car. Why come to our little bathroom? I get hit on all the time. Propositioned for sex. Offered to be paid like I'm a prostitute. Always starts off the same—they ask for sex first, like intercourse. 'Give you a hundred dollars for you to fuck me'—like that's a lot of money. When I say no, then it's like 'How 'bout fifty for a blowjob? Twenty-five for a hand job? Come on, I'll be quick.' Bet they are quick, but . . . my mama, God rest her soul, didn't raise no whore or whatever it is we're supposed to call them these days."

"Sex worker," I say in my most helpful voice.

"*Sex worker*," she says. "*Jesus.* Everybody's so goddamn sensitive. Wouldn't want to hurt a whore's feelings, now would we?"

"Did he say anything else?" Blade asks.

"Who?"

"Melvin."

"Oh. He didn't say a whole lot, but he hung around a while, just kind of lingered. Didn't buy anything. He did use the bathroom, but . . . I don't know . . . Seemed like he was like waiting for something or someone."

"Did he act upset?" I ask. "Was he sweating or out of breath? Have any marks on him?"

"You mean like he . . . did something to . . . He did seem sort of agitated. And he did go to the bathroom before he came in, so . . . he could've washed up or something. The door was supposed to be locked but he got inside it. Like I say . . . I don't want to falsely accuse anyone. But . . . it was all very weird. He kept mentioning the time like . . ."

"Like he was trying to establish an alibi?" Blade asks.

"I didn't think so at the time. Not sayin' I do now. Just that it was weird. I mean, he had a phone. I can get asking like once to see if the time zone changed or something, but he mentioned it like several times. Probably nothin', but . . ."

"Anything else about him or—" Blade says, but stops abruptly as the little bell on the door jingles and Sheriff Jack Bullock ambles in.

"Buy y'all a cup of coffee?" he asks.

TWENTY-TWO

"They've got good bacon, eggs, and grits too if y'all are hungry," Bullock says.

Blade and I are sitting in a booth with him at the little diner across the street from the laundromat.

He is both younger and heavier than what I think of as a Southern sheriff. He's in his early thirties, though his baby-fat face makes him look even younger. And though he's only about five-eight or nine, he's got to be tipping the scales at somewhere close to three-hundred pounds.

He wears black pointed-toe snakeskin cowboy boots, which give him a few inches of added height but accentuate his rotundity, dark blue jeans, a light blue button-down, and a black leather belt with a big silver buckle partially hidden beneath the blousing of his shirt. The right side of his belt holds a holstered Glock, the left an agency radio on a clip. His classic cattleman's off-white straw cowboy hat and black aviator-style shades are on the bench seat of the booth beside him.

"What can I getcha, Sheriff?" the middle-aged waitress asks, her pen poised just above her pad.

"Just three coffees today, Betty," he says. "Still tryin' to talk our guests into some of Xavier's bacon and eggs."

"They knew how good they were, wouldn't be no talkin' into it needed."

"That right there is the gospel truth," he says.

She moves away.

"Y'all be sure to let me know if you change your minds."

"Thanks," I say.

Blade says, "Your secretary told us you weren't available today."

As usual, Blade and I naturally and without intention fall into our respective bad cop–good cop roles.

"I wasn't," he says. "Now I am. One of the things I had this morning took less time than I had scheduled for it and another got canceled altogether. My dance card freed up a bit so I thought I'd take you two for a spin."

"Do you not want us talkin' to Sharon?" Blade asks.

"Why, no ma'am, and I recall saying I'd be happy to wait until y'all were done."

"And we really appreciate that," I say. "As well as you working us in."

"Not a problem, Burke," he says. He then looks at Blade. "Let me ask you something, Alix. You from around here?"

Blade nods.

"Then I'm sure you've heard the expression 'you catch more flies with honey than vinegar.'"

"Yeah?"

"Just wonderin' why you're so hostile?" he says. "You asked to see me and here I am. And I didn't make you come to me. I came to you. And we're not meeting in my office or some interview room, but my favorite diner. And I've offered to buy your breakfast."

She nods. "I appreciate all those things," she says. "But

maybe all my encounters with law enforcement haven't been positive."

"I get that," he says. "I do. More than you know. But I could say the same thing about—" he hesitates a beat and she leans forward, every muscle in her body tensing "—PIs." She leans back and relaxes. "And yet I didn't start out hostile with y'all, did I?"

"You're the one with all the power here," she says. "And yesterday one of your deputies ran us off from a public place on the side of the road."

"Well, now, Alix. You know as well as I do that that wasn't just any public place. And I'm pretty sure Walt didn't run you off, but if he gave you the impression that you couldn't stand on the side of the road, I'll have a talk with him."

The diner is small and old-fashioned and dingy in a way that probably only registers with outsiders, and it appears to have been furnished and decorated with the random remainders of other restaurants that went out of business.

In limbo somewhere between the breakfast and lunch crowds, we are one of only three tables in the checkerboard joint.

Attempting to match Bullock's folksy politeness, I say, "We don't want to step on any toes here. We just want to help find the missing mom and her child."

"We have the same goal there," he says. "And I'll tell you this—and it's the truth—I'd be happy as a pig in slop if y'all found them. I'm pulling for you. And I'll help you in any way I can."

"That's not usually the reception we receive," I say.

"Well, I mean it. I really do. I don't care who finds them, who gets the credit for it. I'd just like them brought home safely."

"That's all we want," I say. "And we appreciate you being willing to talk about the case with us and all your support."

"Because of TV and movies, people think that an agency like mine won't accept help from state or federal law enforcement agencies," he says. "It's just not true. Hollywood always shows interagency fighting. State and feds don't come in and take over. They offer assistance. And I gladly take it. Same goes for private—citizens or licensed PIs like y'all. Now, I won't let y'all or anyone else harass the residents here or disrupt the peaceful way of life we have here. But if you are lawful and respectful, you won't have any issues with me."

"We're lawful and respectful," I say.

He glances at Blade, a wry smile crossing his thin lips, pushing up his chubby cheeks.

"I'm respectful once you get to know me," she says.

He laughs.

"I hope you find them," he says. "I really do. But I can tell you this—it won't be in my county."

"What do you—"

"They're not here," he says. "That's what I mean. If you find them it won't be in Palm County. We've looked everywhere. I don't know what happened to them, but whatever it was it involved them bein' taken far away from here."

Betty brings our coffee. "Creme and sugar are on the table. Let me know if y'all want anything else."

"Miss Betty," he says, "I think I will have a second breakfast this morning. And go ahead and bring them some too. You know when they see mine they're gonna want their own."

"You got it, Sheriff."

She moves away and we thank him.

"You know what happens in every case like this one?" he asks. "'Specially when it gets some publicity from true-crime podcasts and these so-called citizen sleuths get involved—the law enforcement agency working the case is accused of either involvement or incompetence."

I nod. He's right. It's a pattern. In almost every open, unsolved case the true-crime community covers, the cops involved are suspected of corruption, coverup, conspiracy, or incompetence. I see it on Reddit and in documentaries and hear it on podcasts. People with no evidence at all hurl accusations at the authorities who are in charge of the case. The same thing has been done in the coverage of Kaylee's disappearance.

"Neither is true in this case," he says. "We've conducted an exemplary investigation."

"But the land around where she went missing hasn't been searched," Blade says.

"Not true," he says. "The morning after they went missing and for several days after, we conducted a thorough search of the properties. And not just my small department. We had help from Search and Rescue, surrounding county sheriff offices, FDLE. We had K-9 units and drones. See, that's the thing . . . these web sleuths or whatever think because they can't just go on private property and search, that there's corruption or coverup. I'm tellin' you—it has been thoroughly searched. Given the exigent circumstances, we didn't even have to have warrants. And the property owners cooperated. I made it clear to them that we were looking for the missing mother and her child and nothing else. If we found a marijuana field or some such, we wouldn't make any arrests. Now, we couldn't just leave it. We'd have to confiscate it, but we wouldn't jam them up over it. They agreed. They cooperated. Just to be safe and because I try to do everything with exemplary excellence, I went to the judge and got a warrant anyway. It's a hell of a lot easier to get one to search open property like that than a private residence. And given the circumstances, we got one with no problem whatsoever."

"So you didn't search the private residences?" Blade asks.

"There are only two for miles and miles and there was no evidence indicating Nora or Emma were inside them. We searched every other structure though—old buildings, barns, storage sheds. They're just not out there."

"That's a lot of land," I say. "And the woods are dense and thick, hard to traverse—let alone search properly. What percentage of the property do you think has actually been searched?"

"That's a good question," he says. "One I don't have an exact answer for. I'm not gonna sit here and bullshit you. If I don't know something, I say I don't know. But my guess is it's somewhere in the neighborhood of between sixty and seventy-five percent."

"Which is a lot," I say, nodding, impressed.

"But not all," Blade says.

"True," he says. "But in all that we covered, there was not a single sign, not one scrap of evidence that they had ever gone out there. Not a footprint, not a shoe, not a phone, not a torn piece of fabric. Nothing. And the dogs confirm what I'm telling you. They didn't get a single scent out there, but they did get one closer to the car."

"What did they get?" I ask.

"We gave them scent articles we got from the car and from their room where they were staying," he says. "They tracked their movements to the edge of the woods—like they were hiding right past the tree line—but then they went over past the car, down the shoulder of the road for about a quarter mile or so then stopped."

"Like someone picked them up," I say.

"Exactly," he says, nodding vigorously.

Betty brings our breakfast—something she does more quickly than she did our coffee—and all three of us begin eating before she even leaves the table.

I notice that we all take the same approach to our breakfast —mixing the eggs, grits, and bacon together and eating them between bites of buttered toast.

"What do we have to do to search the other forty percent of the property?" Blade asks.

He shakes his head. "Nothing you can do. And it's more like twenty-five percent. The owners have said enough is enough. They don't want any private citizens out on their land. And let me tell you this—if we had a hard time accessing those pieces of the property during our searches, what makes you think a young mother with a small child could? I'm tellin' you, they're not out there."

"What if you're wrong?" Blade says.

He finishes chewing and swallowing the bacon, eggs, and grits in his mouth and chases it down with a big swig of his coffee. "Then I'm wrong and I deserve the criticism I've received, but the chances of that are minuscule. Not of me being wrong. That happens all the time. But of them bein' out there."

"So," I say, "the landowners won't let private citizens search their property, but what about you? Will they let your office? Or would you consider getting another warrant and searching again?"

"Let me tell you, Burke," he says. "I'm not opposed to that eventuality. I'm not. But it could only ever happen if we got new evidence that they're out there, and I'm tellin' you they're not. In order to get a judge to give us a new warrant, we have to have new evidence to justify it. And it can't just be that we haven't found them anywhere else. That's not enough. So . . . you find me evidence that they're out there—and you gather it in a lawful and respectful manner—and we'll take another look, but until that happens we won't be conducting any other searches out there."

TWENTY-THREE

"Did you believe any of what he was sayin'?" Blade asks.

We're back in the car headed to the property near where Nora broke down. I'm driving. Blade is on her phone looking up who owns the land.

I shrug. "Some of it. Maybe."

"Sounded like a bunch of bullshit to me," she says. "Polite, folksy bullshit. I ain't sayin' they're out on that property. I hope they aren't because if they are, they're dead, and I'm hoping we can still find them alive. But I guarantee they haven't searched a fraction of the area he says they have. And he's protecting those damn landowners. Bet they make sizable contributions to his campaign when he runs."

"Yeah, I wonder what they're hiding and why he's helping them to hide it."

"Wonder if what he said about the dogs is true?" she says.

"If it is . . . sounds like they got picked up. And based on what Sharon said, sounds like that creepy truck driver could be the one to have done it."

"But then why stop at the gas station at all?" she says.

I shrug again. "Yeah, looks like he'd keep truckin'. But who knows why sick fucks do the shit they do. Maybe he wanted to clean up and create a sort of alibi. The thing with the time is suspicious."

"Yeah, but it could all be innocent and he's just a weird dude."

"Or he could be the kind of killer who likes to insert himself into the case. What the hell was she even doing up here?" I ask. "There's nothin' here."

"Well, wherever she was headed she didn't make it. Maybe she was meetin' someone in Jefferson or somewhere. Maybe she was with someone who was takin' her to his dungeon."

"And what, leading her in his car, hers breaks down and she and Emma get in with him?"

"Maybe," she says, "I don't know. Seems more likely than some kind of killer—serial or otherwise—just happenin' by at the right moment. I mean, what are the chances? 'Specially in a rural-ass area like this."

"You gettin' anywhere?" I ask, nodding toward her phone.

"I can tell you what owns it, but not who owns it," she says. "It's owned by a holding company, so technically Full Sail Limited owns it, but I don't know who owns Full Sail. Gonna take some more diggin'."

The large wrought-iron gate entrance to the property is down a long dirt road, the pine-tree-lined sides of which hold numerous posted signs and security cameras.

By the time we reach the gate, Holt is waiting for us.

He's out of his big black truck and standing just on the other side of the gate.

"The road you're on is private," he says when we park and get out, "so you're already trespassing.

Above the dark shades he's wearing, his thin gray hair rises and falls in the breeze.

"We'd just like to talk to you for a moment," I say.

"Got nothing to say and you're trespassing—doesn't matter the reason."

"We'd just like to set up a meeting with the landowner," I say.

He shakes his head. "Not gonna happen. Now, I really don't want to have to call the sheriff, but if you don't get back in your vehicle and vacate the premises now, I'll be forced to."

I lift my hands in a placating gesture. "Okay, okay. We're going."

"Nothing personal," he says. "Just the rules. You two have yourselves a good day. And like I said before, I wish you all the luck in the world finding that young mother and her little girl, but this is not the way to go about it. Wherever they are, it's not here. All you're doing is wasting time. I hope you have a better strategy than this. I'd hate to think that they're somewhere counting on y'all to find them and you're doing this."

When we're back in the car, Blade says, "That went better than I expected."

"The upside of always havin' low expectations," I say. "But how could it've gone worse?"

"He's very polite and mannerly—"

"Yeah," I say, "but 'fuck off' is still 'fuck off' no matter how mannerly you are when you say it."

At the end of the dirt road, we take a right onto the rural highway that leads back to town.

"Sure," she says, "but if you're the one it's being said to, it's nice for it to be all pleasant and shit. But it wasn't only that . . . We didn't get into any violent fisticuffs and we didn't have the cops called on us, so . . ."

"Well, hell," I say, "my expectations weren't nearly low enough."

"I keep telling you—"

A hard impact by some sort of vehicle on the passenger side crumples the car, shatters the glass, deploys the airbags, and then we are rolling.

We flip over into the other lane, careen into and then over a metal guardrail, and land upside down in a creek bed, black water flooding into the car.

We are held upside down, suspended by our seatbelts, our heads and upper bodies submerged, as the car fills with the murky water.

Dazed and dizzy, I cough and begin to choke as water goes up my nose.

Reaching down around the airbags, I feel for the seatbelt release. It takes me a moment to find it and I can feel myself running out of air.

I press the plastic button but nothing happens. I press it again and again. Still nothing.

And I begin to panic.

I can't see Blade. I can't see much of anything through the dark water, which stings my eyes so badly I have to close them anyway.

I reach over and feel for Blade.

She's there in the seat beside me, but she's not moving.

I grab her arm and shake it, but get no response.

I feel around for her seatbelt release and then I realize what I need to do.

My lungs are burning and I don't know how much longer I can hold my breath.

Leaning over and feeling in the first of Blade's pockets I can find, I grab one of the many knives she carries, pull it out, open the blade, and saw through the straps of my belt.

As soon as I'm free, I turn around, get up on my knees on the inside roof, and take a quick breath.

Then I reach down and cut Blade out of her seatbelt.

Maneuvering around the airbags, crumpled car, and creek water detritus, I get through the missing passenger window, then pull her free from the car.

Dragging her through the creek bed onto the bank, I lay her down and begin CPR.

A few moments later, as I'm doing mouth-to-mouth, she begins to cough and spit out water.

"What the fuck, dude?" she says when she catches her breath. "You know good and well I'm not into boys. Get off of me."

TWENTY-FOUR

"Y'all might be just a tad bit paranoid," Sheriff Jack Bullock is saying.

Blade and I are sitting on the back of an ambulance, an EMT making sure we're okay after we declined to go to the hospital.

Bullock is standing in front of us.

"What do you think it is?" Blade says.

"Simple hit and run," he says. "An accident. Guy panics and runs away. Happens all the time. Could be drinking. Could have warrants. Or maybe on that fight or flight thing he's a flier."

"That makes more sense to you than it bein' intentional?" Blade says. "We had just left talkin' to Holt about—"

"I told you to find more evidence and we'll get a warrant and have another official look, not pester the landowners."

"We just wanted to meet the owner and have a little sit-down with him."

"Or her," I add.

"Or her," she says.

Bullock says, "Well, I can tell you it has nothing to do with Holt. He'd never be involved in anything like that. He's a decent, honest man who just loves the land. And do you have any idea of the timing it would take to pull out and hit you in that exact spot?"

"We do," I say. "Shows coordination and precision and—"

"And some bad fuckin' intentions," Blade says.

"That kind of thing doesn't happen here," he says. "Think maybe y'all need your heads examined. Sure you won't go to the hospital?"

"We look like we got health insurance?" Blade says.

"Y'all look like a couple of half-drowned rats," he says, "but—"

Blade says, "You think a regular vehicle could hit us like that and then just drive away?"

"Now it's a special vehicle?" he says. "Like what? That truck from *Jeepers Creepers* with the rusted damn snowplow thing on the front?"

"It was massive," I say. "All I remember is a big black blur."

"Could it have been a semi?" Bullock asks.

Blade's eyes widen. "It's possible," she says nodding.

"Think about the angle it had to hit us to drive us up onto and over the guardrail," I say. "It's an unnatural angle."

Bullock looks back over his shoulder at the little dirt road that winds around the creek on the opposite side of the road. Because of the creek and the bridge, it doesn't intersect the highway directly across from where we went over the guardrail into the creek. Whatever hit us had to do so at a fifteen- or twenty-degree angle.

"A vehicle turning left or right onto the highway wouldn't hit us where it did," I add.

Bullock looks back and nods. "That's the most convincing thing y'all've said so far. But either way—accident or not—hit-and-run is a crime and we're gonna find the person who did it. Y'all can count on that."

TWENTY-FIVE

I'm playing Candy Land with Alana that night when there's a knock at my door.

"I don't want to go," Alana says.

"You don't have to," I say. "That's not Mommy."

"*Yay*," she exclaims.

Because I play with Alana and she mostly gets my undivided attention, she never wants to leave.

"Let's play again," she says.

"I have to see who's at the door first," I say. "Then we will."

She never wants to stop playing either.

Feeling the need to be cautious or just being paranoid, I'm not sure which, I look through the peephole before opening the door.

To my delight I am pleasantly surprised to see Lexi Miller standing there holding white take-out bags in her hands.

I quickly open the door.

"Grubhub," she says, raising the bags. "Oh, no, your face. Are you okay?"

My face is swollen and bruised from the deployment of the

airbags and I have an abrasion on my right temple—all realities I had prepared her for when I told her about the accident.

"It looks worse than it feels," I lie. "Come in."

She steps in and I close the door.

"I was worried about you," she says, "and wanted to check on you. Figured you might not feel like cooking so I brought you guys dinner. I hope you don't mind."

"*Mind?* You kidding? It's so good to see you. So thoughtful of you to—"

"Hey, Miss Lexi," Alana says. "Want to play Candy Land with us?"

"*Ah, yeee-ees,*" she says with great enthusiasm. "May I?"

"'Course," she says. "Come on."

Lexi looks at me. "Is it okay?"

"Is that a trick question?" I say. "But I have to warn you . . . Alana has never lost."

"Never?"

"Not once."

She places the bags on the counter and hugs me.

I wince at the pain of my right chest and shoulder from the seatbelt cutting into me upon impact.

"Sorry," she says. "What is it?"

"I'm fine. Don't let go. Just a little sore where the seatbelt got me."

"Oh, I didn't even think about that."

"*Gu-uys,* come on," Alana says. "Stop hugging and let's play."

"We're coming," I say. "Just a little longer." To Lexi I whisper, "Don't let go yet."

When we do release each other and she joins Alana at the small kitchen table, I say, "Smells so good. What is it?"

"Thai Basil," she says. "I remembered you sayin' you like it."

"I don't like it," I say. "I *love* it. Thank you so much."

"And chicken nuggets for Miss Alana," she says.

"Can we eat before we play another game?" I ask Alana.

"*Hey*, I have a great idea," she says, tapping her mouth with her small index finger. "Let's eat *and* play."

"That *is* a great idea," I say.

As we're pulling out the food and finding plates, Lexi stops and hugs me again. "I've been so worried about you. You sure you're okay?"

I nod. "Just a little banged up. Thank you."

"How is Alix?" she asks. "Sorry, I just can't bring myself to call her *Blade*."

"About the same as me," I say. "Maybe a little more so. Impact from the other vehicle was on her side. And the reason for her nickname is why we're still alive and kicking."

"Where'd did she get it?"

"The nickname?" I say, lowering my voice. " Because of sexual battery she began carrying a variety of knives and blades with her at a very young age. Don't know who gave it to her. She already had it when we met."

"Bless her heart," she says. "Can you imagine . . . being so vulnerable and so not cared for that you have to carry a blade with you at all times to . . ."

I don't have to imagine, but I don't say so.

"Not the first time I've wished the world was other than it is," I say.

TWENTY-SIX

"I looked into the land ownership you asked me to," Ben says.

It's the next morning and he has just stepped into our office.

"What happened to you two?" he says.

"You should see the other guy," Blade says.

"Is he dead?"

"We were in a little fender bender," I say. "Looks worse than it is."

"I'd appreciate if y'all'd stay in your office today with the door closed," he says. "Some of our clients bring their children with them and I wouldn't want y'all scaring them."

Ben Simmons is a thin, smallish late-twenties man with dark, stylishly short hair whose boyish face and undeveloped appearance makes him look too young to be such an excellent attorney. A fellow survivor, he's the reason we have such a nice office.

"Don't know what y'all are mixed up in, but . . . I'd say be even more careful than usual."

"Why's that?"

"Well, exhibit A, your faces," he says. "And B, whoever owns the land you asked about has gone to a lot of trouble to hide their identity."

"How so?"

"Essentially with an anonymous LLC," he says. "What started as a way to protect property owners from personal liability has turned into a tool for them to hide their true identities, which in turn has led to the enabling of all sorts of bad behavior—like money laundering, being a bad landlord with impunity, and worse. An anonymous LLC is a great way for landlords to keep themselves from having to deal with tenants —especially if they have a property manager. It's a great way for famous or infamous people to conduct business privately. But it can also be used by victims, especially of domestic abuse, to prevent their abusers from finding them. Certain business, community, and political leaders use them to keep a wall between their public and private lives."

"Well," I say, "regardless of the reasons or motives . . . it all comes down to a way of hiding."

"Exactly," he says. "Ownership information remains undisclosed and unpublished to the public. Anonymous LLCs protect privacy, prevent harassment, and preserve confidentiality. And most of the people who use them use an attorney to set them up and be the registering agent, and therefore take advantage of attorney-client privilege. Think about it—a licensed attorney serves as the registering agent. If he or she is served any legal documentation or correspondence, they forward it to the true owner confidentially. And if a summons or subpoena is served in an attempt to identify the true owner, the attorney will attempt to negotiate the summons or subpoena away. If unsuccessful in doing that, they can assert the attorney-client privilege."

"Somebody goin' to a lot of damn trouble to stay hidden," Blade says.

"You have no idea," Ben says. "Florida doesn't have anonymous LLCs. In fact, most states don't. Only Alabama, Colorado, Delaware, Georgia, Iowa, Missouri, New Mexico, Ohio, Virginia, and Wyoming do. So what your guy did was set up an anonymous LLC in one of these states—in this case, Alabama—and is using it as a holding company. That holding company in turn owns the company in Florida, which is an operating company. He owns the holding company in an anonymous state, which in turn owns the operating company here, so . . . the ownership information disclosed here in Florida is that of the anonymous LLC holding company in Alabama. And he did all that to hide his identity from the public."

"What the fuck he hidin' from?" Blade says.

I say, "So it's impossible for us to find out who owns the land?"

"Not impossible, no," he says. "No anonymity is absolute. He still has to have a bank account and pay taxes. His bank and the IRS know who he is. And anonymous LLCs are not immune from lawsuits. A competent attorney could use the subpoena power of the courts in a lawsuit to identify the owner of an anonymous LLC. But none of that is quick, easy, or cheap."

"Well, hell," Blade says.

"Don't despair," Ben says. "I haven't given up yet. I still may be able to find out who's behind this elaborate scheme to stay in the shadows. Just wanted you to know what we're up against and that whoever you're looking for has gone to great lengths not to be found."

TWENTY-SEVEN

"Y'all don't give up, do you?" Jack Bullock says.

We're back in Palm County—this time to take a look at Nora's impounded car. We're standing outside the fenced salvage yard of the county-contracted towing company in the mid-morning sun.

"Did you think we would?" Blade asks.

"Well, no," he says. "But I thought you might take a damn day off after almost meetin' your maker yesterday. Still wish y'all would go see a doctor."

"Looks worse than it is," I lie.

My face is swollen and sore, my bruised eyes won't open all the way, my nose is tender to the touch, and my entire body is stiff and stove-up. Blade is much the same, but her dark skin hides any discoloration. And in addition to having most every ailment I do, she also has some bruised or broken ribs that make it hard for her to breathe.

"You arrested the hit-and-run driver yet?" Blade asks.

Bullock laughs. "Not yet. But we're workin' on it. We'll get him. Guarantee you that."

"What's the story on Nora's car?" Blake asks.

"It has been processed and now it's just sitting out here. From time to time we get those damn citizen sleuths, you know, the true-crime podcast fanatics, sneaking onto the property to look inside it and take pictures and shit. Hell, all you had to do was go online and you could see everything that you will out here today."

"You know how it is," I say. "We'd rather see it in person for ourselves."

"'Course."

"How soon after it was impounded was it processed?" Blade asks.

"I feel like you already know the answer to that," he says. "Obviously, we didn't know this was going to turn into what it has. We get abandoned vehicles on the highway all the time. Figured she'd be back for it soon enough, so . . . it was towed here and sat for a few days. When we didn't find her . . . and I heard that 911 call . . . I asked FDLE to process it for us. I wish we'd've done it right way, but . . . there was just no way to know that . . ."

"We know that," I say. "No one faults you for—"

"The hell they don't," he says. "You must not spend much time online."

"I meant no one who knows police procedures or understands investigations."

"Well, anyway . . . we eventually got it processed. Didn't turn up much, but a few things were interesting. Now, I believe I am going above and beyond to let you two take a look at the car."

"You are," I say.

"But just to show you that I have nothing to hide and that I'm cooperating with y'all as much as I possibly can . . . I'm going to give you a copy of the report from FDLE also."

"Thank you," I say. "That's very—"

"It's mighty white of you is what it is," Blade says.

He shakes his head. "I don't know how to take you."

"As I am, Sheriff," she says. "Just as I am."

"We really appreciate all your cooperation," I say.

"We do," Blade says. "Has anything been removed or—"

"No," he says. "The vehicle is just like it was."

"None of the little podcast pricks have removed anything from it?" she asks.

"Nope," he says. "We keep it locked. None of them—or anyone else—has ever been in it. It's in the section that serves as our impound lot and we've got cameras on it."

"Cool," she says. "Well, let's go have a look."

"Soon as they're ready for us," he says.

In a few moments, the electronic gate, which just looks to be an aluminum-framed section of chain-link fencing on wheels, rolls to the side with a series of metallic creaks and groans, revealing a tall, lanky young man in a pair of gray grease-and-grime-soiled coveralls.

"This way, ladies," he says with a thick Southern drawl.

The bottoms of his coveralls are tucked into a pair of tall, black waterproof boots, which makes him look more like a deep sea fisherman than a mechanic, but as we traipse through the muddy mess of the salvage yard I know why.

Nora's car, an old, faded-gray Buick LaCrosse, sits off by itself in the back left corner of the property marked as Palm County Impound.

As we walk toward Nora's abandoned vehicle, I think of Kaylee's—how long it took for it to be processed, how it wasn't protected, its evidence wasn't preserved, and how it ultimately became a holy relic for fanatical true-crime true believers.

"You can look at anything you like," Bullock says, "just don't touch. Even though it has been processed, we're trying to keep it in as close to original condition as we can. I'll have Stevie unlock it and open it, but look in from the outside. Don't get in it."

We both nod and let him know we agree to his conditions.

The car's interior is worn and faded, its plastic cracked, its carpet sandy and soiled.

Several items are visible in the front seat from where I'm standing near the open passenger door—a pen with a logo I can't make out, a Cloud Nine matchbook, a Footprints brochure, pieces and parts of random toys not unlike some of the ones Alana has at my place, a couple of receipts that are too small and too far away to tell where they're from, a copy of the *Panama City News Herald*, and a plastic convenience store bag with what looks to be an open bag of chips, a Diet Coke, a Diet Dr. Pepper, a water bottle, and a large Styrofoam cup.

Stepping around the open back door, I lean over and peer into the back seat.

Random clothes that appear to belong to both Nora and Emma are mixed in with more toys, a couple of pairs of shoes, two white towels, children's swimming goggles and sunshades, a sticky-looking bottle of sunscreen, and a crumpled cardboard Happy Meal box.

I raise back up and look at Bullock. "Nothing's been removed?"

"Nothing," he says. "Why?"

"Because," I say, "there's no car seat for Emma."

"That's right," Blade says. "There's not."

"Which lends credibility to them leaving the scene," I say, "but willingly—like someone they know picked them up or they caught a ride with someone."

"The *wrong* someone," Blade says.

"Taking the car seat lends at least a little credence to Nora running away—setting all this up to leave her life," Bullock says.

"I've never given much stock to that theory, but . . . maybe there's something to it."

I nod. "It's possible," I say. "We know she had a stalker ex-boyfriend she was hiding from. I mean, maybe an abductor who happened by would take the time to let her bring the car seat, but it doesn't seem likely, does it?"

"No, it doesn't," Blade says.

"Seems more likely she was picked up by someone she knew who cared for Emma too," I say.

"Can't believe none of us noticed there wasn't a damn car seat," Bullock says.

"Easy to miss what isn't there," Blade says.

"Too true," he says. "Still feel like a fool."

"It's nearly impossible to truly run away," I say, "to walk out of your own life without a trace and stay hidden. The resources you'd have to have . . . And to do it with a small child is even harder. And why do it like this? Why come to the beach and set up this elaborate scheme?"

"Yeah," Blade says. "And she sounds genuinely scared on that 911 call."

Bullock says, "Could just be a good actor."

"It's possible," I say. "If she did choose to run away and is hiding somewhere, she had to have help. Whoever helped her would have to have the resources to take care of her and Emma. Of course, it's only been a couple of months. Guess nearly anyone could hide for that long."

Blade nods. "Yeah. No doubt. It's not the short term that's the problem."

"Still think it's the least likely scenario," I say, "but her taking the car seat gives it some— Unless . . . It's possible that Emma was asleep in the car seat and Nora carried her in it. They could be out there dead in the woods somewhere, Emma still strapped in."

"Did y'all crank it up?" Blade asks.

Bullock shakes his head. "Just hauled it here and then later to the FDLE crime lab, then back here. Why?"

"Just wonderin' if it runs or if it had been sabotaged in any way."

"You ladies want me to put some gas in it and crank it for you?" the lanky young man from the salvage yard asks.

"Should have gas," I say. "From where Willie poured some in it on the night of."

"Well, we'll add some of our own anyway," Bullock say. "Would you mind, Tim?"

He shakes his head and walks away.

"If it cranks, what does it prove?" Bullock says.

"Cranks or doesn't crank," she says, "won't prove anything, but . . . it'd suggest shit . . . so it'd be good to know."

A few minutes later, Tall Tim pulls up on an ATV, a gas can and toolbox strapped to the back.

As he pours gas in the car, Blade studies the case file we have.

"Not gonna ask where you got that," Bullock says.

"Good," she says. "Saves me from havin' to say none-ya."

"Looking for anything in particular?" he asks.

"Just goin' back over everything related to the vehicle," she says. "The reports, the . . . I'm comparing the pictures that were taken with what we see now. Shit like that."

He nods. "I gotta say . . . Y'all are better than I expected. More thorough, more . . . Better at this than you'd think."

Blade continues flipping through the file without acknowledging what he said.

I give him a quick nod. "One of our secret powers is always bein' underestimated."

In another moment, Tim has the car cranked. All it took was pouring gas in it and turning the key.

"So," Bullock says, "not sabotaged."

"Yes, it was," Blade says, "just not in the way I thought it might be. Look at this."

She flips the folder to a particular page and holds it open as she holds it up for us to see.

The page she shows us is a photocopy of a receipt.

"She filled up her car with gas at 9:37 that night," she says. "Even if she had driven nonstop until she broke down on the highway where she did, she wouldn't be out of gas. She'd still have plenty—probably a half-tank or more. And we know she made other stops, so she wasn't drivin' around that entire time anyway."

"So where'd the gas go?" Bullock asks.

"Well, it didn't vanish into thin air," she says.

"Someone siphoned it out at one of her stops that night," I say.

"Question is . . ." she says, "did some random thief just steal some gas from her that night or did her abductor do it and follow her until she broke down?"

"We need to retrace her movements that night," I say. "Find out where it happened and who did it."

TWENTY-EIGHT

"The car seat being missing and the fact that someone siphoned her gas to make her break down in order to abduct her seem to contradict each other," I say.

Blade nods.

We are back in my car, which is what we're using since hers was totaled. I'm driving. She's looking through the case file.

"But they don't necessarily have to," I say. "The abductor, kidnapper, killer—whatever he is—could've been known to her and pretending to be her friend. He could've been in the car with her or supposed to meet her and just wanted to get her into his vehicle, under his control."

"Could've been a stranger who stopped by and offered her a ride," she says. "Someone pretendin' to be a good Samaritan would have no problem with her bringin' the car seat."

"I keep thinking of Kathleen Johns," I say.

"Who?"

"The young mother who said the Zodiac kidnapped her and her infant daughter."

"Oh," she says. "Yeah. Could've gone down something like that."

On the evening of March 22, 1970, Kathleen Johns was traveling from San Bernardino to Petaluma with her infant daughter. She pulled over to the side of the road when a man in another vehicle motioned to her that something was wrong with one of her wheels. The same man pulled over when she did and offered to fix it for her. But instead of fixing it, he seemingly made it worse. When Johns pulled back onto the highway, the wheel came off. The man stopped again and offered to help, ultimately convincing her to accept a ride to a service station. He then drove her and her baby around desolate back roads for nearly two hours threatening to murder them. Eventually, Johns was able to escape with her little girl. At the police station, she saw a Zodiac wanted poster and identified him as the man who had abducted her and her daughter. Some four months later, the Zodiac mailed a letter to the San Francisco Chronicle taking credit for the crime.

Of course, there's a lot of doubt as to whether the kidnapper was the Zodiac. The story had been in the press, and it wouldn't be the first time that the Zodiac or whoever was claiming to be him in the letters took credit for a crime he didn't commit. The letter writer also failed to provide any details that could've confirmed that it was him.

"I've been thinking a lot about Kaylee too," I say. "I mean, I always am, but . . . so many things about this case remind me of hers."

"No doubt. Me too."

"It's always there," I say. "The ache, the missing, the not-knowing. Like a low-grade fever that never goes away and sometimes spikes to a dangerous degree."

We ride along in silence for a while—her, continuing to look through the file in an attempt to create a timeline of the night Nora and Emma disappeared; me, blinking and concentrating on the blurry road.

After a few minutes of grieving for Kaylee, I return my attention to Nora and Emma.

"Thing is," I say, "the 911 call contradicts her going with someone willingly."

"Yeah, she's scared and runnin' and hidin'. Still think they're somewhere on that property."

"You been able to put a timeline together yet?" I ask.

"Sort of," she says with a shrug, "but there's still some big-ass gaps in it. I's thinkin' we could start at Footprints and retrace her movement from that night as best we can—and while we're there talk to Willie Cooper."

"We can try, but we already know how it's gonna go," I say. "How long do you think we'll get with him before Stone shows up and—"

"Ted is speaking at some religious-political fundraiser in Texas," she says. "And Stone is with him. I just got a notification."

"Sweet," I say. "We should also see if Winston is working at Cloud Nine when we go there. Still need to talk to him."

"Who?"

"The new bouncer who saw Nora talking to someone there the night she had the interview with Rachel."

TWENTY-NINE

A bank of gun-metal-gray storm clouds hovers over the horizon of the Gulf, blocking out the sun and draining the day of most of its color. The normally bright white sand appears a tepid beige and the green waters of the Gulf look almost monochromatic.

"Storm approaching," Willie says, surveying the expanse of Gulf before us.

He's a tall, muscular black man in his mid-twenties with large, warm, bright eyes, an enormous afro, and an infectious smile.

"Still a while before it gets here," Blade says.

We are standing on the mostly empty beach where Willie has just finished a run. Wearing only shorts, the dark skin of his lean, athletic body glistens with sweat.

Willie takes a good look at my face and asks, "You box or do MMA or somethin'?"

"Car accident," I say. "Airbags beat the shit out of me. Submitted my ass with a new technique known as the seatbelt shoulder bar."

He smiles and then looks out at the Gulf again.

"Sure is beautiful and peaceful here," he says. "Even when a storm's comin'. Anyway, like I was saying . . . I lost my way for a while." He shakes his head and lets out a little humorless laugh. "Lost everything. Just now gettin' back—well, gettin' me back. Not sure how long it'll take to get back all the other. Lost my kids, my marriage, all my stuff. All because of—well, I's gonna say drugs, but they were the symptom not the disease. I could tell Nora didn't have anything either, but unlike me she never did. She was a good person. Really good. She was poor and she was on her own with a kid. That was her struggle. I wanted to help her any way I could. Couldn't do much. Don't have much, but . . . did what I could. Made sure no one messed with them, helped out with the little one, became her friend, someone she could talk to. We . . . we had this—people thought we were like seein' each other, but we weren't. We just had this . . . Just hit it off like we'd always known each other. Breaks my heart for her and that sweet little baby that they're . . . that something happened to them."

The Gulf breeze blows Willie's fro, causing the ends to wave in the wind.

Blade says, "Who was messin' with her?"

He shakes his head. "Nobody."

"You said you made sure no one did."

"Just . . . you know . . . young, attractive woman on her own. Lots of people coming and going at this retreat center. Lots of troubled people livin' and workin' here. Just let it be known for them to steer clear of her."

"Tell us about the troubled people livin' and workin' at the retreat," I say.

"Place in the back," he says. "Sort of like dorms. People off the street with no place to go can stay there in trade for working at the center. It's what I'm doin. But there's some bad characters who come through. Usually don't stay long, but . . . doesn't take long for some fools to do a lot of damage."

"Know a lot of those fools our damn selves," Blade says.

"You think . . . you're desperate and don't have many options and you think, I'll stay here a while, do some work in exchange for my room and board, but . . . They . . . they do this thing where they give you an account and they charge you for everything—your food, your room, and anything else they might do for you. But the thing is . . . they charge you more for those things each day than you can possibly make by working there, so . . . It's like they start owning you. You think it's this great deal at first, that these are some amazing people doing great things for those who're desperate or in need, then you realize that . . ."

"It's a racket," Blade says. "We know all about it. We stayed there a while back when we were kids."

His eyebrows shoot up in surprise and he nods.

"Nora felt stuck," he says. "She was here on the same sort of deal, but she got to stay in a different part of the retreat since she had a kid. She wanted to leave, but she didn't have any money and nowhere to go. She was going deeper and deeper in the hole, but . . . That's why it works—'cause they run it on desperate people with no other options."

"Do you think she disappeared on purpose to get out of the scheme?" I ask.

He shakes his head. "I don't think so. Think she would've told me, but even if she wouldn't have, she was legit scared that night. Somethin' bad was goin' down."

"You think anyone at the retreat center had anything to do with it?" I ask.

He shrugs. "Can't say for sure, but I don't think so. If I thought so I'd be up they ass. You feel me?"

The person who says these last two lines seems a like completely different person from the other.

We nod—and when Willie's not looking, Blade shoots me a look, her thick eyebrows arching halfway up her forehead.

"Did she hang out with or even interact with anyone besides you?" I ask.

"Miss Liz helped her with Emma some when she was free," he says. "Watched her while she cleaned the rooms or ran errands. She's over at housekeeping."

"We know Miss Liz," Blade says. "She was there back when we were. She was real good to us."

"Mr. Van-Allen and Mr. Stone seemed to . . . They made sure she was all right. A young woman named Tami who is pregnant used to come over and ask her questions about having a baby and bein' a young mom, but they didn't hang out and it only happened a few times. A friend of hers from back home came to see her."

"Do you remember her name?" Blade asks.

He shakes his head. "No, sorry."

"Was it Shanice?"

He shrugs. "I have no idea. Didn't get a good look at her. And I could be wrong. Sorry."

"Anyone else?"

"She interacted some with the staff and the guests but not much and only in . . . a professional capacity."

"Can you tell us about the night she went missing?" I ask.

"I had gone for a run and done a hard workout," he says. "I's just kickin' it in my room, reading and dozing a little when she called. I had a hard time understanding her. Terrible reception, man, and she was talkin' ninety miles a minute. But I made out that she ran out of gas and that she was on her way to Jefferson. I went out back to the shed and grabbed one of the gas cans we use for the mowers and weed eaters and took off toward Jefferson—hoping she meant the little town and not some store or person named Jefferson. I tried calling her back on the way there, but just kept getting her voice mail. One time when I was leaving her a voicemail she called and left me one."

"Mind if we listen to that?" I ask.

He frowns. "Sorry, I didn't know this was going to turn into this whole big thing. I thought they'd be back in a few hours. I just didn't . . . Anyway, I deleted it. It was just more of the same. Sounds a lot like the 911 call that's out there. When I got close to where I finally found her car, she called again and it came through. It was worse signal than before—probably 'cause we were both out there where it's bad. As I pulled up, I saw that a cop was already there searching. She told me to stay away from him and she wouldn't let me know where she was. I didn't understand, but I did what she asked me to. I had no idea what was going on, and the people who wash up at Footprints are . . . usually in trouble or on the run. Thought she might have a warrant or a BOLO on her. I knew she was a good person and I wanted to help her any way I could. Didn't want to get her jammed up. Me and the cop looked around for a while, then decided that she had left the area. I knew she hadn't—or that's what I thought at the time—so I put some gas in her vehicle and left the keys in it. After the cop left I called her again, but she didn't answer. I walked and then drove around for a while yelling for her to come out, that the cop was gone, but she never did and she never called me again or answered my calls. Eventually, I came back here, hoping she'd show up later or call me back, but she never did either. I wish I had done more, but I don't know what else I could've done—besides maybe just keep searching all night. Just wish I had known what was really going on. Still wish I did."

"Any idea why she was out in Palm County on her way to Jefferson?" I ask. "Did she ever mention anything like that?"

"No idea why she was out there, but . . . seems like I remember her sayin' somethin' about that area or . . . maybe it was written down somewhere. She was always writing in her notebook."

"Speaking of . . ." Blade says. "Where are her things? Still in her room or . . ."

"No," he says. "Already someone else staying in her room. We packed everything up in boxes and put them in the storage shed in back."

"Could you get them for us?" I ask. "It'll help us find them faster if we can look through their things."

He narrows his eyes and looks out at the slow-approaching storm. Eventually, he begins nodding slowly. "I can do that. I'll do anything I can to help find them. I don't know when I'll be able to do it, but I'll do it. It'll have to be late at night when no one is around. Probably take the stuff out of the boxes and put them in something else—storage bins or something. Leave the boxes so it's not obvious the stuff is gone. And I'd like to put it back as soon as y'all've had a chance to look at it."

THIRTY

"Oh, my God, it's so good to see you two," Miss Liz says. "But what happened to your face?"

Liz Jansen is a warm, kind mid-sixties white woman with longish bottle-blond hair, thick thighs, and an oversized caboose. Relatively flat chested, she has the figure of an old-fashioned glass Coke bottle.

She hugs each of us, holding the embrace for a long moment and patting us with genuine affection.

Blade winces and her breathing changes.

"We were in a car accident," I say. "Looks worse than it is."

"I've read about y'all in the paper," she says. "I'm so, so proud. To bring that little girl back to her mama . . . I sure hope you can do the same thing here."

"We're gonna do our best," I say.

"Probably been better if they brought y'all in sooner," she says, "but . . ."

We are at Pier Park, a large outdoor mall on the west end of the beach, during Liz's lunch break.

Anchored by national chain department stores, Pier Park has trendy and touristy shops, a wide variety of unique restaurants, an IMAX movie theater, and a small amusement park with a giant SkyWheel.

"Y'all mind if we walk around a little, let my lunch digest?" Liz says.

"Not at all," I say.

We walk beneath the covered sidewalk toward the pier, passing a touristy T-shirt shop. Up ahead, live music, a female singer and acoustic guitar playing country covers, pours out of Tootsie's. Tootsie's Orchid Lounge is a bar and country music hall that began in Nashville back in 1960 when Hattie "Tootsie" Louis Tatum, a singer/comedienne with Big Jeff & The Radio Playboys, purchased a bar called Mom's and changed the name. The person playing must be from Nashville. As much as I've listened to and played with all the locals, I think I can usually identify them after hearing only a few notes.

"I don't want to," Liz says, "but I have such a bad feeling about Nora and poor little Emma—the sweetest and prettiest baby you ever did see. It breaks my heart more than I can say, but for there to be no sign of them after all this time . . . I keep wondering what would be worse . . . them being dead or in some monster's basement dungeon. I keep askin' myself which I'd choose—being dead or being raped and tortured with the chance of being found and saved."

Blade shakes her head. "Some fates worse than death for sure," she says. "But maybe if we can find them fast . . . it'll be somethin' they can recover from."

"God, I hope so," she says. "I pray for her every day."

"What can you tell us about them?" I ask.

"Nora was a good mom—especially considering what she came from. Really didn't have any good examples growing up, but she was determined to give her little girl everything she never had—in terms of love and nurture and stuff. She knew she'd probably never be able to provide her with much in terms of material possessions. But she also knew that wasn't what was most important. She was always reading, studying, making notes in her notebook. Never seen someone so intent on self-improvement. I didn't have much extra time, but I tried to help her with Emma as I could—keep her a little here and there so she could work or do things she needed to or just give her a little break. It's so hard being a single mother."

"Do you know where she went or what she did while you kept Emma?" I ask.

She shrugs. "Not really. A job interview, maybe. Or to put in applications. I think she took Tami to get prenatal vitamins and stuff like that one time. She mentioned something about writing or something, but I don't know if she was doing that. I wasn't able to do it much—just a few times—and most of those Nora didn't go anywhere, just cleaned up or sat at one of the outdoor tables and wrote."

"She mention having any problems with anyone?" I ask. "Anyone harassing her or—"

She shakes her head. "Not that she mentioned. We didn't talk a lot. I'd come in and say I've got half an hour or whatever it was, go do what you need to. I did get the sense that she was sort of hiding out here—but from someone back home. Not anyone here."

"What was her relationship with Willie like?" I ask.

"He's such a good guy," she says. "He was like a big brother. He was very good to her. There was definitely a spark there, but I don't think they did anything about it. And it may have been just on her side. I've worked at Footprints a long time. Seen a lot of people over the years. I'm a pretty good judge of character and what's really goin' on. Don't know if it would've turned into something else, but so far Willie was just a great friend to her. They weren't romantic. Pretty sure the idea of that frightened her."

"With Willie or in general?" Blade asks.

"Oh, in general for sure," she says. "She adored Willie. Think it had to do with her previous relationship. Or all her previous relationships."

"Usually the way it works," Blade says.

We reach Front Beach Road by Margaritaville and stop.

"I'm parked back here," Liz says.

"Is there anyone else we should talk to besides Tami?" I ask.

"I don't know that you'll be able to find her," she says. "She left Footprints a few weeks ago. Went home to have her baby, I think. I'll see if I can find her for you. But they weren't close. Sweet Nora just helped her out a bit. As far as anyone else . . . She really kept to herself. Took care of her daughter, worked hard, read, and wrote."

"What about anyone who took a special interest in her?" I ask.

"Anyone creepy or suspicious," Blade adds.

"That's half the people in the dorm," she says. "Y'all know that. But I never noticed anyone watching or following her or anything like that."

I take out one of our cards and hand it to her. "If you think of anything else . . ."

"I certainly will," she says as she takes it. "And you two stay in touch. It was so good to see you."

She hugs us and starts to turn to leave.

Blade says, "What about Ted?"

Liz stops and turns back toward us.

"How much interaction did Ted have with her?"

The color drains from Liz's face. "Um, well . . . Not much, I imagine." Her hands and voice shake, and she appears to be in the first stages of panicking. "He stays very busy. Always traveling. Can't imagine he interacted with her any more than anyone else who stays at the center. I've really got to go. You two take care and stay in touch."

THIRTY-ONE

"So we don't know exactly what time they left, but at some point durin' the night in question, Nora and Emma leave Footprints," Blade is saying.

We are back in the car. I'm driving. She is reading from a timeline she created. We're not sure if the Palm County investigation includes a timeline, but the copy of the Bay County file that Pete gave us doesn't have one—something that matches the general and pervasive thinness of the file and probably the investigation.

"As best I can tell," she says, "her first stop was Cloud Nine."

"Well, let's head there," I say.

The traffic on Back Beach is light—even for off-season—and we make good time.

"You see how Miss Liz reacted when I asked about Ted?" she says.

"I did."

"Somethin' there," she says.

I nod. "Could just be that he makes her nervous. She knows not to talk about him."

"Yeah, or he could be behind Nora and Emma's disappearance."

"Or that," I say.

She returns her attention to her timeline as we head up the overpass and onto the Hathaway Bridge.

"I'm not sure how long she stayed or if she went anywhere else in between," Blade says, "but less than an hour later, she fills her car up at Dodge's."

"Okay," I say. "So she leaves the beach, drives into town, stops by Cloud Nine. Then an hour later she's still in town."

"Right. We know from the Dodge's receipt. We know other things from that receipt too—like she filled up and it was less than three hours before she called 911."

"Car like hers," I say, "full or nearly full of gas, you could drive around for three solid hours and not run out of gas."

"She should've had a half or more," she says.

"Unless . . . Are we sure she put it all in her car?"

She nods. "Store clerk statement and surveillance footage. We don't have the footage, but it's in the case file notes and there are a few stills captured from the video."

"So she was sabotaged—most likely from siphoning. It'd be nearly impossible to put a hole in a gas tank. Wonder why she didn't stop and get more gas when the low fuel light came on."

"Could've thought she had more than she did," she says. "Maybe she was lookin' for a gas station when she ran out—didn't know how desolate it was out there. And she was only a couple of minutes from a gas station. Or maybe she didn't have any money."

I nod again and think about it. "All reasonable, even likely possibilities."

"We only know of one more stop she made," she says.

"Couple of eyewitnesses have her at the Twisted Spoke Saloon about an hour after she filled up at Dodge's."

The Twisted Spoke is a biker bar on the beach. It's rough and rowdy, even dangerous. Not tourist friendly. Actually, not friendly to anyone. And not the kind of place I'd ever expect someone like Nora to go.

"According to them she was only there about a half hour or less," she continues, "so that leaves another hour and half unaccounted for before she's broken down on the highway outside of Jefferson, trippin' her balls off, scared as hell, callin' for help."

"She could've met someone at Cloud Nine or the Twisted Spoke who . . . Or they could've seen her, siphoned the gas out of her car and started following her."

"The hell she doin' goin' to places like these?" Blade says.

"Doesn't fit with who everyone says she is."

"Damn sure don't."

THIRTY-TWO

"I seen her talkin' to that punk-ass bitch Dallas Hale," Winston is saying.

We are in Cloud Nine talking to Winston Fry, the bouncer who saw someone talking to Nora when she was here. We now know that someone was Dallas Hale and that he's a punk-ass bitch.

"Man, I hate that motherfucker," Winston says. "Thinks he's a playa, wormy little fuck."

Like Declan and the other bouncers employed by Cloud Nine, Winston is a very large man, and though he has less muscle than Declan, he's every bit as big if not bigger. Everything about him is thick—his meaty hands, his plump cheeks, even his speech.

"First time I seen them together," he says, "was right out front."

That's where I wish we were right now, but Winston is working the door and has to remain inside. And though the music is loud and the dancers are distracting and the dark environment isn't conducive to conducting an interview, the real reason I don't want to be inside Cloud Nine at the moment is that Ashlynn is working and that's something I'd rather not see. Watching her work the pole is uncomfortable enough, but seeing her work the customers is nearly unbearable.

Two young white frat-boy-looking guys come in and Winston checks their IDs with a small flashlight he holds like a knife he's about to stab someone with. When their IDs check out, he places an orange band around their wrists and directs them to the counter beside him to pay the cover charge.

While he works, I notice Blade checking out the dancers and shooter girls—and doing so with a directness and intensity of interest few of the male customers exhibit.

"See anything you like?" I ask.

"Don't see anythin' I *don't* like," she says. "But if I had to choose . . . that thick dark-haired girl over there with the big, natural breasts and the ghetto booty . . . Could have tons of fun with her."

"Well, maybe when your ribs are better—"

"*Shee-it,*" she says, "when love don't feel like it should . . . you know what we do."

I nod and smile.

"Her fine, thick-ass self can make me hurt so good *any*time she likes."

The house music is dance versions of popular songs, and the constant mechanical pounding of the four on the floor beat is making my face hurt even worse.

"Where was I?" Winston says as he steps back over to us. "Oh, yeah. That weasel-ass bitch Dallas Hale. Girl you're lookin' for come out from talkin' to Miss Rachel in the back and his little douche-ass follows her out into the parking lot. I was out there on the phone. My shift ain't started yet. Ol' worm-ass Dallas has himself a lawn service business and he acts like he's . . . bitch has a riding mower and a weed eater and thinks he's a fuckin' mogul or some shit. He may deal or somethin' too. I don't know, but he always has lots of cash on him and the little dick motherfucker always tryin' to lend a nigga money. He drops a lot of cheddar up in here, but he's also always offerin' to lend you money—dancers, workers, customers. He always sayin' how low his interest rates are, but . . . *shit*, they ain't *that* low. He did his normal thing . . . went up checkin' on her. *'Hey, girl, you a'right? You seem upset. Anything I can do for you?'* They talk for a few minutes. He tried to get her to come back in and have a drink with him, but she said she had to go. He glanced over at me a few times 'cause I kept easin' closer to them. He didn't put no high-pressure shit on her 'cause I was there, but when she left she had his card with her. Night she went missin' she met him in the parkin' lot. Didn't even come inside. He got in the car with her for a few minutes then . . . he got out. She pulled out and I didn't really think anything of it at the time, but . . . he didn't come back in here. He got in his truck and left. Didn't seem like they left together—she didn't wait for him or anything—but . . . they did head in the same direction, so . . ."

"He here tonight?" I ask.

He shakes his head. "That the other thing . . . little bitch-ass punk has stopped comin' in since then. I don't think he's been back in, 'less he came in sometime when I wasn't workin'."

"Thank you for this," Blade says. "We really 'ppreciate it."

"Hope y'all find that girl, man," he says. "She seemed sweet. Be a bonus if y'all bust his little bitch-ass too."

More customers walk in, and as he steps up to check their IDs, we thank him again for the info and start to leave.

"Yo, niggas, you betta slow yo roll," he says. "Ashlynn tol' me to tell y'all not to even think about gettin' up outta here without havin' a drink with her hard-working ass."

THIRTY-THREE

"Oh, y'all too good to sit down and have a drink with a stripper, huh?" Ashlynn says when she joins us at the small table in the back corner.

"Clock's tickin' on our case," Blade says. "If it was you and your little girl out there, would *you* want us to stop long enough to have a drink?"

"Who has your precious little girl tonight?" I ask.

"Probably *you* later tonight," she says. "She's at a little friend of hers from pre-K, but I don't know how long she'll last."

I nod and smile. "Just let me know. Be happy to have her."

At the three-minute mark of Baby Bash and T-Pain's "Cyclone," the DJ fades it down and fades up Usher and Pitbull's "DJ Got Us Fallin' In Love." No matter the actual length of a song, the DJ fades each and every one at the three-minute mark because the customers getting lap dances in the back room pay per song.

Ashlynn widens her eyes at me and shakes her head. "Bro, that's some serious eye contact you're making with me," she says, smiling, amused.

She is wearing very little and what she does have on is so revealing as to almost not be there. I can't look anywhere but her eyes without risking seeing too much of her.

I nod and smile but don't break eye contact.

"You act like we're actually brother and sister or something."

"To me we are," I say.

"You're a sweetheart, but we aren't even step sibs."

"I'm checkin' your gorgeous ass out enough for both of us," Blade says. "Sometime when I have more time, I want you to introduce me to that thick slice of cake over there."

She nods at the dancer she had singled out earlier.

Ashlynn follows her gaze. "Trinity? She'll love you."

"Can you tell us anything about a regular named Dallas Hale?" I ask.

"Not much," she says. "I stay away from him. I was warned about him from some of the other girls when I first started working here, and I listened to them. Some of the other hard-headed bitches 'round here had to learn the hard way."

"Three ways we gain wisdom," I say. "Reflection, which is the highest. Imitation, which is the easiest. And experience, which is the bitterest."

"Exactly," she says. "What's that? Some kind of philosophy shit?"

I nod. "Some kind."

"What was the warning?" Blade asks.

"Stay away from his creepy little ass," she says. "Don't borrow money from him. Don't take a drink from him. And for fuck sake, don't go out with him no matter how many times he asks or what he offers you to do it."

"What does he—" Blade says, but Ashlynn continues.

"Borrow money from him and he's got his hooks in you," she says. "Take a drink from him and there might be something in it that lowers your common sense and self-preservation. Go out with him and you won't remember what a terrible time you had because he's gonna Cosby your ass."

Blade shoots me a glance, her eyebrows arched.

"Wait," Ashlynn says. "Is that who Winston saw her with? *Fuck*."

"Winston said he hasn't been back in since Nora and Emma went missing," I say.

Her eyebrows shoot up, her forehead crinkling. "Yeah, I don't think he has. Wow. Did he . . . Is he behind their disappearance?"

"He's one of many possibilities," Blade says.

"We'll know more after we talk to him," I say.

"Want me to get him to come here tonight?" she asks.

"Is that a trick question?" I say. "Of course. *Can* you?"

THIRTY-FOUR

"Feel like I been set up," Dallas is saying.

He is at our table less than half an hour after Ashlynn had disappeared into the back, where she had gotten his number from one of the other dancers and called him to say she needed a loan.

He's a young, smallish white guy in his early to mid-twenties, who could easily get his clothes from the boys section of the department store. Average to plain looking, he has short blond hair and blue eyes.

"We just have a few quick questions for you," I say. "If it makes you feel better we'll borrow some money from you."

He shakes his head. "I don't know . . ."

Though the incessant thumping of the monotonous dance music is loud, it's not so loud that we can't hear each other. The clients have to be able to hear the dancers when they chat them up and entice them into paying for some private VIP treatment in the back.

Blade says, "If you have nothin' to hide—"

"Everybody has *somethin'* to hide," he says.

"I mean relatin' to Nora."

"Let us buy you a drink and enjoy the scenery while we have ourselves a nice little conversation," I say.

"Never say no to a free drink," he says.

"Prudent policy," I say.

I motion for both the cocktail waitress and the shooter girl.

We order drinks and while we wait for them, we get Dallas a table lap dance and a shot.

Even before the shot hits his system, he shows no inhibitions about getting a lap dance out here in front of everyone. He's in his element and he knows what he's doing. He uses both his hands and his mouth on the shooter girl right up to the point of having a bouncer intervene, but never crosses that line —something I'm sure is not the case when he's with a dancer in the champagne room.

I can't watch, and as I'm looking around I notice Blade is avoiding the creep show also.

The unseen DJ fades "Rapture" by Iio into a dance version of "Rapture" by Blondie. It's a nice move and I look at the mirror the DJ booth is behind and nod appreciatively.

A few minutes later, after the shooter girl has finished her dance and moved on to another table, our drinks arrive, and I raise my glass and say, "To finding Nora."

I can't bring myself to mention Emma to him.

All three of us clink glasses and take long pulls on our weak, watered-down drinks.

"I hope y'all find her," Dallas says. "She owes me money. That's not the only reason. But . . . I won't be able to help you."

"Just knowin' she borrowed money from you helps us already," Blade says. "Gives us insight into her . . . ah, situation when she went missin'."

"How much did she borrow?" I ask. "What'd she borrow it for? How'd it go down?"

"Look, I've got a good business," he says. "I'm very blessed. God has been good to me. I give back by helping others. I provide a service. And I do it for people who banks and even payday loan places won't touch. Charge a lot less than those places too. I saw her in here one afternoon, looking all upset and . . . kind of desperate. I checked on her. Gave her my card. Told her to give me a call if she ever needed anything. She said was fine but . . . as I expected, she called me about a week later and asked if she could borrow some money. We met here—out in the parking lot. Didn't even come in. I gave her the dough and she took off. A few days later, I hear she's missin' and I think, *Never gonna see that money again.* That's it."

"What did she borrow it for?" I ask.

He shrugs. "No idea. But she didn't seem like a druggie."

"How much did she borrow?" I ask.

He shrugs again. "Can't remember exactly. Wasn't much. Few hundred."

"She seem upset? Worried? Scared?"

"High?" Blade adds.

He shakes his head. "None of those things. She was chill."

"What exactly did she say?" Blade asks.

"What they all say—that she'd pay me back in a few days. Famous last words."

"Were those her last words?" she says.

"To me? Maybe. She may've said thanks. Can't remember."

"Did you see her again after that?" I ask.

He shakes his head. "They say she went missing later that night. I tried callin' her a few times after I heard she up and vanished, but she never answered."

"Did the police interview you?" I ask.

"Cop stopped by the house and asked a few questions."

"Did they make you provide an alibi?"

"Just asked where I was that night, that kind of shit."

"What'd you tell them?" Blade asks.

"The truth," he says. "I's at home all night. Buddy of mine came over and we built a fire in the backyard and drank Bud Light and ate oysters. Did shots too. We got fucked up. Passed out. Didn't leave the house until the next morning. For work."

THIRTY-FIVE

Later that night, as Alana watches YouTube videos of adults and children opening, demonstrating, and playing with new toys—something she loves to do—I sit beside her on the couch reading Nora Henri's journal.

We had met Willie after leaving Cloud Nine and gotten her things. Blade had taken everything else to go through and left me the journal and notebook to read.

I'VE GOT to do everything I possibly can for Emma. She's all that matters now. It's up to me to make sure she is safe and well taken care of. It's my job to make her feel loved and secure.

How could my mom have left me? How could any parent ever leave any child? I can't begin to fathom what must be so deeply wrong with these selfish, wounded, fucked-up people. I could never leave Emma. Not ever. No matter what. She is my everything. My reason. My mission. I would gladly die for her, but what I want to do is live for her, give to her the life I never got to have.

Having Emma and being her mom has made me realize more than ever before that my mom leaving me had nothing to do with me. It was all her. Her issues. Her shortcomings. Her lack. I feel sorry for all she missed. I lost everything, sure, but so did she.

EMMA ASKED me today when we're going home. How do I tell her we have no home to go to? How could I have already failed her so miserably? I want to give her everything and I'm giving her so little. How will I ever dig out of this hole on my own? I need help. I need . . . I need a fucking family is what I need. A decent one who helps each other.

MOST OF HER journal entries are about Emma, about what it's like to be a mother, about her hopes and fears, dreams and nightmares, relating to Emma and their future.

I'LL NEVER BE the person I want to be, the mother I need to be for Emma, if I don't let go of and heal from my past traumas. I've got to let go, to forgive and release—for me. For Emma. I don't want to pass the pain I have onto her. But if I don't let my wounds heal, that's exactly what I'll do. I wasn't cared for like I should've been. I can't blame them. They did the best they could. But I have to do better. I can do better. I'm going to break this generational curse.

MY PHONE RINGS and I glance at the screen. It's Blade. I step away from Alana and answer it.

"Hey," I say.

"Found anythin' interesting?" she asks.

"Just getting started," I say. "Going through her journal first, then'll move on to her notebook. So far the journal is mostly about Emma and the kind of mom she wants to be to her. Sounds like she went through a lot of the same shit we did and she wants to recover from it and be a great mom to Emma."

"And then something like this happens," she says. "I know they're probably dead, but goddamn I don't want them to be."

"I know. Really want her to get the chance to be the mom she wants to be and for Emma to have the life she wants her to. Anything in her things?"

"Mostly just stuff that goes along with that," she says. "Self-help books and lots of clothes and Emma's toys. Nora's clothes are all old and worn but Emma's are new and nice. And there are a lot of them."

"If we all just did better than what was done for us . . ." I say.

"Exactly," she says. "And some of us are."

I glance over at Alana, who is snuggled up with her big blue bunny watching her video with a strong sense of safety and security and love and without a care or concern in the world.

"Ashlynn has done it," I say.

"Yeah, but with a village—of which you're the damn mayor. You do so much for that little girl. But I didn't think you just talkin' about as parents."

"I didn't. Meant do better than what was done for us in every way. Leave this shit-show a little better than we found it."

"Should put that on our business cards," she says. "Speakin' of shit . . . How much of Dallas Hale's bullshit did you buy?"

"Less than none. We need to take a closer look at him. What I want to know is how closely the cops looked at him and the other suspects. I called Pete and left a message. I'm waiting for him to call back."

"You already know how much," she says. "Dallas's name isn't even in the file. By the way, who *are* our suspects?"

"Too many to name," I say. "A bunch we don't even know about yet."

"Okay, but who so far?"

"Well, the little prick we're talkin' about," I say.

"Yeah?"

"Willie. If for no other reason than he was out there that night. And he was involved with her—at the very least as a friend."

"I was thinkin' about that," she says. "Someone like Willie or anyone stayin' at Footprints . . . would've had to kill them and bury the bodies. Not like they could keep them—they've got no privacy, no place of their own."

"Unlike Dallas," I say.

"Then we got Ted and Fred Stone."

"They sound like a couple when you say it like that."

"I want a different video, Luc," Alana says. "And some chocee milk. And *get off the phone*."

"Okay," I say, using the remote to select a different video for her. "I'll be off in just a minute and I'll get you some more chocee milk."

"Who else?" Blade asks.

"The trucker," I say. "The boyfriend. The foster family. The landowner."

"Yep," she says, "or it could be some rando who happen to be passin' by or a rattlesnake or motherfuckin' aliens."

"A galaxy full of suspects," I say.

My phone beeps and I pull it away from my ear to check it.

"Pete's calling me back," I say. "Better take it."

"We'll shake some more trees and rattle some more cages tomorrow," she says. "Get that little angel some chocolate milk and give her a kiss from her Aunt Blade. And tell Pete I said fuck the *po*-lice."

She disconnects and I switch calls.

"Hey man, thanks for calling me back," I say.

"No problem. How's it going? Y'all solved it yet?"

"Not yet, but maybe you can help us do just that."

"Hell, if I can do it, I'll solve it myself and get me a big promotion and some nice headlines like y'all get."

"What can you tell me about Dallas Hale?" I ask.

"He's a little piece of shit predator. Why? Is he connected to Nora's case in some way?"

"How hard did y'all look at him during the original investigation?"

"We didn't," he says. "But like I said, we handed it off to Palm County pretty fast. Everything we have is in the file I gave you."

"There's nothin' in it," I say.

"See previous answer," he says. "It was never our case."

"Can you find out what Palm County has?" I ask.

"Probably not without raising some red flags and ruffling some feathers, but I can try."

"Anything you can get us will help," I say. "I really appreciate it. But don't do anything to jeopardize your job. The sheriff over there, Jack Bullock, is pretending like he's cooperating, but he hasn't given us much of anything."

"What is Dallas Hale's involvement?"

"Nora met up with him the night they disappeared," I say. "He says he lent her money and then they went their separate ways."

"He did it," he says. "I guarantee it. Creepy little piece of shit. Can't tell you how many complaints we've had against him. Just haven't been able to make a case yet. He's a serial date raper and a little loan shark."

"If Palm County had investigated or interviewed him, wouldn't they have reached out to your department?"

"Should have. Common practice when investigating a perp in someone else's county. Doesn't mean they did, though. A county sheriff has more power than anyone else on the planet—and the ones from small counties have about zero accountability. But I'm tellin' you . . . If Hale was anywhere near them on the night of their disappearance, he's involved. He's on my radar and I'm gonna get him. And if he had something to do with this case, I'll get him for it too."

THIRTY-SIX

We meet Jerry Melvin, the trucker who called 911 about Nora's car being in the road, at a truck stop near the interstate outside of Mariana.

It's the next morning and we're driving to Dothan to interview Nora's ex, and the truck stop near Marianna is virtually on the way.

Just sixteen miles across the Florida-Alabama line and about eighty miles from Panama City, Dothan is Alabama's eighth largest city with around 70,000 people. Named after the biblical city where Joseph's brothers sold him into slavery, Dothan's farms are responsible for producing a quarter of all the peanuts in the country.

Marianna, a small town of about 6,000 residents near the tip of north Florida, was built on the Chipola River and founded by Scottish entrepreneur Scott Beverege, who named the town after his daughters Mary and Anna.

Jerry Melvin is a short, lean, muscular middle-aged white man in need of a haircut, a shave, and a shower. Beneath his Braves baseball cap, his gray hair spills out in longish, greasy, unruly strands, and the grimy-looking gray stubble on his neck and face is unkempt and out of control.

He's in old, faded jeans, a denim shirt, and scuffed and marred once brown work boots, and he smells of BO, stale cigarette smoke, and dirty hair—even from a few feet away.

We are standing near his truck in the large parking lot, the activity of the busy truck stop buzzing around us, as up on the interstate a steady stream of vehicles whizz by.

"Can we go inside and buy you a cup of coffee or breakfast or something?" I ask.

He shakes his head. "Don't have time. Need to hit the long dusty again. I can spare a few minutes—and they're all yours."

"We appreciate your time," I say.

Before I can say anything else my phone rings. I glance at it and see that it is our client, Candace Landis.

As I'm deciding to call her back after we finish with Jerry, a text from her appears on the screen. *Answer my call. It's an emergency.*

"I'm sorry," I say. "I have to take this. Won't take but a second. You two go ahead and start without me."

I answer the call as I'm stepping away from Blade and Jerry.

"Are you in your office?" Candace says. "I have an emergency and I must see you today. I can drive down and—"

"We're actually on our way to Dothan," I say. "We were hoping to meet with you while we're in town anyway."

"Really? Why are you coming here?"

"To interview Tyler Reece and—"

"Oh, well, I wish you would've let me know. In fact, I wish I was getting more updates from y'all."

"We were waiting until we had something significant to share with you, but we'd be happy to give you regular updates on what we're doing. We just didn't know you wanted them."

"Well, I do. How soon can you be here?"

"We'll get there as soon as we can," I say. "But it will be a little while. We're in the middle of an interview with the trucker who called 911 about Nora's car right now and then we have appointments with—"

"Change them or cancel them if you have to," she says. "Just get here as fast as you can."

I step back over to Blade and Jerry and apologize.

"He was just tellin' me about his rig and the kind of hauls he makes," Blade says. "You can go ahead and start about that night."

"Can you tell us everything you remember about the stretch of highway from about twenty miles before seeing the vehicle to twenty miles after?" I add.

He sort of shrugs and purses his lips. "Pretty typical. Gone over it so many times . . . it's seared into my brain. Flat empty road. Probably emptier that night than most for some reason. Bet you I didn't pass more'n a dozen cars in the stretch you're talkin' about."

"Any of them stand out?" I ask.

"An old van," he says. "Painted like the Mystery Machine from Scooby Doo. Paint job was homemade as shit—probably hardware store spray paint, but it was kind of cool."

"Anything else?"

"Couple of trucks with huge Rebel flags mounted in the back of them," he says. "I'm talkin' flags about as big as the trucks they were in—and the trucks were big, almost like monster trucks. And they had those crazy loud-ass muffler kits on them. Between that and the way their ridiculously big knobby tires sounded on the road they were loud as hell. Sure as shit couldn't sneak up on anybody. Oh, and a car—not sure what kind it was, I'm not a car guy, but some kind of sports car —flying down the highway. I'm talkin' flyin'. I was doin' nearly eighty when he passed me, and he flew past and disappeared down the highway in no time. And that highway is straight and flat. You can see for several miles in both directions. Also saw a black stretch SUV limousine."

"Where was this?"

He looks away, squinting and twisting his lips. "Come to think of it . . . wasn't too far from where the car was in the road."

Blade cuts her eyes over at me, eyebrows rising, forehead furrowing.

Ted Van-Allen often travels in just such a vehicle.

"Anything else? Anything suspicious? Anybody walking or biking or pulled over on the side of the road?"

"Passed a man pissin'," he says. "Wasn't even near his vehicle. Not trying to hide the fact or nothin', just lettin' it stream in the moonlight."

"Anything else?"

He looks away and makes the same squint-eyed thinking expression from before.

We wait.

I have been so focused on what he has been saying that the noise and movement of the semis and other vehicles all around us—pulling in, gassing up, pulling out—had faded, but now all that moves from the background into the foreground of my perception. As does the traffic on the four-lane highway and the interstate passing over it.

Finally he frowns and shakes his head. "Not that I can think of."

"Why'd you stop at the little gas station outside of Jefferson?"

"Pee and stretch my legs," he says.

"Not really room there to park your rig, is there?"

"Not really," he says. "I did what the other vehicle did back a ways. I blocked part of the road. But I had my lights and flashers on."

I say, "The night clerk, Sharon Rolland, said she had to convince you to call 911 about the car in the road."

He lets out a harsh, humorousness laugh. "So I keep hearin', but that's not true. I asked her to do it while I went and used the john. She said I needed to do it since I was the one who had seen it. So I did. No big deal. I don't know if the clerk is makin' it into this big thing or it's comin' from the cops or all the online bullshit, but it's ridiculous. She didn't have to talk me into it. I just asked her to do it while I peed, so it'd be done sooner. Also didn't want to hang around any longer than I had to. Was in a hurry."

Blade says, "Why didn't you just call from your truck when you first saw it?"

"There again, no big mystery or conspiracy. I don't use my phone in my truck. Never have. Never will."

I'm pretty sure he was driving his truck when he took our call about meeting with him, but don't say anything. Best not to antagonize witnesses or suspects while they're giving you information.

"Look," he says, "I've got to go, but just so you know . . . my buddies refer to my truck as the Pussy Wagon. If I told you the number of chicks I've had in my truck—in the sleeper and in the front—it'd blow your mind. I like to fuck and I do a lot of it. And I've never had any trouble gettin' laid. I don't pay for pussy. And I certainly don't abduct young girls in the night. I don't have to."

"Well, all right then, playa," Blade says, a mocking amusement in her voice.

"Hey," he says, "I like black girls too . . . so if you ever wanna climb aboard the love truck express . . ."

"Tempting," she says with subtle but obvious sarcasm, "but I actually drive a pussy wagon myself."

"*Oh*," he says, as if seeing something clearly for the first time. "Really? Wow. I wasn't picking up a dyke vibe from you."

"Then your gaydar definitely needs recalibrating. 'Cause, sugar, the force of my queer vibe is undeniable."

His tone-deafness to Blade's obvious orientation makes me wonder what other signals he misses—like how many of the mind-blowing number of chicks he's had in his Love Truck Express were actually saying *no* while he was hearing *yes*.

THIRTY-SEVEN

"I'm sure you've heard all the shit that's been posted about me online," Tyler Reece says, "but I'm not a stalker and I didn't have anything to do with Nora's disappearance. I care for her deeply and hope you can find her and her baby, not just for their sake but so she can clear my name. My life's been a living hell since all this happened."

"Bless your heart," Blade says.

Tyler Reece is not what I expect. He's smart, thoughtful, well dressed and well spoken. A cross between classically handsome and boyishly cute, he's in his mid-twenties and has short brown hair and deep brown eyes.

We're in his office at *Fake News*, a satirical independent online publication whose mission, according to its website, is to battle dangerous disinformation with wit and wisdom.

"Sure," he says, "I know. Nobody cares how it affects me. And I get it. I do. What I'm going through is nothing compared to what Nora and Emma are going through, but it's not nothing. It's . . ."

"Hell," Blade says. "A living hell."

For whatever reason—probably personal dislike more than anything else—she has chosen to take a confrontational approach with Tyler. She nearly always gets there with everyone anyway, but she doesn't always start there.

"How would you like it if everyone accused you of something horrible that you didn't do?" he says. "That would be bad enough, wouldn't it? But then what if they stalked and harassed you all the time—and felt justified in doing so because they believe you're a stalker, or worse, a murderer."

"Take us through it?" I say. "Why do people believe you stalked and harassed and murdered Nora?"

"Because it's online and people are stupid and believe the weirdest, most ridiculous shit," he says. "There's no restraint anymore, no skeptical inquiry, just gluttonous consumption of confirmation-biased bullshit."

"You talkin' about politics, pop culture, and religion, or your love life?" Blade says.

"Applies to both," he says. "It's an online bread and circuses blood sport, and aren't we entertained?"

"Okay, let's forget about all that for a minute, the opinion of strangers and all the online BS," I say. "What about the people close to Nora? The people who know you both?"

"I made some mistakes," he says. "I did. I went too far, but . . . the thing is . . . Nora is wounded. She's got a lot of baggage from the shit her parents and foster parents did to her. I'm from a good family. A loving family. I thought I could save Nora. That's what I was trying to do. She was scared to let someone really love her. True intimacy freaked her out. I knew what we had was amazing and rare and only comes around so often and I also knew that she wanted it, wanted me, us, but was just too scared to let herself have it. So . . . when she ran . . . I chased her. I'm speaking figuratively here. So please don't take it the wrong way. I thought if I just kept loving her, kept pursuing her, I'd prove to her that she . . . that she could trust me. I thought her trust issues would be no match for my love. So I made some grandiose romantic gestures. Was I too intense? Yes. Was I a little controlling and co-dependent? Yes. But just a little and just for a little while. As soon as I saw it was futile, I stopped and I let her go. Most of what I did was online—videos on Facebook, YouTube, and in our magazine. I wrote and posted poetry for her, wrote an entire article detailing why we should be together. I showed up at unexpected places and proposed. It was all innocuous enough, but people thought it was too much, too . . . And then when she went missing they went crazy with it and read into it all these dark, malevolent meanings. Everything, and I mean everything, has been blown way out of proportion. We never, not once, had a physical confrontation. Never once were the police called. She never felt scared or frightened of me in a physical way. She never worried for her safety. Her fear was of intimacy, of letting someone love her. Now, I still love her, still care for her, but I let her go a long time ago."

Blade starts to say something, but he interrupts her.

"I've got family and friends, bosses, classmates, even exes lined up to testify as to my character, telling anyone who'll listen that I could never hurt anyone, especially Nora, but nobody is listening."

"Where were you the night they went missing?" Blade asks.

"Well, that's the thing," he says. "I don't have an alibi."

"I didn't ask if you had an alibi," she says. "I asked where your ass was."

"Mostly just driving around. Not doing much of anything. I was feelin' particularly blue and lonely. I turned off my phone, turned on some music, and drove around for hours."

"Can't believe people're pointin' the finger at you," she says. "'Cause that's not suspicious at all."

"I know," he says. "But at least you know it wasn't premeditated. If I had known ahead of time that I was going to kill her, I'd've created a better alibi."

"Hard to see with statements like that that people actually suspect you," I say.

"See what you did there?" he says. "You made a statement where the literal meaning is the opposite of the actual one. Are you a monster? Are you a killer?"

"Opinions vary," I say. "But I don't think I'd be flippant or sarcastic about killing someone I was accused of killing."

"You're right," he says. "It's a stupid thing to do. Not all our defense mechanisms are helpful."

"Yeah," I say, "I'd say most of 'em aren't."

"But that's all it is," he says. "I swear it."

"Have the police interviewed you?" Blade asks.

He shakes his head. "No, they've interrogated me. And more than once. If I was lying, they'd've caught me in it. If I was hiding something, it would've been found. Between them and all the damn web sleuths."

It's a good point. He's probably been looked at as much as anyone. Probably more. Maybe a lot more.

"So if it wasn't you," I say, "who was it?"

"I have no idea," he says. "I keep thinkin' . . . There really are only three options, right? She died accidentally—in the woods or wherever, and their remains just haven't been found yet. She ran into a very bad man—a serial killer or someone like that—meaning, a stranger did it. Or, and as I understand it this is the most likely, someone she knows did it. So if it wasn't me—and it wasn't—who else is close to her that would want to hurt her or . . ."

"Who?" I say. "Give us a name."

"To me . . . if it's someone close to her . . . and given the fact that her baby was taken too . . . What about the father of her child? What if this isn't about Nora at all, but Emma? What if what you're lookin' at here is a child abduction?"

THIRTY-EIGHT

As we are leaving, Eudora Pryce, the editor of *Fake News*, calls us into her office and asks us to close the door.

"What's your opinion of our boy?" she asks.

She is a regal middle-aged woman with an air of intellectual sophistication about her. She's thin and wears a sheath-type dress that shows it. She's sitting behind a large, seemingly solid wooden desk that's out of place with everything else in her office—and the building.

"We want to hire him if he ever decides to leave journalism," I say.

"Smart, isn't he? I'm pleased you noticed. But did you believe him?"

"We try to just gather information," I say, "take it all in and compare it to everything else we hear. See what comes of it. See how it fits together and see what doesn't."

"Sure," she says. "A fact-finding expedition. It's very similar with how we develop a story, but . . . surely you formed an opinion as to him and the veracity of his claim."

"I found him convincing," I say.

She turns to Blade. "And you?"

"I'm always convincing."

Eudora Pryce laughs and gives Blade an appreciative nod and expression. "I've looked into you two, your agency, and I like what I see. I've made a decision to trust you—one I hope I shan't regret."

"You shan't," Blade says.

Eudora smiles appreciably again. "Tyler is innocent," she says. "Of both the stalking allegations and having anything to do with whatever happened to Nora and Emma. I'd rather this not get out . . . but he's a . . . bit on the spectrum. Never been diagnosed or anything, but . . . that's why he behaves the way he does. His expressions of love and care for Nora were sweet and . . . well, lovely when you realize . . . his condition. It's why he often turns his phone off or leaves it behind and goes for drives at night. As I say, I don't want this to get out. I'd never want to embarrass him or . . . But I wanted you to know."

I nod. "Thank you."

"There's something else I want you to know," she says. "Something I want to entrust you with in hopes it might help in some way for us get our girl back."

"*Our* girl?"

"Not many people know this," she says, "but Nora works for me too."

"*Really?*" I say, my voice rising with surprise.

"Completely anonymously, of course, but yes. She's a good writer and shows signs of being a good reporter. Have you read our little magazine?"

I nod. Blade shakes her head.

"Read any articles by Regina Wright?"

"That's Nora's pseudonym?" I ask.

She nods.

"Wow," I say.

"What?" Blade asks.

"We just got a lot more suspects," I say.

"Why?"

"Her specialty is corruption and—"

Eudora says, "Her focus is always on the abuse of power. She reveled in revealing it. Local, state, even national misuse and abuse of power—from cops to congress persons, religious to business leaders. She's exposed a lot of greedy bastards with their pants down and their hand in the cookie jar."

"So if someone found out who she really is . . ."

"Thought you should know," she says.

"How likely is it that someone could find out?" I ask.

"Difficult but not impossible. Nothing's impossible to find out these days. Just depends on motivation and resources."

"I'm surprised to find a publication like this here," I say.

She laughs. "In Alabama?"

"In a small town in Alabama," I say.

"Well, we're mostly an online presence so we could be anywhere. I live here, so . . ."

"How do you . . . There don't seem to be a lot of ads. How do you fund it?"

"My late husband," she says, rubbing the large wooden desk affectionally. "This was always our dream. He was from here. Moved us back here when he got sick. We never had much money, but he carried a lot of life insurance and when he died . . . this is what I used it for. He worked in insurance. This was his desk."

I nod. "I'm sorry. How long ago did he—"

"Three years ago this November."

We are all quiet a moment.

Eventually, Eudora says, "It's possible that some corrupt cop or politician or business person found out who Regina Wright really was and went after her, but . . . it's far more likely that someone who felt threatened by what she was working on when she disappeared was involved—and with what she was working on . . ."

"What was she working on?" I ask.

"She was looking at extremism," she says. "In particular domestic terrorism, but how supposed so-called mainstream politicians, organizations, and media manipulate, use, and benefit from it."

"Well, fuck," Blade says. "Why not just paint a giant target on her back?"

"It was totally her choice," she says. "Wasn't an assignment I gave her. She . . . she always looked at the abuse of power, how people in positions of trust misuse and abuse the power entrusted to them and the consequences that has on those they are entrusted to protect and care for. I think it had to do with how she was raised. She was orphaned as a small child and came up in the foster care system and various children's homes."

Blade and I both nod but don't say how well we know what that experience is like.

"Do you know any of the details of what she was working on most recently?" I ask.

She shakes her head. "Not really. She usually wouldn't show me anything until she really had something—at least a good first draft. And I believe she was just in the research phase."

"Did you tell the authorities about this?" I ask.

"Tried to," she says. "That sheriff over the investigation . . . Bullock . . . but he wasn't interested. For all I know, he could be the subject of the investigation. That's why I wanted you two to know."

THIRTY-NINE

When Shanice Wright opens the door, she looks confused and scared and then she bursts into tears.

"She's dead, isn't she?" she says.

"Sorry," I say, "no. We're just here to talk to you. We didn't mean to . . . I'm so sorry."

"I just thought . . . why would you come in person unless it was to tell me . . . to give me the bad news."

Like the last time we saw her, she is dressed to reveal plenty of caramel skin. Her legs look even longer and more muscular, and her taut body looks as if she spends more time at the gym than anywhere else, though I believe that's not the case.

"We should've thought about that," Blade says. "Our bad. Can we come in?"

"Oh, yeah. Sorry. Come in. Imani is napping so . . ."

"We'll keep it down," Blade says.

The apartment is small and sparsely furnished but neat and clean.

We sit at an old metal kitchen table with three wobbly chairs.

"Can I get y'all anything?" she asks. "All I have is water."

"We're good," Blade says as we both shake our heads.

"Have y'all come to give me an update? Have you found anything?"

"We're making progress but we've just come with a few more questions," I say.

"Oh," she says, her disappointment obvious, "okay."

"What can you tell us about Emma's dad?" Blade asks.

"Nothin'," she says. "Nora never talked about him."

"You have no idea who he is?" I ask.

"She wouldn't tell me," she says. "She wouldn't tell anyone. Guarded the secret like . . . I don't know. I couldn't tell if she was scared or ashamed or embarrassed, but . . . she never would say. She didn't put his name on the birth certificate, didn't try to get any child support from him, and never even hinted at who it might be."

"Who was she seeing around that time?" I ask.

She shakes her head. "No one. She was in school, working hard, focusing on her writing."

"You must have some ideas," Blade says.

"Not really. We were still living with Satan's spawns at the time. We were on constant lockdown. Couldn't do shit."

"Then what about there?" I say. "Anyone living there at the time who she might have—"

"What about ol' Harold Landis?" Blade says. "Is he a—"

"He's not that kind of creep," she says. "He's a greedy fuck. Shady as shit. He's way more into money than sex. I think. Least that's always the vibe I got from him. And Nora never said he . . . did anything . . . you know like . . . inappropriate and shit."

"And you can't think of anyone else?" Blade says. "Any other possibilities at all?"

She starts to shake her head, then stops. "Wait. There was a

. . . Wow. If they did . . . they were stealthy as fuck. They seemed to like each other, flirt a little, but I never thought they acted on it. Don't see how they could have. That evil bitch watches all her inmates like a hawk and she's got cameras everywhere. But somehow they must've found a way. Props to them."

"What's his name?" I ask.

"Jesse," she says. "Jesse Strickland." She smiles and nods approvingly. "He's a sweet kid. Probably why Emma's such a good-natured baby. He's young—younger than us. Would've been about eighteen when they . . . If it's him. He's also one of Candace's chosen ones, so she would'n't like that. Not at all. If she found out she'd blame Nora, not Jesse."

"We're on our way to see her next," I say, "so we'll find out what she knows."

"You shouldn't do that," she says. "You should stay as far away from Candace as you can. I mean it. Find Nora if you can, but stay the hell away from her. I'm warning you."

"We can handle Candace's middle-aged ass," Blade says.

"It's a mistake to go see her, but if you make that mistake, don't make the mistake of saying anything about Nora and Jesse. Don't even hint at it. No tellin' what she'd do."

I nod. "We'll find out what she knows without revealing anything," I say.

"But . . ." Blade says, "we're back in the same position as before. It's another dead end. 'Cause if Jesse is the father . . . or even if he isn't . . . he didn't have anything to do with whatever happened to Nora and Emma."

FORTY

"Y'all took your sweet time getting here," Candace says.

If possible, she looks even more matronly and middle-aged than when she came to our office to hire us. The dark circles beneath her eyes are larger, deeper, and darker, the lines on her face, the redness in her eyes, and the hunched tension in her shoulders all more pronounced.

"Sorry about that," I say. "Just because we're working Nora and Emma's case. Really making some headway."

Her huge home—the result of numerous add-ons to an already large home over the years—is disorganized and in disarray, mostly from the detritus of an inordinate number of children. Most of the once nice furnishings are threadbare and worn, and every surface of the dwelling seems covered with a sticky patina of grime.

The culprits of the unkempt condition of her home are conspicuously absent, their runny noses and sticky fingers with them on a church outing to a local amusement venue with an arcade, bowling alley, and skating rink all under one roof.

"Well, it's . . . I told you it was an emergency. Seems to me you'd've dropped everything and come running. I'm not accustomed to employees acting like this, but . . . no matter. Not now anyway."

"What do you mean?" I ask.

"I will no longer be requiring your services and I need a full refund immediately," she says. "No, you know what. Not a full refund. Subtract the fee for the days you've worked so far."

"We're not Walmart," Blade says. "We don't issue refunds. That's not how this business works. I explained it to you when you hired us. We're on this until we find them. We're not gonna stop. We've also already done a ton of work on the case—spent a lot of time and money. We have no funds to refund you with."

She shakes her head, the resolve on her face entrenching even more. "That's not acceptable."

"It has to be."

"We're making real headway with the case," I say. "We're going to find them."

"My mind is made up," she says. "Decision is final. And I must insist you refund my money."

"Who is Emma's father?" I ask.

She stops. "What? What does that have to do with— Never mind, it doesn't matter and I don't know anyway. Just hand over my money and leave."

"Oh," Blade says, "you think we carry it around with us?"

"I don't know what you do and I don't care, but I'll tell you this—if you don't hand it over to me peaceably, my husband will come and collect it from you. And that is something you really don't want."

Blade shakes her head. "They haven't yet invented a car salesman who scares me."

"Well, he should," she says. "Him and the men who work for him. Please, I'm begging you . . . for your sake. Please deal with me."

"We are dealing with you," I say. "And we're working as hard as we can to find Nora and Emma."

"You know what I mean," she says. "Give me my refund now or suffer the consequences. Last chance."

Blade says, "Does your church and your donors know how dangerous your husband and the people who work for him are?"

"Get out of my house," she says. "Right now."

"No, dear," Harold says, walking in with two heavies, both of whom have their guns drawn and pointed at us, "don't make them leave. Not just yet."

FORTY-ONE

Blade lowers her right hand and lets it linger around her waist, just above her black leather jacket and the 9mm holstered beneath it.

I speak to get them to look at me instead of her.

"This how you sell so many cars?" I ask. "Sort of heavy handed, isn't it?"

"My wife gave you every chance to do this the easy way, but you wouldn't take it," Harold says. "So now we're gonna do it my way."

He is a shortish, round, potbellied man, a halo of dyed black hair around the dome of his bald head. He's wearing black slacks and a silk button-down with several of the top buttons undone and a splash of curly gray chest hair spilling out.

"*Hey,*" the heavy closest to Blade says. "Lift your hand up away from your waist. Now."

She does.

The two men with Harold are huge but have far more fat than muscle. They are dressed in all black, including black tennis shoes. As if a uniform, they are wearing nearly identical black leather jackets over black T-shirts and sweatpants.

The heavy closest to Blade steps over and removes her firearm, making the same mistake most do and missing her many blades.

The heavy closest to me motions for me to raise my hands and I do. He then pats me down, obviously surprised and disappointed to find me not carrying.

"Do you have to do this here, Harold?" Candace says.

"Makes it easier," he says. "We got total control of the situation *and* the environment." He looks back at us. "Y'all saved us a trip. We were headed down to Panama City to do this today, but . . . We sure appreciate y'all showing up here."

"Whether you were going to do it at our place or yours, what exactly is *this*?" I say.

"I'm pretty sure my wife already explained it to you," he says. "You're fired."

"We've had clients dissatisfied with our work before," Blade says, "but *damn*. First time they've pulled a gun on us over it."

"Language," Candace says.

"Lady," Blade says, "if that little *damn* was too much for you, you might want to skedaddle on up outta here now."

"The weapons are just negotiating tools," Harold says. "Make sure you do the right thing. Now, my wife asked you for a refund and you refused her. I'm simply asking the same thing and I'm makin' it so you can't refuse."

In her best Brando, Blade says, "He's makin' us a deal we can't refuse."

"Who was that supposed to be?" I ask.

"You know *exactly* who," she says. "It was a pretty good one too."

I nod and say, "Yeah I know *who* it was—Billy Crystal

doing an old Jewish man—I just don't understand *why* you're doing it."

"Man, fuck you, that was an Oscar-worthy performance of Marlon fuckin' Brando."

"Enough of that silly shit," Harold says.

Blade looks at him and says, "Language."

He actually laughs. "We know what you're doing. You're showing us that you're calm, cool, and collected, that our guns don't scare you. Well, good. I don't care if you're scared or not. But know that these guys will gladly put a bullet between your eyes and bury you in the backyard, and not being scared won't change that. Now, it's real simple. Give me my money and you can go."

"Harold, we look like we walk around with that kind of cash?"

"Wouldn't surprise me," he says. "Be a nigger-rich thing to do."

"Wondered how long I'd be in Alabama before somebody called me a *nigger*," she says. "And I ain't never been rich—nigger or otherwise. You see any bling hangin' 'round my neck, rims on my car, gold in my teeth? Speakin' of cars . . . mine got totaled a few days ago—when we almost got killed for lookin' for your daughter. I was hoping . . . with you being the used car lot king of Alabama and all . . . you could hook a sister up with a nigger-rich-lookin' whip."

"My money or your life," he says. "I can't explain it, but the situation is far more serious and desperate than I can say. We'd do anything to get that money back. We have to have it. It's a matter of life and death."

"Well, we don't have it on us," she says, "so what we gonna do?"

"Where is it?"

"Under my mattress at home," she says. "Where else would it be?"

"No way you have that much cash under your mattress," he says.

"Why?" she says. "Be a nigger-rich thing to do."

He looks at me. "Where is the money?"

"She's fuckin' with you," I say. "What's left of it is in the bank."

"What's left of it best be most of it," he says. "Here's what's gonna happen. Teddy is gonna take her to the bank to get the money."

"Which one is Teddy?" I ask, nodding toward the man next to Blade. "Heavy One or Two?"

"She's gonna withdraw the money and bring it back here where you'll be with a gun pointed at that smart mouth of yours. If she gives Teddy any trouble, she's dead. If she doesn't come back with the money in . . . half an hour, you're dead. But —and this is what I want to see happen, sincerely—if she gets the money and brings it back here, you two walk."

Blade begins to stay something, but he stops her.

Glancing down at his watch, he says, "The clock is ticking. You have twenty-nine minutes and thirty seconds left."

FORTY-TWO

"Can't imagine what you must think of us, Mr. Burke," Candace is saying. "I'm truly sorry about all this." She nods toward the heavy holding the gun on me. "If you knew what was going on you'd understand. We're not criminals and thugs."

"Well," the heavy says, "I am."

The three of us are sitting at the kitchen table. The heavy, who is across from me, has his elbow on the table, his gun pointed at the center of my chest.

I'm not sure where Harold is, and it's only a few minutes until Blade and Teddy are supposed to be back with the money.

"I meant me and my husband," she says.

"You can keep telling yourself that all you want to, Mrs. Landis, but only criminals employ criminals and thugs like these guys."

"I save children," she says. "I take them in off the streets, out of the worst of circumstances and love and care for them. I'm a good person."

"Maybe," I say. "Maybe this whole thing is like a balance

sheet and the good you do outweighs the bad, but I don't see it that way."

"I'm not tryin' to work my way into heaven, Mr. Burke. I already have my spot. Jesus saw to that. I do the good I do because I have the love of God in my heart. But sometimes . . . havin' nothing to do with you or your choices, bad things happen, bad people come into your life and you must use other bad people to deal with them."

"Who is Emma's father?" I ask.

"What?"

"Do you know?"

"Why do you want to know?"

"Because I'm trying to find your daughter and granddaughter," I say. "And the way to do that is to look at all the possibilities."

"You're still tryin' to . . ."

"We told you when you hired us we wouldn't stop until we find her," I say. "Those weren't just words."

"But we fired you," she says. "And it's not necessary any longer."

"Do you know who the father is?"

She shakes her head.

"No idea?" I ask.

She shrugs. "Not really. Some suspicions, but . . ."

"Who do you think it might be?"

She shakes her head again. "I don't know. And I won't say who I think it could be."

"Is it Harold?"

"*What?* God, no. He would never do anything like that. He's a good, decent man. He's not a sick—"

"Then who?"

"Let's get her back and ask her," she says.

"That's what I'm trying to do," I say.

"What *we're* tryin' to do," Blade says, appearing behind the heavy and pressing her .9 to his enormous head. "Slowly, place the gun on the table and put your hands behind your back, or the contents of your fat head are going to join whatever the hell that is smeared all over the table."

He nods slowly and complies. I reach over and grab the gun.

"Where's Harold?" she asks.

"Not sure. Teddy?"

"Tied up in the car."

"Please don't hurt us," Candace says.

"We're not going to hurt you," I say. "Why would you even think—"

"The company she keeps," Blade says.

"I just thought you might be angry about what Harold and the boys did."

"We ain't none too happy about it," Blade says. "I can tell you that. But you can calm your tits. We're the good guys. We're not going to return stupidity for stupidity. Where's your husband?"

"We're just trying to save Nora and Emma. That's all."

"Where's Harold?"

"Running around trying to get the rest of the money together," she says.

Blade looks confused.

"Did someone contact you with a ransom demand for getting Nora and Emma back?" I say.

She nods.

Blade nods slowly as she thinks about it, then shoots me a look and gives me a respectful raise of her chin, impressed I came up with that.

"Please let us have the money back," Candace says. "We need it—need every cent we can get. Please let us go and don't contact the police. They said they would kill them if we do."

"All y'all tryin' to do is get them back?" Blade says.

Candace looks confused. "Of course."

"Why didn't you just tell us?"

"They said not to tell anyone."

"How much did they ask for?" I say.

"Fifty thousand."

"By when and how are you supposed to get it to them?"

"They said get it together by tonight and they'd contact us with where to bring it to get them back."

Harold walks into the kitchen. "Are y'all going to help us or get them killed?"

He has a gun in his hand, but it's not pointed at anyone.

"We're trying to find them," I say. "Save them. We're not going to do anything to endanger them, but . . . the chances that this is legit are—"

"You don't think they have them?" he asks.

"Hell no," Blade says.

"Did they offer you proof of life?" I ask.

Harold shakes his head. "I asked to speak to them, but they just said do what they told me and I'd see them soon enough."

"When did they contact you?" I ask.

"Day before yesterday," he says.

"If someone kidnapped them for ransom, they wouldn't wait over a month to reach out to you about it," I say. "Think about how much attention this case has gotten in local and regional and social media. And you have a high profile and are seen as having a lot of money."

"I'll give everything we have to get them back," Harold says, "but I don't want to just hand over fifty Gs to some petty criminals for nothing."

The way both Harold and Candace are speaking and

acting contradicts what Shanice has said about them. They seem genuinely concerned about both Nora and Emma and willing to do whatever it takes to get them back safely.

"But how do we know for sure?" Harold says. "What do we do?"

"It's just money," Candace says. "We give it to them and do exactly what they say just in case they have them."

Harold nods. "You're right. If they don't have them or have done anything to them . . . we'll deal with them later. I'll hunt them—"

The power goes out and the room is suddenly shadowed in darkness.

I jump up and move over to the wall behind me, ducking down and pressing my back against the cabinets, gun up.

The gun feels strange in my hand—the familiarity of an old friend, the discomfort and danger of an old enemy.

A distorted voice in a bullhorn says, "We have night vision goggles on. We can see you. You can't see us. Lie face down on the floor and if you have a weapon put it on the floor in front of you and slide it forward. You have one chance to comply or we will shoot you."

I do as he says.

I can hear others moving around, presumably doing the same.

Then the flash of a muzzle and a deafening gunshot fills the room, ricocheting around the hard surfaces.

My ears are ringing.

Candace is screaming.

Harold is saying, "Wait. Wait. Don't shoot. We'll do whatever you say. Please. Just tell me what you want."

The distorted bullhorn voice says, "Fat boy didn't do what I told him and now there's a big fuckin' hole in his head. Now, do what I tell you or you'll have a hole in your head too. As for what we want . . . We want our money."

"Do you have Nora and Emma?" Candace asks.

"'Course we don't have them, you stupid bitch. We just wanted you to have some cash on hand when we came calling. Now, Harold is going to take a couple of us to get the money while a couple of us stay here with guns pointed at the back of your heads. If any of you move or even breathe too heavily, I'm gonna scatter your brains all over this disgusting tile floor. Understand?"

"We understand," Harold says. "Just don't hurt us. I'll take you to get the money now. You won't have any trouble from us. I swear it. Just come get your money and leave. Let us live. Please."

FORTY-THREE

Lying on the Landises' kitchen floor in the dark, an unseen gun pointed at my head, I can feel my rage rising.

My adrenaline-spiked blood is racing through my veins, pounding in my ears, causing my muscles to twitch, my hands to shake.

Based on their breathing, there are two guys in the kitchen with us—and one of them has severe adenoid issues. His labored breaths are incessant rattling, wheezing, nasally half-snores seemingly designed to be a psychological torture device.

"HEY," the one behind me says. "We said no moving."

He steps over and presses his weapon into the back of my head, his adenoidal-addled breathing directly behind me now, hovering over me like the low rumblings of an approaching thunderstorm.

I lie as still as possible—everything in me wanting to whip around, grab the gun, and shoot him in his face with it, if for no other reason than to shut his adenoids up.

I begin to see colorful shapes in my head, oblong blobs

expanding and contracting as if my brain were a lava lamp. And I can feel myself losing control.

I'd be tempted to try to take his gun away if he were the only one in the room, but it'd be too easy for the other one to shoot Blade or Candace or both while I wrestled with this one for his weapon.

What I hope doesn't happen, what I'm fighting against with all I have within me, is that my rage takes over and I lose control and do it anyway, regardless of the results.

I begin reciting the steps in my head.

Admitted we were powerless over rage and that our lives had become unmanageable. Came to believe that a power greater than ourselves could restore us to sanity. Made a decision to turn our will and our lives over to the care of God as we understood God. Made a searching and fearless moral inventory of ourselves. Admitted to God, to ourselves, and to another human being the exact nature of our wrongs.

I focus on my breathing, which I slow and deepen.

Don't do it. Let go and relax. Let the tension melt out of your body. No good can come from an anger episode. You'll just get people killed. And some of them will be the wrong people.

"Why're you breathing like that?" the guy closest to me says.

The other guy from the opposite side of the room says, "Nigga, your ass got some nerve talkin' 'bout anybody else's breathin'."

"*Ha . . . ha,*" he says without humor. "Fuck you."

"Man, just chill. Nobody's movin'. They got to breathe. What we care how the fuck they do it?"

I try to remember everything I can about the voices—approximate ages, accents, dialect—so I might be able to identify them later.

In another moment, Harold and the other man reenter the room.

"Okay, let's go," the distorted bullhorn voice says. "Count to one thousand slowly before you get up or call the police. Understand? If you call them before then, we will come back and kill all of y'all—including all the fuckin' orphans. Understand? That's not an idle threat. Don't test me. And Harold . . . you fucked over the wrong people."

A shot rings out. A body drops to the floor. And Candace screams and begins to cry as the men rush out of the room.

FORTY-FOUR

"What a mess," Effren Daniels says. "So glad the children weren't home."

"Pretty sure that was by design," Blade says.

Effren Daniels is a thirty-something African American investigator with the Houston County Sheriff's Office. Immaculately groomed and stylishly dressed, he's tall and skinny with long, thin, tapered fingers.

We are sitting in his unmarked outside of the Landises' house as Crime Scene continues to process the house and the property around it.

He interviewed us earlier individually, then called Pete Anderson of the Bay County Sheriff's Office to check us out.

We've all been kept separate, so I'm not sure where Candace and Terry are, but they're no longer here. Harold's and the other heavy's bodies had just been taken away.

"You think they knew this was goin' down tonight?" Effren asks.

Blade shrugs. "Not sayin' that exactly, but they knew they

were gathering the money and waiting for instructions . . . and they had to figure they'd have to get rough with us."

He nods. "That fits. And y'all got the sense that they thought they were payin' a ransom for their foster daughter and granddaughter?"

We both nod and say we did.

"And as far as you could tell . . . the victim did everything they asked and they still shot him?"

"Yep," Blade says.

"Everything they said and did made it seem like this had nothing to do with Nora and Emma," I say. "Like they were just using their disappearance to stage a robbery. Seemed personal with Harold. Told him he fucked over the wrong people before they executed him."

Effren nods and seems to think about it. "He's in a shady business with shady people and carries it out in a shady way. People think he owns all these lots, but he doesn't. He sets people up in business and takes an exorbitant amount of the profits while also charging high interest on the loan to start the business. A lot of the lots go out of business, but Harold always does okay on the deals. Just shifts the cars to another lot he sets somebody else up in. Lot of people feel like he's done them wrong. And from what I can tell, he has."

"Sounds like to me this was a robbery and a hit," I say. "Maybe the hit part was in the spur of the moment or maybe it was planned, but . . . someone told him they had his daughter and granddaughter and wanted a ransom so he'd gather the money and have cash on hand when they came to rob him. Did they steal anything else?"

He nods. "Some jewelry, coins, and bonds that were also in the safe. But . . . get this. Man like Harold, business he's in, way he does things . . . got to be paranoid, right? He had hidden cameras everywhere. We got most everything until the power went out—including the vehicle and shots of all three guys before they put on their night vision goggles and shit. They'll be in custody inside a week. Probably a lot sooner."

"If I'd've known that," I say, "I could've saved myself a lot of effort listening to their breathing, accents, dialect, and voice types."

"Y'all know who they are?" Blade asks.

He nods. "Recidivists with rap sheets as long as my . . ." He glances sheepishly at Blade. "As long as something very long. They're exactly who we'd expect to pull something like this. The question is . . . who hired them to do it and how long will it be before they give them up."

"The second part of that question is easy," I say. "Not long."

"True," he says. "But no matter who the answer to the first part of the question is . . . I'd be shocked if it had anything to do with the disappearance of Nora and Emma, so y'all better keep lookin' hard as you can for them."

FORTY-FIVE

I've just gotten out of the shower and poured myself a drink when there's a knock on my door.

It's late and Ashlynn isn't working tonight so she has Alana, and I wonder who it is.

It has been over two full days since I've heard from Lexi, and I hope but seriously doubt it's her.

Leaving my drink on the kitchen counter, I walk over and open the door. Lexi is standing there in her work clothes looking tired and somewhat sad.

"Come in," I say. "Are you okay?"

She nods as she walks in, but her expression contradicts it.

"Would you like a drink?" I ask. "I just made me one."

"Sure," she says. "Whatever you're having is fine."

She drops onto the couch while I go to the kitchen and pour her a black cherry cider in a mason jar like mine.

"What's going on?" I ask. "You seem—"

"I'm just exhausted," she says. "Long, tough day at work."

"Sorry to hear that," I say as I hand her the drink and sit on the coffee table in front of her.

I hold up my glass and she clinks it without meaning it.

We both take a few sips in silence.

"I was hoping it would be you," I say, "but I didn't think it would be. Figured when I didn't hear from you the past few days I wouldn't again—I mean, not like this."

She frowns. "Yeah, sorry," she says. "I wanted to do this in person. But I should've texted or somethin'. Sorry."

I want to ask her *Do what in person?* But I know.

"How was your day?" she asks. "How are you?"

I tell her.

"Well, damn," she says. "Your day was a fuck-ton more stressful and eventful than mine. Shit. That's so . . ."

"If it had gone just a little different," I say, "I wouldn't've been here to answer the door tonight. And you wouldn't have to do what you're going to do in person."

She nods slowly and frowns again. "I'm very glad you were. Even though I don't want to be doing this. I'm tired . . . I am, but . . . it's the weight of this . . . that's more of . . ."

"The weight of us or of what you're about to do to us?" I ask.

"Both. Actually."

"Well, I appreciate you not just ghosting me. Means a lot that you came to do it in person."

"I . . . I don't want to be doing it. I . . . It surprises me just how much. But . . . as much as I'd like to see you, to . . . see where this might go . . . I can't. I wish things were different. Been wishin' nothin' but that, but all those wishes haven't changed anything. I'm not allowed to see you. And even if I had a different job and I was allowed to . . . I just think . . . given your choices . . . it's not going to be long before you're back inside. That breaks my heart to say, but . . . I truly believe it. Think about tonight. If the cops in Dothan had handled it a different way or if you had had to fight or kill those guys—I could be here violating you back to prison instead of . . ."

I nod slowly and give her an understanding expression. "I know. And I understand why you have to do what you're doing. I really do."

"And it's not just getting sent back to prison to finish out your sentence," she says. "It's not just all the wasted time and potential and life. It's all that can go wrong in there. It's a dangerous place. You could get killed. You could get hepatitis or some other horrible disease. You could lose your temper and beat up somebody and get more and more time added to your sentence."

"I know. I don't want to go back. Ever. I don't. And I'll do everything I can not to. Everything. And as far as me and you . . . I wish things could be different, but . . ."

"I really feel like I need to get you reassigned to another probation officer," she says, "but it's going to be hard to do without making it look like you did something inappropriate. And I also don't like who they'd assign you to. He's very quick to violate offenders back to prison. You wouldn't last any time at all."

"I promise you I won't be a problem," I say. "Please don't put me in a situation where . . . I'll act as if we've never exchanged a single word not about my custody. Please. I can't go back. I can't."

"I'm going to do my best to take care of you, but . . . when I see how you're acting, the chances you're taking . . . it makes me wonder why I'm tryin' so much harder than you to keep you out of prison."

"I'll do better," I say. "I will. I'll be more cautious. I had no idea what we were walkin' into tonight."

"That's the nature of that business."

"I know," I say, "but I can't abandon Blade and we can't

stop looking for Kaylee. Or Nora and Emma. I'll figure out a way to do better. I will."

She shakes her head and sighs. "You break my heart," she says. "I care about you. I can't stand here and watch you sabotage your own life."

"I don't think that's what I'm doing," I say, "but I certainly understand why you can't . . . move forward with anything. But . . . please don't forget . . . we haven't really done anything yet. Not much anyway."

"You're right," she says. "I've crossed a few lines, but haven't gone *too* far over them. This has mostly to do with how I feel and what I want."

"I think it's important that we keep that in mind," I say. "I think the guilt and regret you feel aren't commensurate with what you've actually done."

"I've just never done anything like this and I never thought I would," she says. "This is first day of training stuff—never get involved with one of your probationers. Not in any way. I crossed a line I didn't think I was capable of crossing."

"But like you said . . . you didn't go very far across it. And now you're shutting it down, so . . ."

"You're right," she says. "I've got to remember that and trust that everything will be okay."

"You can trust me," I say, standing. "I'll only ever do good by you. You have nothing to fear from me, so don't waste any time worrying about something that's not going to happen."

She seems hesitant to do so, but eventually stands too. "I'm gonna do my best not to. I do feel I can trust you."

My heart is hurting. I feel sad and disappointed and more alone than I did just a short while ago. I walk her to the door, not wanting to prolong this any longer.

I open the door and she steps out. "Are you parked close by?"

She nods and gestures to her car, which is not far away. "Right there."

"Take good care of yourself," I say. "From now on when I see you—no matter where it is—I'll be nothing but a professional probationer."

"I feel like I'm making a huge mistake," she says.

She then turns and kisses me. What starts out as a kiss goodbye turns into a long, intense kiss that includes a passionate embrace.

When the kiss is concluded we step back from each other, and breathlessly, wordlessly she stumbles to her car.

As she drives away, I step back inside and close the door.

FORTY-SIX

"What's wrong with you?" Blade asks.

We're in our office the next morning waiting for Ben, who had texted us to say he had news about the property Nora's remains are believed to be on.

I shrug. "Nothin'. Just tired."

"I've seen you *just tired* plenty," she says. "This is more than that. This is either weight of the world or girl trouble."

"Weight of the world?"

"You know how you get when you read too many newspaper articles."

"Have you noticed the state of the world?" I say, in part to try to distract her from the fact that it is, in fact, girl trouble that has me down. "The west is on fire. The east is flooded. Superstorms are a common occurrence. Civility is out. Conspiracy theories are in. Democracy is dying—everywhere, including here at home. Fascism is fashionable. Facts are called fake news. Science is suspect. Ignorance has been weaponized. The worst of us are doing truly horrific things—with the support of hordes of sycophants. We live in a world of ideological echo chambers that filter out all but the most blatantly biased. People are suffering and dying in unprecedented ways and numbers, and no one gives a fuck."

"So you and Lexi broke up?"

"We were never anything that requires a breakup," I say.

"But whatever y'all were, y'all ain't no more?"

I nod.

"I know you don't want to hear this, but . . . that's the best possible outcome of that particular self-destructive walk on the wild side."

"Have no desire to talk about it," I say. "Where is Ben?"

"You need anythin', you let me know," she says. "My recommendation is we go out and get you laid as soon as possible."

Mercifully, Ben walks through our open door.

"What's wrong with you?" he asks when he looks at me. "State of the union or state of the heart?"

"*See?*" Blade says.

"What've you got for us?" I ask.

"Nothing good," he says.

"Let's have it," Blade says.

"It's hidden very well—through a series of different corporations and organizations and holding companies—but . . . bottom line . . . the land is owned by a kind of religious-political action group. Separation of church and state is a fuckin' myth. This group, the Tree of Life and Liberty, is into all sorts of activities. They have a think tank, grassroots political support systems for the candidates they choose, conferences and conventions—some more political, some more religious, but always a mixture of both—an online network, a weekly email, a podcast, a YouTube Channel, a fundraising machine like you can't imagine, and various worldwide outreach programs that support their geo-religious-political cases all over the globe."

"Sounds like they're pretty damn public," I say. "Why go to so much trouble to hide their ownership of that piece of land?"

"They have very definite public and private sides—and coinciding activities—and like so many dark money political pacts, they hide who's really behind everything even in their public and visible activities."

"Interesting," Blade says.

"It gets more so," he says. "The organization has regional chapters. It's the regional chapter that manages this particular piece of property, and its many board members and officers include the previous and current mayor of Panama City, at least two Bay County commissioners, several wealthy businessmen in town, two judges, the head of Footprints in the Sand, Theodore Van-Allen, and Jefferson Chief of Police, Jack Bullock."

"Fuck me sideways," Blade says.

"Once I found out who owned it," Ben says, "I was able to take a closer look at the landowners and what they're up to. And I found out what may be the real reason they want their identity concealed. Every group has a spectrum of ideology, involvement, etc. Well, this group has some true believer extremists like the kind who stormed the Capitol. The heavily armed kind who use intimidation and force and violence in the name of their so-called righteous cause. The best I can tell, this piece of land is the meeting place, training ground, and head-quarters for a very well-funded and well-armed militia."

FORTY-SEVEN

"Remember what Nora's editor at *Fake News* said," I say.

"Who? Oh, yeah, Eudora somebody."

"Pryce," I say. "Nora was working on stories about political extremism. Her notebook confirms that. I don't think it was an accident she was staying at Footprints and that she went out to that piece of property."

"Ted had Fred Stone kill her because she was going to uncover his involvement in nefarious neo-Nazi militant extremism?"

I shrug. "Not sayin' that exactly, but . . . working on this story could've gotten her killed. Not sure I buy Stone as a hitman."

"I'm not sellin' him as a hitman," she says. "I'm just sayin' I think we just figured out what happened to her and who's responsible. These are weekend warriors playin' soldier for a cause. Offin' a poor mixed girl threatenin' them would be an honor."

"You'd think Emma would give them pause," I say.

"Yeah, but . . . what are the chances?" She drifts off a

moment, shaking her head. "What do we do with somethin' like this?"

"I've been wondering that too," I say. "We can't take it to the Palm County sheriff. FDLE could do an investigation, but . . . I don't think they will on what we have."

A Florida sheriff is the chief law enforcement officer in his county. There is no authority higher except for we the people at the ballot box. However, if a sheriff is involved in criminal activity, FDLE—the state cops—can investigate and the governor can remove and replace the sheriff if need be, but there's a high threshold for anything like that to ever be done, and it is very rare.

"This just jumped way above our pay grade," I say. "It's so much bigger than anything we can do about it."

"We need more evidence so we can turn it over to FDLE," she says. "I think we've got to sneak onto that land and—"

"We'd get caught almost immediately. So many cameras and they watch it so closely. And even if we didn't, which we would, do you know how long it'd take the two of us to search it? We're talkin' months."

"*Fuck*," she says. "How come they holdin' all the cards?"

"Who? The rich and powerful?"

"*Fuck.*"

"Wait," I say. "There might be a way to . . ."

"What? What is it?"

I start to say something else but stop as I glance at an incoming text. And then another. And then another.

There on my screen, from a number I don't recognize, are photos of me and Lexi on my doorstep in various stages of making out—touching tenderly, embracing, kissing passionately.

"What is it?" Blade asks.

I show her.

"*Goddamnit*, Burke," she says. "I told you, didn't I? *Fuck*. Who they from?"

"Don't recognize the number," I say. "Probably a burner. No message so far. Just the images."

"The images *are* the message," she says.

Before I realize what I'm even doing, I hurl my phone at the far wall, jump up and begin knocking things over and breaking things.

Within a matter of minutes, I have wreaked havoc on our office.

There's a knock at the door, which I didn't even know was closed, and a voice on the other side asks if everything is okay.

"We're fine," Blade says. "Everything is under control. Give us a few minutes, but everything's okay."

Blade walks over to where I'm sitting on the floor shaking.

"You back?" she asks.

"Huh?" I ask, looking up at her.

I glance at the door.

"I jumped up and closed and locked it when you started," she says.

"Sorry," I say.

"Tell that to your cell phone," she says.

I follow her gaze over to the far wall where about a quarter of my phone is sticking out of the painted Sheetrock.

FORTY-EIGHT

"What the hell, man?" Ben is saying.

"Sorry," I say. "I . . ."

"I'm sorry," he says, "but if anything like that happens again . . . y'all are out."

"It won't happen again."

Ben, Pete, Blade, and I are at lunch at Little Village just off Beck Avenue in St. Andrews. We are sitting beneath the palapa, the huge, open-sided thatched roof covering out back on the water, eating fish and shrimp tacos, the breeze blowing in off the bay providing a pleasant outdoor atmosphere.

It feels like an intervention.

Little Village is a cool place with a great vibe—an island food restaurant, a beer and wine bar, a live music venue, and a shop featuring fair-trade, eco-friendly gifts and clothes from little villages all around the world.

"We all know that's not true," Blade says. "But we'll cross that bridge when we burn it."

"I'm working my ass off," I say. "I'm doing better."

"You are," she says. "No question. And who knows . . .

maybe it won't happen again inside there. Just sayin' we have bigger shit to deal with right now."

Ben remains silent, a frown on his face.

Pete says, "Are y'all payin' today or did your client take all his money back?"

"We're payin'," Blade says. "What I look like? A mother-fuckin' ATM? Didn't let that bitch anywhere near our money. Sliced his ass up and took his little gun long before we ever made it to the bank."

"Then I think I'll have seconds," he says.

"Finish firsts first," she says. "And earn them by helpin' us out."

"With what?"

"With what to do next," she says.

"Nothin' you can do," he says. "You can't get on that land without more evidence and if there is any evidence it's on that land. Classic catch-22."

"Got to be somethin' we can do," I say.

"Let me think about it for a minute," Pete says.

We all eat while Pete thinks. Pete eats too, and I suspect he's doing more eating than thinking.

"Okay," he says. "I know what you can do. You can get me more tacos."

"I'm'a stick my boot up your taco," Blade says.

"Way I see it," he says, "you can take what you have to FDLE. If you get it to the right person, they may look into it, but . . . the problem is you won't be giving them enough evidence to really do anything. They won't be able to get a warrant to search the property—not with what you have."

"So we've got to keep diggin' for evidence," Blade says.

"Sure," he says, "but it's gonna be hard to find."

"Another option would be to take what you have to the media," he says. "Hope a reporter will do some digging, run some stories, bring enough attention that law enforcement will have to get involved. 'Course they could just kill the new reporter like they did the other one."

Ben says, "The laws in this country are set up to protect the innocent, but they wind up protecting the guilty more. Far more."

"They protect the rich and powerful," I say. "The entire system does."

"But only for so long," Pete says. "Almost always catches up with them."

"Takes way too long," I say. "And I wonder how many it actually catches up with. Bet it's a much smaller percentage than any of us want to think."

"I know it is," Blade says. "Fuckin' hate feelin' so powerless and little."

FORTY-NINE

Alana has quite a selection of entertainment options at my place—dolls, games, action figures, Barbies, castles and houses, balls, kids-classroom-type musical instruments, and lots of books—and though we most often play make-believe using our imaginations, I like for her to be surrounded by the comforting and familiar.

I'm playing the triangle and she's playing what she calls the shakaracas when there's a knock on my door.

When I set my instrument down on the coffee table, she stops playing too.

"No interest in being a one-man band?" I ask.

She doesn't answer. Instead, she grabs a crayon and returns to a coloring book she had abandoned about an hour before.

I open the door to see Lexi standing there looking haggard, her eyes red and face puffy from crying.

Before either of us says anything, a large black man in a navy blue suit steps from the side and looks menacingly at me.

Stepping out onto the stoop with them, I pull the door closed behind me. I look at Lexi in shock. "What the fuck?"

"Why are you doing this?"

"Doing what?"

"Let's step inside," the man with her says.

"I'm babysitting my four-year-old niece," I say. "Please don't involve her in this. Let's stay out here."

"What do you want?" Lexi asks.

"Just to keep her safe," I say. "Whatever y'all came to do, you can do out here."

"No, I mean why did you send me the pictures?" she says.

I shake my head and frown. "I didn't send you any pictures," I say. "I'd never do anything like that. If it's the same pictures I was sent, then I couldn't've taken 'em. I'm *in* them."

"I figured your partner did it so y'all could blackmail me," she says.

"I would never do anything like that," I say. "Neither would she."

"I didn't think so, but when you wouldn't answer my calls or respond to my texts . . ."

"I threw my phone through the wall when I got the pictures," I say. "Got a friend comin' by in a few to replace my screen. 'Til then my phone is useless. You really thought I sent those to you?"

"No. Not at first, but when you wouldn't respond I went a little crazy. I didn't want to believe it. But then I just freaked out and went a little nuts."

"I know you don't know me that well," I say. "And I know I'm an ex-con, but . . . apart from my tendency to lose my temper and do damage while in a rage state, the only harm I practice is self-harm. When I get my phone fixed I can show you the—"

"Can I take a look at your phone now?" the man asks.

I reach back and open the door just wide enough for me to

look in and check on Alana. She's coloring and having a conversation with herself. I leave the door cracked.

I slowly pull my phone out, which is in my pocket out of habit, and hand it to him.

He examines it closely, then hands it to her. She looks at it quickly, then hands it back to me.

"I'm sorry for thinking what I did and for showing up here like this with him," she says. "But when I couldn't reach you, all I could think of was how much more these photos could hurt me than you. Worst that'll happen to you is you'll be assigned to another probation officer. I'll lose my job and my career. I panicked and I'm sorry."

"I understand," I say. "I'm sorry I lost it and broke my phone. Maybe if you had known me better or longer you'd've known I could never do anything like that, but . . . given everything . . . I can certainly see how you could jump to that conclusion. I just wish you'd've asked me instead of—"

"I tried," she says. "Many, many times."

I nod and frown. "Well, I need to get back in and check on Alana."

"Who could've done this?" she asks.

"Don't know," I say, "but I plan to find out."

FIFTY

Later that night, with Ashlynn and Alana sound asleep in my bed and me tossing and turning and overthinking everything on my couch, Pete calls.

My phone has been repaired for a few hours—long enough for me to listen to and read Lexi's original voicemails and texts and her more recent apologetic ones. So far I have only responded with a text that said: *It's over now and all good. No need to keep apologizing. Just let it go.*

"How fast can you get downtown?" Pete asks.

"Fast," I say. "What's up?"

"Tell you when you get here. Come to the parking lot behind the old Fiesta."

"On my way."

"And see if you can reach Blade," he says. "I didn't have any luck."

I jump back into my jeans, throw on my T-shirt, slip into my shoes, grab my keys, and am out the door in under a minute.

I take 9th to Foster to Beach Drive, calling Blade as I do. In less than six minutes, I am climbing out of my car downtown.

Like the streets I've taken to get here, downtown Panama City is empty, appearing abandoned.

When I pull in behind the old Fiesta, I see a Panama City PD patrol car with its lights flashing, a black Ford F-150, and Pete's unmarked.

The Fiesta and the Royale Lounge across the brick courtyard from it was the gay bar back in the day and the best bar in town. Now, only the courtyard and the Royale building remain, and it's a glassblowing shop called Hot Glass.

By the time I park and get out of my car, Pete is standing there.

"Did you get Blade?" he asks.

I shake my head.

"Me either."

"What's going on?" I ask.

"PCPD friend of mine pulled over Dallas Hale," he says. "He's got an unconscious nearly underage girl in his truck, all sorts of illegal drugs, and he's over the limit. Basically he's fucked. He's desperate and motivated to talk. Figured I'd give you and Blade a chance to talk to him before we book him."

"Thanks man. I really appreciate that."

"You ready?" he asks. "Can't wait any longer for Blade."

I nod. "Let's do it."

The night is quiet and cool with only a hint of moisture in the breeze winding its way around and in between the buildings. The emergency lights from the cruiser intermittently wash out the oak trees of McKenzie Park, the back of Hot Glass, the dentist office across the way, and the first floor or two of St. Andrews Tours with an eerie splash of electric blue.

We walk over and pull Dallas out of the back of the patrol car. We then lead him to the front of his truck. His hands are cuffed behind him and he's wasted and he stumbles several times—and would've fallen if we hadn't held him up.

Holding him up is no problem. As before, I'm surprised at how small he is.

When we have him in front of his truck, we stop, which blocks the view of the PCPD officer.

He leans against the grill and steadies himself, looking like a little boy too young to drive.

Beneath his tousled blond hair, his blue eyes are bloodshot.

"You are so fucked," Pete says. "But you can help yourself be less fucked. Do you want to do that?"

He nods. "Yeah. 'Course."

"You remember Lucas Burke?"

"Yeah, I remember. Lookin' . . . for that girl . . . Nor—a."

"That's right," he says. "Tell us what you really know—all of it—and I'll help you out in this jam you're in."

I wonder if what Dallas heard was *I'll help you out of this jam you're in*, which is not what Pete said, but what it was meant to sound like.

"I'll tell you . . . everything I know," he says. "It's just . . . not much. Can you uncuff me?"

His speech is as unsteady as his feet are.

"No."

"Okay. Okay. It's just hurting my wrists and my arms are going to sleep."

"The sooner you tell us what you know, the sooner we can get out of here," Pete says.

"Yeah, okay. I told you the truth before. I did. I just . . . didn't tell you every single little thing."

He isn't exactly slurring his words, but he is stumbling over certain syllables and *s*'s are kicking his ass.

"You said you lent her money and went your separate ways," I say. "That you spent the rest of the night in your backyard with a buddy drinking and eating oysters around a fire."

"None of that . . . is a lie . . . exactly," he says. "But . . . I left out a little. Not much, but a little."

"So let's have it," I say. "All of it this time."

He looks at Pete. "And you'll help me out?"

"I will. You have my word."

"I met her in the Cloud Nine parking lot like I said. Gave her the money. She started askin' me questions. Was I a member of the Sons of Liberty and shit like that. What could I tell her about the Sons of Liberty. I's like . . . have a drink with me and I'll answer your questions . . . so . . . She said where and I said Dubois's—little place on the west end of the beach. She said okay 'cause she was headin' up to Jefferson anyway."

"You left out a lot," I say.

"I didn't have anything to do with what happened to her," he says. "So . . . I didn't leave out nothin' too big like that . . ."

"So y'all leave Cloud Nine separately and drive out to Dubois's?" I say.

"Yeah. She's all friendly and shit and I'm like you want to party and she said yeah, sure, sugar. And I'm like, hell yeah. It's on. So I gave her a little party package and we—"

"What did you give her and how did you give it to her?" I ask.

"Party package is a little concoction of my own makin'."

"You gave it to her and she took it, or you slipped it in her drink when she wasn't looking?"

"Hey, she said she wanted to party. If a girl says she wants to party, she wants to party. She's up for it, you know?"

"So you slipped drugs into her drink without her knowing," I say.

"She said she wanted to party," he says again.

"Then what happened?" I ask.

"When I wouldn't tell her what she wanted to know and tried to make a move on her, she jumped up and left."

"And you followed her," I say.

"No. *Fuck no.* She wasn't worth the effort. You can ask the bartender or anyone else there that night. I went over and talked to my buddy. His name is Hank. We shot a couple of games of pool then bought some beer and oysters and went back to my place and built a fire and had ourselves a good ol' time. That's it. I swear on everything. I never saw her again. I didn't do anything to her."

"Except drug her and send her out into the night alone," I say.

FIFTY-ONE

"So she sounded like she did on the 911 call because of what that little creep gave her," Blade is saying.

I nod.

We are on our way back out to Footprints to talk to Ted again.

"But that's all he did. He didn't follow her and do something else?"

"His story checks out with the bartender and the buddy he was with."

"Damn, I hate that I missed it," she says.

"Were you asleep?"

"Phone was on silent," she says. "I's at Jackie's havin' some of the best sex of my life."

Jackie Dunaway is Blade's on-again, off-again girlfriend who has mostly been off-again of late.

"Then I'm glad it was," I say. "Wouldn't want to interrupt that."

"Yeah, I wouldn't've been worth shit anyway," she says. "Still . . . would've loved to see that little punk-ass bitch squirmin'. Glad he's finally gettin' what's been comin' to him. Please tell me Pete's not gonna help him too much."

"Some, but not too much," I say. "He's still going down. He just won't go down quite as hard."

"The girl that was with him okay?"

"Yeah, he was takin' her to do whatever he was going to do to her. Nothin' but the drugging and abduction had happened yet."

"Least there's that," she says. "He ever admit to what was in his little concoction?"

"Not really," I say. "He mentioned Molly, Special K, and didn't deny that it had GHB."

"God, I hope they hurt him in prison," she says.

We ride in silence for a while, her wish hanging in the atmosphere between us.

As we near Footprints, Candace calls.

I put her on speaker.

"How are y'all doing?" she asks.

"We're okay," I say. "How are *you?*"

"I'm . . . I've been better, but . . . I'm still here, still standing, and that's something."

"We're making good headway on the case," I say.

"That's good," she says. "That's real good. I'd like to come down and meet with you today. Perhaps you could tell me about it then."

WE FIND Ted in the chapel, having just finished delivering his mid-morning message—both to the hundred or so in-person followers and the thousands streaming it around the world.

He excuses himself from the handful of stragglers he's speaking to when we walk in and makes his way over to us.

By the time he reaches us in the back corner of the plush sanctuary, Fred Stone is with him.

"Y'all are late for the service," he says. "It's a shame too. You both could've really benefitted from the blessing."

"We feel extremely blessed to miss it," Blade says.

"I only have a moment," he says. "Have a meeting to get to. What can I do for you? Have y'all found that missing mother and child yet?"

"We know about the Tree of Life and Liberty," I say. "And the Sons of Liberty."

"Okay," he says slowly, his tone and inflection conveying *so what?* "Would y'all like to join?"

"We know that you and Jack Bullock and a lot of other high-profile politicians and businessmen in the area are behind it."

"Okay," he says again in the same seemingly confused manner. "It's public record. Do y'all want a gold star for uncovering something that was never covered to begin with?"

"Y'all've gone to great lengths to hide your involvement with that group and ownership of that land," I say. "I wouldn't exactly call it public record."

"Well, it is," he says. "Havin' to take a couple of extra steps to find out doesn't make it any less public."

"We know that Nora Henri was an undercover journalist working on a story on religious and political extremism that centered on you and the group."

"That one's new to me, but I'll take your word for it."

He seems genuinely nonplussed.

"We get that kind of thing a lot," he says. "There are a lot of evil and misguided people in the world working against the righteous causes of the Sons of Light. I hope she was in the latter group. If you don't mind me sayin' so, I'd place you two in that group."

"Misguided but not evil?" I ask.

"From what I can tell," he says. "Means there's hope for you yet."

"What happened to Nora and Emma?" I ask.

"As I understand it, it's your job to find out," he says. "I assure you I don't know."

"She get too close and someone killed her?" I say. "I know it wasn't you, but you could be charged as an accessory, a co-conspirator. It would help you immensely to help us find her and turn over who was involved."

"Is this a joke?" he asks, looking around. "Am I on *Candid Camera*? This is absurd and I'll tell you this—not only will talk like that get you sued for defamation, but . . . if this is something you actually believe, then you are truly terrible at your job and I pray to God that that poor woman and her child aren't just dependent on you to find them and bring them home."

"Last chance to cooperate," I say. "Before we go to the media with what we have."

"The media?" he says. "The *media*. This is laughable. Are you being serious right now? I can't tell. You seem like you are, but . . . surely you know better. No one cares. No one. Take what you have to the media and see what happens. I'll tell you. Absolutely nothing. Do you think any of our supporters believe a thing the media reports? They know the media is our enemy. Do you know what happens when the media does a hit piece on me or us? Our fundraising goes up. I'm talkin' way up. And you know why? Because we share it with them in our newsletters and broadcasts, otherwise they'd never even hear about it. We have our own media and that's all they listen to. Your ignorance and naiveté border on the criminal—particularly for the line of work you're in."

"Even your brainwashed cultish followers care about murder," I say.

"Of a whore unwed mother liberal reporter attempting to destroy us? Are you serious? It's like y'all have abandoned detective work for standup comedy. This is all ludicrous. Hysterical. But—and let's be clear on this—there has been no murder . . . not related to or connected to us. Understand? You have no proof there was, because there wasn't. And if you claim such a thing, you'll not only be sued for defamation, but our legion of followers will make your lives a living hell."

"If y'all didn't do anything to her," I say, "why not let us search your land?"

"It has been searched," he says. "Not only did the authorities do a thorough search, but our foot soldiers searched every square inch of it. I'm tellin' you, that poor woman and her child were never on our land. And you've wasted how much time and money on it? It seems your ineptitude knows no bounds."

FIFTY-TWO

"He's right," Blade says. "Nobody *does* care."

We are back in the car, heading to Jefferson to meet with Jack Bullock.

"He's right that his followers don't care, but . . . not that nobody cares."

"Apathy is our identity," she says. "Our defining characteristic. Nobody gives a fuck. No one can. And if they do they don't know what to give a fuck about."

We ride along in silence for a long moment after that.

I don't want to believe that she's right, that Ted is right, but part of me knows they both are.

A dark cloud of despair and hopelessness descends on me, and I'd feel completely and utterly alone in the world if I didn't feel so numb.

We meet Bullock at the place on the highway where Nora's car was found. He's waiting for us when we arrive.

We get out and meet him in front of the white wooden cross with Nora and Emma's names on it.

He says, "Van-Allen just called me."

"Figured he would," I say.

"Let me tell y'all something," he says. "I take my oath seriously. I'm a good cop. I'm accountable to the voters of this great county and to the laws of this great state and nation. I . . . If I don't do my damn job, I get voted out of office. If I break the law, FDLE will remove me from office. I was raised to do what's right and I do it. Understand? And I'm tellin' you, that woman and her child are not on this property. They're just not. We've searched it. Twice. Now, after what Van-Allen just told me, I told him we should let y'all search it. It'd be a colossal waste of time and it'd take y'all longer than you think, but if y'all will agree not to go to the media with these outlandish conspiracy theories . . . y'all can search this property until your heart's content."

I look at Blade.

Bullock says, "Do we have a deal?"

We nod.

"I hate to see y'all waste a bunch of time," he says, "but the way I see it . . . it won't hurt anything. Not like y'all are the only ones looking for them."

"You say you're a good man, do the right thing," Blade says. "Say you're a good cop."

"I am."

"How can you be part of a fuckin' neo-Nazi fringe militia group and—"

"There's nothin' neo-Nazi about the group," he says. "It's mostly harmless men wanting to feel safe, wanting to know they can protect their families if they had to. I'm in there to keep an eye on them. Somebody gets too extreme, starts talkin' crazy . . . I shut that shit down."

Neither of us says anything, and I wonder if what he's saying is true. I certainly hope so.

"All sounds good," Blade says, "but . . . how many black men in your group?"

"None, but not because they're not welcome."

"Yeah, I'm sure all the Rebel flags and white supremacists' rhetoric makes them feel real welcome."

"There is some of that," he says. "And I'm workin' on it. I'm doin' my part. What are you doing?"

"Not nearly enough," she says. "Not nearly enough."

FIFTY-THREE

"I wanted to make sure you two were okay and to apologize to you," Candace Landis is saying.

We are back in our office, which is still a bit in disarray and disrepair from my outburst.

Unlike before, Blade is behind the desk and I am in the client chair next to Candace's, which I have turned so I'm facing both of them.

"I feel just terrible about what happened. Still can't believe it happened in my home. And I want you to know that I had no idea Harold was in business with people like that. I guess I thought it was sort of a cut-throat business, but . . . I had no idea he was involved with such criminals. Or that he was such a . . . criminal himself. I loved him and I'm very sad he's gone, but I'm also angry at him for what he did and feel like he brought it on himself and that he almost brought it on all of us. I'm so, so grateful to almighty God that the kids weren't home."

"We are too," I say. "And thank you for—"

"What have the police told you?" Blade asks, her impatience and anti-sentimentality getting the best of her.

"That they have the men in custody and they'll be making a statement later today," she says. "They were hired by a Marco Estravados—a man who Harold had to repossess a car lot from and who blames Harold for his downfall."

Blade says, "And are they still sayin' it had nothing to do with Nora and Emma's disappearance?"

"Yes. They said Estravados just used that to motivate us to get the money together and not go to the police."

"Y'all definitely seemed motivated," Blade says.

"Of course we were," she says. "And I still am. Can't believe they're still missing. I'm . . . I can't eat. I can't sleep. I miss them so much. I just pray they're okay. I pray that all the time."

Blade starts to say something but Candace adds, "You seemed surprised."

"Well . . . we understand that you and Nora had had a falling out."

"*What?*" she asks, looking genuinely confused. "That's simply not true, but even if we had . . . I wouldn't be any less motivated to find her and Emma. Why on earth do you think I hired you if not to find them?"

"We were told you might be more interested in finding Emma than Nora."

"Oh," she says, nodding, "you've been talking to Shanice." She shakes her head and frowns. "She's a sad, sad child. All the children we take in are broken, but she's more broken than most. And she's the only one who seemed to get worse instead of better over the years, but if she went missing, I'd still do everything I could to find her. Now . . . you said you were making some headway."

"We really thought we had," I say, "but it seems now like it just led to another dead end. I'm so sorry. I shouldn't've said anything until we were able to confirm it. I was just so excited."

"We *are* making headway," Blade says. "And every lead that doesn't pan out gets us closer to the one that will."

"Oh," she says. "I . . . I allowed myself to get my hopes up."

"I'm so sorry," I say. "That's my fault. I should've never—"

"We've gotten permission to search the area where they went missing," Blade says. "Which is huge."

"I thought it had already been searched," she says.

"Well, yeah, but . . . we don't know how thoroughly. We do now know why she sounded so out of it."

"Really?" she asks. "Why?"

We tell her.

"And this boy who drugged her . . . You're sure he didn't . . ."

"We're pretty sure," I say. "His alibi checks out."

She begins to cry. I stand and grab the box of tissues off the desk and hand it to her.

"Sorry," she says. "I know I'm . . . that I've been through a lot and I'm very emotional right now, but . . . I don't . . . It doesn't seem like we're getting anywhere, and I wonder if they'll ever be found. And I'm broke and I don't know how I'm going to take care of all my children . . . I'm sorry. I'm just over-whelmed."

"We're not going to stop," I say. "We won't. No matter what. We're going to find them."

"Yes, we are," Blade says.

"And," I add, "we're going to give you the rest of your money back to help you with your children."

"Wait, *what?*" Blade says. "We *are?*"

FIFTY-FOUR

The next morning we are back out in Palm County, searching the area where Nora and Emma went missing.

It has taken a while, but Blade's anger at me for unilaterally deciding to give Candace her money back has mostly dissipated.

Jack Bullock was right. It'd be a waste of time—and a lot of it—for me and Blade to try to search the land by ourselves, so we've decided to take a different approach—a search-and-rescue drone and cadaver dogs.

We stand near the cross on the side of the road where Nora's vehicle was found and watch as the drone takes flight and below it the cadaver dogs and their handlers enter the thick woods.

The drone, which Josh Evans, one of our foster brothers, borrowed from Gulf County Search and Rescue where he volunteers, is equipped with thermal imaging so it can pick up the heat signatures of all the living creatures in the area. And though if Nora and Emma are still out here we don't expect them to be alive, it will be nice to know if anyone is out here. The infrared imaging will show Josh where to fly the drone so the 4K camera can then show who is there.

The drone is weather resistant, can travel at speeds of up to forty-five miles per hour, transmit up to six miles, and has side by side infrared and 4K cameras, but only has a flight time of about thirty minutes, so Josh will try to cover as much ground as possible in as short amount of time as possible, then bring it back to change the batteries and send it out again.

"The route we take is a judgement call," he says. "I figured we'd start here where they are most likely to have entered the woods—if they did."

"Sounds good," I say. "And thank you again for doing this."

He's one of only two members of Gulf County Search and Rescue who has received the training and FAA certification necessary to operate the sophisticated piece of equipment.

"I'm not sure how much good this will do," he says. "I've always used it to look for living beings. The woods are thick and it will be hard to see much, but . . . we'll give it a try. Who knows, we might have some good luck."

"We're due some," Blade says.

I watch for a while as Josh maneuvers the drone over the trees, looking at the screen to see what he's seeing, but eventually I drift away, crossing the street.

"What're you doin'?" Blade asks.

"Gonna walk the fence line on this side," I say. "Just because we haven't—and to have something to do."

She gives me a single raised-head nod. "I'll call you if we find anything."

"Probably won't get it. Service out here is shit. I won't be gone long."

The imposing fence is roughly ten feet tall with loops of

barbed wire across the top and is constructed of metal mesh panels with rusted and graffiti-covered sheets of tin behind them attached to enormous creosote wooden posts.

I start to head east, but then turn and head west toward town instead.

As I walk the fence line looking for any places that someone might go under, through, or over it, I think about the case. I do my best to consider and question everything we know so far.

I begin by wondering who's lying to us, then quickly decide to assume everyone is and ask what that might mean.

What would it mean if Candace is lying? Tyler? Willie? Shanice? Ted? Fred? Bullock? Sharon? Jerry Melvin? Dallas? Eudora?

I go through what I can remember of what each one has said and what it would mean if each statement were untrue.

I feel like a new insight is about to form when my phone rings.

It's Lexi. I answer it.

"Hey," she says.

The service is bad. She may have said more than just *hey*.

"Hey," I say, my voice flat.

"What're you up to? I can barely hear you."

I tell her.

"Oh . . . wow. Cool . . . [garbled] hope y'all . . . them soon."

I don't say anything, and we are quiet a moment as I continue walking along the fence, scanning it and looking up and down as I do.

"Has anyone contacted you about the pictures?" she asks.

"Not yet," I say. "You?"

"No. It's . . . me crazy."

"We'll hear from them," I say. "Nothing to do until then. Worrying about it, obsessing over it won't change anything."

"Can't compartmentalize as . . . as you," she says.

I don't think that's what I'm doing, but don't say anything.

"I miss you," she says. "I feel like I've . . . a huge mistake."

I still don't say anything.

"Say something," she says.

"You did," I say.

"Well . . . how . . . can . . . unmake it?"

"I don't know," I say. "Oh, wait, I thought of a way. Get in a time machine and go back and not come to my house with muscle."

"That . . . so stupid. I . . . lost it and . . . crazy desperate. I'm so sorry. I'm rarely that nuts. I swear."

I come to a place in the fence where a piece of the wire mesh and the tin behind it have come loose or been cut. It's a small area—about two-and-a-half feet tall and a foot-and-a-half wide—but someone could certainly crawl through it.

Because of the way the two pieces hang down, you can't tell it's an opening until you're right up on it.

"Hey, I've just found something," I say. "I've got to go. Can I call you back later?"

"Sure."

I end the call and turn to see how far away from where Nora's car broke down I am.

I've walked farther than I realized. I'm so far—a mile-and-a-half or more—that because of a curve in the road I can no longer see Blade or Josh or anyone at the scene.

Placing my phone in my left pocket and pulling out a pair of latex gloves from my right, I snap them on and bend down and pull on the fence.

By pulling the wire mesh up and pushing the sheet tin back, the woods behind the fence are easily accessible.

Is there any way Nora and Emma came this far? Could they have found this access point and gone inside?

One sure way to find out.

I get down on my hands and knees and, holding up the wire mesh with one hand and pushing the tin with my other, crawl through the rabbit hole.

FIFTY-FIVE

Upon entering the property, I'm in a thick stand of trees and understory growth, but after taking several steps, I'm in a field.

This is it.

I pull my phone out and call Blade.

"I think I found the field she mentions in the 911 call," I say.

"Where? Where *are* you?"

I tell her before we lose signal.

"So she walked up the road a mile or so and then went into the woods—just on the other side of the road."

"If I'm right," I say. "Remember on the 911 call her saying something about lions or tigers or something?"

"Yeah, but they don't have that kind of game over there."

"Somewhere on this property is what's left of an old mom-and-pop zoo. Remember?"

"There wouldn't be anythin' like that there now, would there?"

"I don't know, but . . . it makes more sense than anything else—"

"Except for her hallucinating," she says.

"I'm gonna look around and see what I can find," I say, "but at least we now know that it was possible for them to get in here."

"Should we bring the dogs and drone over there?" she asks.

"Just let them keep doin' what they're doin'. I'll look around over here. I'll call if I find somethin'."

"It's not like they need me over here just watchin'," she says. "I'll come help you."

"Okay," I say. "I'll come back out so you'll see where to get in."

A few minutes later, she is pulling onto the shoulder and hopping out of my car.

"You really think she found this little hole in the fence?" she asks.

I shrug. "No idea, but at least we know it's possible. Think it's worth checking out."

"Lead the way," she says.

I do.

In a few moments, we are back in the field.

More of an opening or clearing than a field, the area, which is bordered on all sides by pine trees, is roughly the size of about half a football field—far too small for most people to consider it a field.

"It's small," she says, "but it could be what she was talkin' about for sure."

"I think it's the most likely candidate in the area."

"Which way?" she asks.

"From what I was able to find online, the old zoo was that way," I say, pointing west toward town. "It shouldn't be that far away."

"Good, cause my black ass wasn't designed to walk through the woods. What kind of animals they hunt out here anyway?"

She looks around, overplaying her fright and paranoia. "Not sure."

"Hope it's not some *Jurassic Park* shit."

"I feel fairly confident it's not."

We walk west, through the field and into the woods beyond, the dense terrain of the forest floor difficult to traverse.

"You really think she walked through all this carryin' a baby?" she asks.

I shrug. "It's hard to imagine, but if she was trippin' and terrified—of something real or imagined . . ."

"Yeah. True."

We walk for another ten minutes or so, moving slowly through the jungle-like underbrush of the thick pine and oak tree forest.

Eventually, we reach the end of a hardwood hammock, and as we emerge on the other side we encounter a fallen billboard with the huge, faded face of a tiger on it.

"This is it," she says. "Has to be. She said something about both sides in the 911 call—she came down both sides of the road. Broke down on the other side and then came over to this side. And the tigers . . . She wound up here."

Surrounding and beyond the collapsed billboard is just more dense forest.

"I was thinking this was the zoo," I say, "but it must just be an advertisement for it."

"Look," she says, pointing at the bottom of the billboard.

There, in small red-faded-to-pink, nearly invisible letters, it reads: Mason Family Zoo 1 Mile Ahead.

"This is a potential crime scene," I say. "We need to notify Bullock and FDLE."

She nods. "But since we're already here . . . Let's look around for a few minutes."

"Carefully," I say.

As we approach the slanted sign and the fallen, rotting posts that used to hold it up, I say, "There's no smell."

"Huh?"

"Of decay and death. I was thinking this may have been the end of the line for them, but . . . doesn't smell like it was."

On the back side of the billboard there's a hollowed-out place in the dirt next to what's left of the structure, like someone sat in it for a while leaning against the frame. And beside it in a nest of leaves and grass is a cellphone.

"They were here," I say.

"They damn sure were," she says. "And we just got another big step closer to findin' them."

FIFTY-SIX

Over the next three days, while the area is being thoroughly searched, FDLE processes the phone and we are largely kept out of the loop. We wait like everyone else to hear what the results of the searches are and if the phone actually belonged to Nora. Pete has told us what he can, but he doesn't know much because Palm County hasn't shared much. Local news outlets have reported that the hole in the fence was believed to have been made by kids sneaking onto the property to hunt, but that's the only place we've heard it.

Finally, the wait is over.

Jack Bullock has called a media briefing and we are here for it.

"If she ran in there and died because she was trippin' on what Dallas slipped her, he needs to be charged with their murders," Blade is saying. "And if someone else killed them, he needs to be charged as an accessory."

"You won't get any argument from me."

We are standing in the back of the Palm County Sheriff's Office conference room waiting for the briefing to begin.

The folding chairs of the theater-style seating hold mostly media, which includes Tyler Reece and Eudora Pryce.

Candace sits front row center.

"I thought there would be more press here," I say.

Most of the media is local or regional. As far as I can tell there are no state or national outlets represented.

"Victims aren't white, blond, and blue-eyed enough."

I nod. "I just thought with a break in the case like this . . ."

"This is so frustrating," she says. "Just waiting to hear what the hell they found."

"Won't have to wait much longer," I say.

"You think they found them?" she asks. "Mean their remains?"

I shrug. "Feel like they wouldn't've been able to keep that a secret."

"We the reason they even know where to search," she says. "Should've let us be involved."

"We knew that was never gonna happen."

To our surprise, Bullock had acknowledged our work on the case in alerting his agency on where to search in the initial statement he released on the day the phone was discovered.

The door to the conference room opens and Bullock walks in holding a manila file folder. He quickly strolls to the front and stands behind the podium, flanked on either side by the US and Florida flags.

Clearing his throat, he opens the folder and places it on the podium in front of him. He then looks up and pauses, seeming to take in the room.

"Good afternoon," he says. "I'm Jack Bullock, Sheriff of Palm County. As you know, my office with the assistance of the Florida Department of Law Enforcement and local Search and Rescue have been searching a parcel of property off Highway 321 in Jefferson County known to most people as the Harvest

Hunting Club or the site of the old Mason Family Zoo. We have been looking for the remains of Nora Henri and her baby Emma. We were directed to search there because of the work of Baker and Burke Investigations, the firm that recently reunited Amy Littleton with her family."

"Wow," Blade whispers. "More free publicity."

"He didn't have to say any of that," I say. "That's very generous of him."

"Investigators from Baker and Burke discovered an access in the fence of the property and a cellphone inside believed to possibly belong to the woman who went missing from a spot approximately two miles east on Highway 321. After a thorough and exhaustive search of the area, we can confirm for you today that, though Nora and Emma have not been found, they were, in fact, on the property at some point and the cellphone recovered there does belong to the missing woman."

"So they were out there but now they're not," Blade says.

"So all we did was find another piece of the puzzle," I say.

"Yeah, but that's how it gets solved," she says. "We found the Dallas-drugged-her piece. We found the where-she-saw-tigers piece. Now we just gotta find the next piece."

Bullock is closing his statement by asking for anyone who has any information to come forward and saying that he won't take questions at this time.

Several reporters begin asking questions anyway, but Bullock ignores them and walks away from the podium. On his way out, he asks us to stop by his office before we leave.

"Hopefully the phone will help with the next piece," I say to Blade.

"Won't help *us* with that."

"True."

"Maybe that's best, though," she says. "Maybe we should let the cops take it from here. 'Cause somebody gave the client back most of her money and we need to find some payin' work. Something Bullock may've just helped us with."

"I can't quit any more than you can," I say.

"Oh, I can quit. That's the difference between us. I know what it takes for us to survive. Plus . . . it'd be different if no one was lookin' for them, but the cops are all over the case now. And FDLE. They got resources we ain't."

"But who's found all the leads so far?"

She frowns and nods and shoots me a *you got me on that one* look.

"Us," she says. "Well . . . more like *you*."

"Definitely *us*," I say. "And the biggest came from Pete lettin' us talk to Dallas."

"Takes a village," she says. "But . . . village got to eat. We either got to get a day job and do this shit as a hobby on the side or run this bitch like a business and do professional work for payin' customers."

"I know you're right," I say, but then stop as a text comes through on my phone.

It's from the same number that sent the pictures of me and Lexi.

Want to buy some pictures?

Sure.

Actually, it's bartering I have in mind. I know you haven't got money. And it's services I want anyway.

Let's meet to discuss.

You do a few jobs for me and I'll destroy the pics. You don't and I'll post these online and give them to the media. Your girl-friend loses her job and her reputation.

Where do you want to meet? When?

I'll let you know. Stay tuned.

FIFTY-SEVEN

"Thank you," Candace is saying. "Sheriff Bullock has made it clear that you two are to thank for these latest developments."

She is standing in front of us, having just walked over when seeing us while exiting the room.

"We're doin' all we can to find them," I say.

"I know you are. And the fact that you kept workin' on it after refunding most of my money . . . Shows real character and . . . where your heart is."

Not sure what to say, we just nod and smile politely.

"I think we're closer to finding them than we've ever been," she says. "And it's because of you. But . . ."

I wonder what the *but* is. Can't imagine what she could be dissatisfied with.

"But?" Blade says.

"I can't let you do what you're doin' without paying you," she says.

Blade nods and smiles. "And we appreciate that."

"But your children," I say. "They need—"

"Turns out Harold had life insurance."

Blade looks at me and says, "*Harold had life insurance.*"

"Y'all come see me when you can and we'll figure out the details. I'm back in the house."

"We will," I say. "Thank you."

"No," she says, and pauses for a moment. "Thank *you*."

"I TOLD you I don't care who gets credit for it, I just want it done," Bullock is saying.

He is sitting behind his desk and we are standing just inside the open door to his office.

"We appreciate you acknowledging our contributions," I say.

"Least I could do."

"No," Blade says. "We've seen far less."

"Well, anyway, y'all deserve it. Y'all've impressed me. Y'all do good work. And who knows? Maybe it'll help y'all get more work."

"Thank you," I say.

"I really thought we were going to find them out there," he says. "Not sure . . . I really have no idea where they could've gone from there or—"

"You sure they're not out there?" Blade asks.

"I wouldn't've said so at the press conference if I wasn't one-hundred percent. We thoroughly searched every inch of that property. We used dogs and drones and search and rescue and even ground penetrating radar in any suspicious spots. They're not out there—above or below ground."

"Did y'all turn up anything at all that might . . . Any tracks? Blood? Prints?"

"Not a damn thing," he says.

"But you're convinced they were out there."

He nods. "Yeah. Nora's phone had her prints on it and we

found a few partials on other surfaces she touched. They were there. But they're not now and I don't have a clue where they might be."

"What did the phone reveal?"

"Lab still has it," he says. "But I'm not sure it's gonna give us much—if anything. Anyway, I've got to get back to work, but I just wanted to thank y'all again and tell you that if you come up with any theories or find any other evidence, give me a shout."

FIFTY-EIGHT

"We just got shown the door," I say as we walk out of the building.

"Thank you, we owe you, but *see ya*," Blade says.

We see Pete in the parking lot and walk over to him.

"If they are found it's going to be because of you two," he says.

"Wouldn't it be pretty to think so?" I say.

"That's a line from something," he says, "but I don't know what."

"Half of what he says is," Blade says.

"What aren't they telling us and the public?" I ask.

"Tell me what the line is from," he says.

"Hemingway," I say. "Last line of *The Sun Also Rises*."

"Oh. Not what I was thinking. They really don't have much. The phone. There's some calls and texts that . . . may help some. I don't know. You never know. But it looks like she and Willie were talking and texting more than he said. Not sure what's in them, but get the feelin' they don't make ol' Willie look too good."

"We know he was out there," Blade says. "Been easy for him to . . ."

"To do what?" I say. "Whatever happened to them, it didn't happen there—or if it did their bodies were moved, and if they were taken . . . He has nowhere to take them. He lives at Footprints."

"Maybe that's where he took them—back to Ted."

"Why would he help us?" I ask. "Give us her things?"

"To avert suspicion off his ass. And we don't know he gave us everything."

"True."

"Aspects of this remind me of Kaylee's case," Pete says. "Wonder if they'll ever be found."

"Oh, they gonna be found," Blade says. "Kaylee too. And we gonna be the ones to do it."

FIFTY-NINE

That night I listen to Nora's calls again—both the 911 call and the voicemail she left for Shanice.

Since Nora hadn't been hallucinating about the tigers, maybe there were clues in other things she said that will give us some idea of where she might be or who might have her.

911 Operator: "911. What's your emergency?"

Nora: "Yes, I'm in the middle of a field."

The connection is bad and Nora is speaking fast and breathlessly. It sounds like she is moving—walking or running—and that her head is turning, as if looking around, moving her mouth closer to and farther away from the phone.

Nora: ". . . Escaped. May . . . My . . . baby. Runnin' from . . . [garbled] and he . . . shot . . . somebody. We're out here goin' toward Jefferson . . . outskirts on both sides. No . . . cell serv— My car ran . . . gas. Stolen. There's two . . . cars . . . truck . . . out here. Guy . . . [garbled] chasin' . . . me . . . out . . . hiding . . . tigers . . . like . . . frond . . . Empty . . . through the woods. Please help . . . Please . . . come out here . . . Hurry."

911 Operator: "Okay, now run that by me once more. I didn't—"

Nora: "They . . . to be . . . not . . . talkin' to him. I ran . . . into . . . like me, but . . . the hole."

911 Operator: "Oh, okay. Someone ran into someone? Is that—"

Noises in the background are loud and distorted—maybe someone saying or shouting something, maybe gunshots.

Nora: ". . . [garbled] . . . of the only . . . or some . . . know. Guy is . . ."

More loud noises—maybe the backfire of a vehicle, maybe a gunshot, or maybe someone yelling in background.

Nora: "Not . . . way . . . but . . . over . . . tricked . . ."

911 Operator: "Where are you? Do you need an ambulance?"

More background sounds—maybe someone yelling something, maybe the phone being dropped or moved around quickly or bumped into something.

Nora: ". . . for . . . to . . . me . . . so . . ."

911 Operator: "Ma'am, what is your location? Do you need an ambulance or—"

More garbled sounds—maybe from Nora, maybe from someone else farther away from the phone.

Nora: "Uh huh."

911 Operator: "Can you tell me where you are? Do you need an ambulance or the police?"

Nora: "Yeah . . . no . . . I need the police."

911 Operator: "Okay, can you tell me where you are? Is anybody hurt?"

More garbled noises and loud sounds.

And then it sounds like Nora drops the phone, picks it up, moves it around, then disconnects the call.

911 Operator: "Ma'am? Ma'am? Ma'am?"

No response.

911 Operator: "Ma'am? Ma'am? Ma'am? Are you there? Ma'am?"

A few more noises like maybe the call hasn't been disconnected, and then nothing.

911 Operator: "Ma'am? Ma'am? Ma'am?"

After listening to the 911 call recording, I pull up the voicemail Nora left for Shanice and play it.

". . . call . . . back. Need your . . . Don't . . . do . . . Out . . . gas. We're . . . Jefferson . . . sides. No . . . cell . . . two . . . truck . . . . out. Field. . . me . . . out . . . hiding . . . Help me . . . Take . . . Emma . . . wo— Please help . . . Please . . . call . . . Hurry."

I'm about to play it a second time when there's a knock at my door.

I walk over and open it to find Lexi standing there.

"Hey," she says.

"Hey."

"Can we talk?"

"You don't have to ask," I say.

"I mean unofficially . . . personally."

I nod.

"Can I come in?"

"Sure. Sorry. Come in."

She walks in and I close the door. "Can I get you a drink or something?"

"I'm fine. Thanks."

We go over and sit on the couch.

"I made a mistake," she says. "Well, a couple of them. The biggest was my reaction to the blackmail photos, but even before then . . . pullin' the plug on us so soon was . . ."

"A mistake?" I ask.

She smiles. "It was. Don't you think?"

"I thought so at the time."

"It's just . . . textbook of what I'm not supposed to do. I was trained not to do this. And I could lose my job. I was scared. To be honest, I still am. But . . . And then the whole pictures thing and not being able to get you. It was the perfect storm and it sent my paranoia into overdrive. I freaked out. I . . . I was stupid, but . . . put yourself in my position and think about the circumstances and then not being able to reach you . . . I'm not saying there's any excuse, but I am saying that . . . I think it just might be . . . at least . . . forgivable. Could you forgive me for what I did and could we see each other again? I'm not saying . . . you should . . . You don't have to trust me. All I'm asking for is the chance to build trust. I just feel like . . . From my perspective . . . seeing you is worth the risk. And I'm wondering if from yours, seeing me is?"

I think about it.

"Is it?" she asks.

"It is," I say.

"*It is?*" she asks, her voice rising.

I lean in and kiss her, which is what I'm doing when Logan Owens and his goons walk in, though I know I locked the door.

SIXTY

"Hold on," Logan says. "Let me get my camera. These are even better than the others."

I should've known that Logan Owens, my so-called victim, was behind the blackmail photos, but I thought it might have to do with Nora's case.

Lexi and I both jump up, but both Logan and his body-guard Clyde have their pistols drawn and pointed at us, so there's nothing we can do but stand there.

I can feel the anger-infused adrenaline flooding my blood.

"You've already met Clyde," he says, jerking his head toward the huge black man with the big belly and plenty of muscle who had been with him at the Lie'Brary the night of my last gig.

"Clyde," I say, nodding to him.

When I look back at Logan, I can see just how much he's enjoying this. Beneath his bleached-blond hair, the expression on his pale face is one of sick pleasure, his strange light blue eyes wide with wild delight, his bright red lips forming an insipid smile.

This time Logan and Clyde are joined by another man—a thick, dirty-looking white man with coarse black hair and thick glasses.

"And this is Tripod," Logan says.

I glance over at him, as my pounding heart rattles my ribcage. "Tripod."

"You and Tripod have some shit in common," he says. "More after tonight. He just got out of prison."

"Always nice to meet a fellow convict," I say.

"Tripod hasn't just got the biggest dick I've ever seen . . . he's the horniest bastard I've ever met."

"So," I say, "his nickname only tells half the tale."

I'm trying to calm myself down by talking, but it's not working.

Logan nods. "Yeah. You're right. Should be Horny Tripod or some shit like that. Anyway . . . For the past few years he's only been fuckin' his fellow prisoners' asses and he's jonesin' for some female companionship bad. And as fate and good fortune would have it, he really likes the look of your girl. 'Course he'd like the look of any girl right now, truth be told, and he's more partial to young pussy, but . . . And it's just an added bonus that she works for the Department of Corrections."

I try to think of options for getting out of this, but I can't come up with any.

I can't get to my phone without them seeing me. Lexi can't get to the gun in her purse without them seeing her. They could shoot us before we could do anything.

I can feel my rage rising.

"But our sexuality is fluid, right?" Logan is saying. "He may have gotten such a taste for inmate ass while he was in prison that he'll want to fuck yours when he finishes with hers. You just can never tell about these things."

Think. What do I do? What can I do?

I'm so grateful Alana isn't here.

"But I digress," Logan says. "Since I have these photos of you two . . . and you'll do whatever I say or I'll make them public and send them to her boss . . . ol' Tripod here's gonna have a date with the lovely Lexi. The only question is . . . do we want to watch? I mean, he can do her out here or take her into the bedroom. It's really up to you. We've seen his work before, but I have to warn you . . . it's . . . It isn't . . . comely."

"If you think pictures of us kissing is going to make me fuck him, you're even more delusional than I thought," Lexi says.

"Oh," Logan says. "Okay then. Guess we'll just be goin'. But wait . . . we don't just have the pictures. We have guns too. We have guns pointed at you and you have . . . well, you have nothin'. Besides . . . Tripod prefers resistance, don't you, big boy? So the more unwilling you are the better. Bet the big bastard's hard as hell right now just thinking about you fighting back at first."

Placing my hand in front of my mouth, I look back at Lexi and whisper, "Go for your purse when I rush them."

"What's that?" Logan asks. "Let's not have any secrets, okay? Let me guess—and Tripod, don't let this hurt your feelings—y'all were sayin' you'd rather die than have Tripod fuck her. Is that right? But the thing is . . . that's not what it's between. The choice isn't between getting fucked or getting killed. Because I can tell you . . . a little thing like a heartbeat isn't going to dissuade Tripod from gettin' what he came here to get. He's very determined."

"You ready?" I ask Lexi.

"Wait," Logan says. "Tell you what . . . Let's . . . do this. You both want the girl, right? So . . . let's see which one of you is worthy of her. Neither of you have a weapon . . . unless you count Tripod's big dick . . . so . . . If you can stop Tripod from getting to the lovely Lexi . . . we will let you. We will not shoot you. In fact, I'll put my gun away. And Clyde, don't shoot him. Even if by some miracle he can best Tripod, okay?"

"Okay, boss."

"Tell you what . . ." Logan says. "I'll sweeten the pot too. If you can beat Tripod . . . you can have the pictures and that will be the end of the whole matter. You're not gonna get a better deal than that anywhere."

As he puts up his weapon, I rush Tripod, lunging at him, knocking him to the floor, getting on top of him, pounding his face with my fists.

The release of the rage feels even better than I expected and soon I have his blood on my quickly swelling hands.

It's a few more moments before I realize he isn't fighting back.

I stop and look down at him.

He's still conscious, just choosing not to fight back.

Blood is flowing out of his broken nose. Beneath the abrasions on his skin his face is swelling fast, and it won't be long before both of his eyes are black.

Confused, I turn toward Logan.

He's standing there with a huge self-satisfied smile on his face, recording the whole thing with his phone.

"And . . . cut," he says. "Great take. I think we've got what we need. Great work, everyone. Really nice."

Clyde points his gun at me and motions me off of Tripod with it.

I climb off him, hands throbbing, head pounding, heart aching.

"Okay," Logan says, "so . . . we've got pictures of you two that will cause the lovely Lexi to lose her job and be publicly disgraced, and we have video that will send Burke back to prison. We'll be in touch."

SIXTY-ONE

"So the whole thing was a setup," Blade says. "Just to manipulate you to commit what will appear like on the video unprovoked battery on someone."

I nod. "He can send me back to prison anytime he wants to," I say. "And if Lexi tries to defend me, to explain what really happened . . . he will use the photos to discredit her."

We are in the car together, headed back to Dothan to meet with Candace.

"*Damn, damn, damn,*" she says. "Don't often see you get outthought, but creepy little Logan playin' chess to your checkers."

I shake my head. "No doubt."

"The bitch about it is . . ." she says. "What's worse? Him usin' it to send you back to prison or . . . what he'll blackmail you to do to keep from goin'?"

"Hard to imagine anything worse than prison," I say. "But guarantee whatever he'd want me to do for him would be."

"Shit man," she says. "You are so *fucked.*"

"Can we talk about something else?" I say. "I'd like to find

Nora and Emma before I go back. Hell, I'd like to find Kaylee, but at least Nora and Emma."

"Well, let's do that."

I nod.

"Where the fuck are they?" she says. "Thought for damn sure they'd find them out in that zoo thing. Or at least somethin' out there would give us a clue to where they are."

Something sort of wriggles at the fringes of my consciousness. It has been there before, but I can't quite pin it down.

"I keep having a thought tryin' to form but I can't get it to develop," I say.

"About the case?"

"Yeah."

"Want me to shut the fuck up so you can think?" she asks.

Before I can respond, her phone rings. It's Pete and she puts it on speaker.

"Hey, just wanted to give y'all a heads-up," he says. "Palm County is asking for our help in an arrest over here in the Nora and Emma case."

"Who?" I ask.

"William Floyd Cooper," he says.

"'Course they are," Blade says. "He the only black man involved."

"What do they have?" I ask.

"Not much from what I can tell," he says. "Some texts from her phone. Seems he lied about the nature of their relationship and how much and how late he spoke to her the night she went missing."

"That's very thin," I say.

"Not for the only black man involved," Blade says.

"Maybe they have more," he says, "but if so they're not sharing it and they didn't use it to get the warrant."

Blade says, "Threshold to arrest a black man—'specially the only one involved—is a lot lower than normal."

"That's all I got so far," he says. "Just wanted y'all to know. Will let you know if I hear anything else."

"Thank you, man," I say. "We really appreciate it."

"Yeah," Blade says. "And fuck the *po*-lice," she adds before ending the call. To me she says, "Think there's anythin' in it?"

I shrug. "Think if he had killed them for whatever reason—and we haven't seen anything like a motive yet—it would've been out there in the woods. He had nowhere else to take them."

"That we know of," she says.

"True. And he could've just taken them to another part of the woods or some old, abandoned building that no one has looked in yet. But . . . I can't see it. Nothing in his post-offense behavior seems the least bit suspicious."

"Maybe he took them back to Footprints and Ted has them somewhere," she says. "Or he or they just helped her get away from Candace and Tyler and they're alive and well somewhere."

And then it comes to me.

"What?" she says. "What is it? You just thought of somethin', didn't you?"

"Before I found the hole in the fence of the hunting lease and old zoo, I was thinking through everything everyone has said so far and asking what it would mean if they were all lies."

"Come again?"

"I was going through witness by witness and asking what would change if what they had told us were lies."

"Most of it probably is," she says. "Everybody lies."

"Okay, Dr. House, I'm not talking about in the usual ways. I mean if the evidence they gave us, the statements they provided and the information in them, were intentional lies to mislead us."

"Okay," she says. "And?"

"You said what if Willie or Ted or someone helped Nora and Emma run away from Candace and Tyler," I say. "And that's certainly one of the main and most popular theories floating around online. She just stepped out of her life and never looked back."

"Some fools say the same thing about Kaylee," she says.

"Exactly."

"And it's no more true of her than it probably is of Nora."

"Right," I say, "but why Candace and Tyler?"

"Huh?"

"Why did you say it would be Candace and Tyler she'd be tryin' to get away from?"

"Who else she got to get away from?"

"Why do you think she would want to get away from them?"

"Because of the control and domination and stalking."

"According to them there wasn't any," I say. "And they both seem credible to me. And each has character witnesses who say they really cared for Nora and Emma and were good to them."

"But Shanice said—"

"Exactly," I say. "Shanice said. And what if she were lying?"

"Why would she?"

"Good question. Can you pull up her voicemail and play it again?"

She does, turning up the volume of her phone as loud as it will go.

"... call ... back. Need your ... Don't ... do ... Out ... gas. We're ... Jefferson ... sides. No ... cell ... two ... truck ..

. out. Field. . . me . . . out . . . hiding . . . Help me . . . Take . . . Emma . . . wo— Please help . . . Please . . . call . . . Hurry."

"Okay," she says.

"Why would Nora call Shanice when she's so far away and can't do anything for her?"

"Scared. Panicked. Didn't know what else to do."

"Maybe," I say. "Or maybe she wasn't so far away. Maybe she was a lot closer. Maybe she was keeping Emma for her."

"Huh?"

"No one we've talked to has mentioned seeing Emma that night," I say. "Not a soul. And everyone we've talked to about Nora says she wouldn't endanger Emma. Wouldn't take her to the places she went to that night. Wouldn't leave her in the car while she was at a strip club or a bar with a weird little perv."

"So you sayin' Shanice was babysitting for Nora that night."

"It would explain why there wasn't a car seat in Nora's car. And . . . I could be wrong about this, but thinking back . . . I don't think Shanice has mentioned us finding Emma once. I think she's only talked about Nora being missing, what Nora did that night, us finding Nora. Listen to the voicemail again," I say. "Especially the last few seconds."

She does.

"Nora says 'Take', then there's a beat or two, then she says 'Emma.' What if the part that cut out was 'care of'? 'Take care of Emma.'"

"Motherfuck almighty," she says. "That could be it. Think we may need to go by and see her before we go to Candace's."

"I'd like to talk to Candace about her before we—"

"Call her," she says. "Shit, I will."

She calls Candace and puts her on speaker.

"We'll be a little later getting there than we thought," I say.

"And we've got some news for you, but I have a quick question for you."

"Okay," she says. "What is it?"

"What can you tell me about Shanice Wright?" I ask.

"Not a lot," she says. "I haven't seen her for quite some time. She wants nothing to do with any of us—except for Nora of course. She's a very sad and troubled young woman. She's always been . . . We tried to help her, to reach her, but we never could get through to her. She's always been . . . disturbed, but . . . losing her baby . . . sent her way, way over the edge. Why do you ask?"

SIXTY-TWO

Like before, when Shanice Wright opens the door to see us standing there she looks confused and scared. Unlike before, this time I know why.

She is holding the baby she calls Imani, who we now believe to be Emma.

"Whatcha'll doin' here?"

"We wanted to give you an update," I say. "There's a man about to be arrested in the case."

"Can we come in?" Blade asks.

She nods. "Sure."

She turns and walks back into her small, sparsely furnished apartment and we follow.

Like the other times we've seen her, she's dressed to reveal. Previously I had wondered how she could have the figure she does after just having had a baby, but now I know she never had one.

On the drive over, Candace told us how Shanice had miscarried and how Nora had been worried about her and had moved in here to keep an eye on her. And how Nora let

Shanice keep Emma sometimes because it seemed to do her such good.

"Is it Tyler?" she asks.

"It's a Panama City Beach man who was staying with her at the retreat center," I say. "Name is Willie Cooper."

"He was decent to her," she says. "He didn't do it."

"Do what?" Blade asks.

"Whatever was done to her. He's one of the good guys."

"Mind if I hold Imani?" Blade says. "She is so precious."

"Why you wanna hold her?" she asks.

"She's just so adorable. I don't have any children yet, but I've been jonesin' for some lately."

"Oh yeah?" she asks, suspicious.

"Yeah, you're so lucky to be a mother. And you're such a good one."

"Well, have a seat," she says. "You can give her a bottle. It's time. Y'all both sit down. Let me grab her bottle."

As we sit, she steps over into the small kitchen and opens the refrigerator.

When she closes it, she is holding an old blued .38 Smith and Wesson revolver instead of a bottle.

"Y'all know, don't you?" she says.

"Know what?" I ask.

Blade says, "What is there to know?"

"Y'all don't think she's mine. But she is. She's all mine. I'm her mama. She's my little baby girl. Nora always told me if anything happen to her, take care of her little girl."

"What happened to Nora?" I ask.

She shrugs and shakes her head. "Don't know. I figured it was Candace or Tyler, but maybe it *is* that Willie guy."

"How can you not know?" Blade asks.

"How can *y'all* not know?" she says. "Y'all the damn detectives."

"How do you have Emma and not know where Nora is or what happened to her?" I ask.

"Her name is Imani," she says. "That became her name when she became mine."

"Sorry," I say. "Imani."

"I went down to see them. I missed them so much. Nora asked me to watch her while she went out to do something . . . and that's it. She never came back. Y'all know the rest. On the message she left me she asked me to take care of Imani if she didn't make it. She didn't make it."

"So you have no idea what happened to her?" Blade says.

"Right."

"There's no need to point the gun at us," I say. "We're on your side. Nora wanted you to have her. You're her mama now."

"I am," she says. "I'm hers and she's mine."

"She's lucky to have you," I say.

"We're lucky to have each other," she says. "God knew what he was doing. He took my baby only to give me a new one."

We nod.

"I'm not gonna let anyone take her. I'd rather us both go to heaven together than that happen."

"Nobody can take her from you," I say. "She is yours. You are hers. It's what Nora wanted. Nobody's gonna take her. Nobody's even going to know. We would never take your child from you. Would never go against Nora's wishes."

"I wish I could believe you," she says. "I don't want it to end this way."

"You can," I say. "This isn't the end. This is the beginning. Y'all've got your whole lives in front of you. Together. She needs you. You need her. No one else can raise her. Only you. Don't do anything to mess that up."

"You're just sayin' that," she says. "You want to take her from me."

"I'm not," I say. "Who else would get her? Candace? The state? No. She has to be with her real mama—the mama Nora wanted her to be with."

"When Nora didn't come home that night and then she called and left that message . . . I knew she was never comin' back. I took Imani down to the beach. We walked to the pier. I pledged to take care of her, to be her mama and her to be my daughter forever."

"That's beautiful," I say. "And it's all that matters. Don't let anything change that."

"But . . . I can be her mama and she can be my daughter forever . . . in heaven."

She raises the gun and points it at Emma's head.

I lunge for the gun, kicking the couch back and knocking over the coffee table as I do.

Crashing into Shanice, I knock her down as I grab the gun, which goes off.

As Shanice and I crash to the floor, Blade, who has lunged too, is grabbing Emma, keeping her from falling with us.

SIXTY-THREE

"But she's mine," Shanice is saying.

She is delusional, broken, sad, pathetic, perhaps damaged beyond repair.

How is it possible for human beings to get to this state? Is it nature? Nurture? Some strange combination of them both?

It's dispiriting to witness.

"No," Candace says. "She's Nora's, and we're going to find Nora and give her back to her."

We are still at Shanice's little apartment. Joined now by Candace. Waiting for Effren Daniels, the Houston County Sheriff's Office investigator.

Candace is on the couch holding Emma, who is still upset. Shanice is across the room in a kitchen chair, Blade standing watch beside her. I'm standing across from all of them, forming a conversation triangle.

"She *was* Nora's," Shanice is saying, "but Nora left her. God gave her to me."

"Do you know where Nora is?" Candace asks. "Have any idea?"

She shakes her head but doesn't look at Candace. "She was . . . so messed up. Wherever she was and whatever she was doing . . . she wasn't thinking about her little girl. She was high as hell and—"

"She had been drugged," I say.

"Oh."

"She would've gotten back to Emma if she could have," I say.

"You know that's true," Candace says. "She's a great mom. She absolutely adores this precious angel."

I notice that Candace still refers to Nora in the present tense, and I'm glad, though it's hard to imagine it's accurate.

"I didn't know . . . She was trippin' so hard. She hadn't done anything like it before, but I thought maybe she was bein' a stupid party girl and got in a situation that she couldn't get out of. I took Imani to the pier. Pledged my life to her before God and the great sea."

"What else did Nora say to you?" I ask. "Anything that you haven't told us?"

She shakes her head and purses her lips.

"Anything," I say. "No matter how small or if it didn't make any sense."

"Sounded like she said something about Imani's father, but . . . I couldn't make it out. And she may not have said anything about him at all. It was so hard to hear. She was breaking up. And when I could hear her she wasn't making sense. I feel bad now. I thought she was partyin'. I really did. I was mean to her. I thought she had abandoned her child. The last thing we . . . She said she saw a light and I told her to walk toward it."

. . .

"I'LL DO the best I can for everyone," Effren Daniels is saying. "I've got to arrest her, but I'll get a psyche eval and try to get her some treatment. Who knows? Maybe the right meds . . ."

"I'm not letting this little one out of my sight," Candace says.

Shanice has been cuffed and is in the back of Daniels's car.

He, Blade, Candace, and I are standing just inside the apartment with the door open and a clear view of his vehicle. Emma is asleep on Candace's shoulder.

"We've got to get her checked out at the hospital," he says. "And I've got to involve Child Protective Services, but I'll do everything I can for you—and you can stay with her every step of the way. As far as I'm concerned, you're her legal guardian."

"Thank you."

"Do you have any idea who Emma's father is?" I ask.

She shakes her head. "Nora never would say. Eventually I quit asking. She didn't put his name on the birth certificate. I really have no idea."

"Shanice mentioned that it might be Jesse Strickland," I say.

Candace looks surprised but not shocked. Shrugging as her eyes narrow and her lips crinkle, she says, "I guess it's possible. I never would've suspected it, but . . . it happens with foster kids sometimes. They're both young and attractive."

"I'll follow up with him," Daniels says. "We can do a paternity test if we need to. Y'all think he had something to do with this?"

SIXTY-FOUR

While Daniels is busy processing Shanice and Candace is at the hospital with Emma, Blade and I look for Jesse Strickland.

To our surprise, we find him in Panama City Beach.

He's working as the bumper boats operator at an arcade and entertainment center on Front Beach in the heart of all the tourist attractions—go-cart tracks, putt-putt golf courses, batting cages, Ripley's Believe it or Not, and Wonder Works.

"You livin' here now?" Blade asks.

"Yeah," he says, nodding. "Going to Gulf Coast."

He's referring to Gulf Coast State College.

It's off-season and there are only a few people at the arcade, so we talk to him at his workstation.

He's a skinny white guy of average height with thick, wavy brown hair and a shy, socially awkward way about him.

"What brought you here?" I ask.

He shrugs. "Wanted to be close . . ." he says.

"To Nora and Emma?"

"In case they find them or . . . thought I might try to help look for them. I don't know."

"You have any idea where they are?" Blade asks. "Or what happened to them?"

He frowns and shakes his head. "I wish. I . . . I still can't believe they could just vanish like that."

"Did Nora call you the night of her disappearance?"

He shakes his head. "We weren't talkin'."

"Why's that?"

"I . . . It's personal. Private."

Blade shakes her head. "Boy, they ain't nothin' personal and private when a baby and her mama are missin'."

"I want them found, but . . ."

"No buts," Blade says. "You want them found, you tell us the truth, the whole truth, and nothin' but the truth. Don't hold back shit."

"We'll keep it between us," I say. "Nobody has to know if it has nothing to do with why they disappeared."

"Okay," he says. "I want them found—more than you know. I just . . . Anyway, I . . . We weren't talkin' 'cause I thought Emma was mine, but Nora wouldn't tell me. She kept sayin' I was too young to . . . She told me to go to college and get on with my life and . . . she was dedicating hers to Emma. But I wanted to do that too, to be with them."

"Did you come down here stalkin' them?" Blade asks.

"What? No. I wasn't here when they— I just moved here a couple of weeks ago. I didn't . . . have anything to do with what happened to them. I . . . I love them. I want to be with them, take care of them. I could never do anything to hurt them."

"Even if she was with Tyler Reece?" Blade says.

"She wasn't with him. She wasn't *with* anyone. He was into her, but she wasn't into him. Look, I'll take a lie detector test or anything you like. I just don't want y'all or anyone else wasting time on me when I had nothing to do with it."

"Will you take a paternity test?"

"Of course. I'll do anything."

"Where were you the night they went missing?"

"At home with everyone," he says. "They can all vouch for me. Ask Miss Candace. And I shared a bedroom with two other boys . . . We were all up late playing Yu-Gi-Oh."

"Yeah," Blade says, "you ain't the one. Your ass ain't stalked or kidnapped anybody . . . Playin' Yu-Gi-Oh. *Shee-it.*"

SIXTY-FIVE

That night I fall asleep reading in bed, placing the paperback copy of Marcus Aurelius's *Meditations* on the bedside table after dropping it on my nose a few times.

I awake a few hours later from dreams of Nora and Kaylee, jump out of bed, and get dressed.

I call Blade several times while I'm getting ready and leaving and again as I drive toward Palm County.

After getting her voicemail several times, I finally leave a message.

"Hey, I had an idea. I was calling to see if you'd like to go check it out with me, but hopefully you're in the middle of an extended scissor session with your dream girl. Not sure if anything else would justify you not answering my calls. Anyway, I was thinking . . . Remember how the tigers were real and not some hallucination Nora was having? Real as in painted on a sign, not actual tigers. And I keep thinking . . . what if everything she mentions on all the calls was real and not hallucinations? Remember how Shanice said Nora said she saw a light and Shanice told her to walk toward it? What if she really did see a light? Could've been the trucker or another car or maybe a house or something. I think we need to be out there —where she was— at night to see what it was really like and to see if we see any lights. Anyway, that's it. It's probably nothing, but I'm riding out there now to see if I can see what she might have seen. Okay. Call me back if you get this tonight. If not, I'll fill you in in the morning on what I saw—if anything."

Less than twenty minutes later, I'm crawling through the hole in the hunting lease fence again.

Once I'm inside, I click on the flashlight I brought and look around, then turn it off again and scan the area.

I don't see any lights.

Turning the flashlight back on again, I walk the same path toward the old zoo sign.

The path has been trodden by all the cops and search and rescue personnel and is easier to traverse.

Several minutes later, I arrive at the fallen zoo sign and look around.

Clicking off the flashlight, I scan the area from both sides of the sign—even sitting where we think she had on the back of the frame where we found her phone.

There is no light in any direction except for the moon and stars above. And even when I can hear a car passing on the highway, I can't see its headlights from here.

Disappointed, I stand up and start to head back toward the car, but then stop.

We didn't find her here, so she was probably somewhere else when she saw the light—if she even saw a light.

I decide to continue in the direction she was heading when she made it this far.

As I shift my weight I see a tiny light through the trees in the far distance.

I walk toward it.

I stay close to the fence line as much as possible and stop occasionally to turn off the flashlight and look around.

I arrive at what's left of the old zoo, which isn't much, and switch off the flashlight again.

The light is gone again. Nothing. No illumination but the moon and stars.

I continue on, deciding to go all the way to the end, climb the fence, and walk back to my car along the shoulder of the road.

As I near the end of the property, I see it again.

The light from the gas station and convenience store spills over the fence and through the trees in a way that looks warm and inviting.

I pull out my phone and call Sharon Rolland, the night clerk on duty the night Nora went missing.

"Sorry to call so late," I say.

"I was up," she says. "No problem. Bit of a night owl."

"Are you at the station?" I ask.

"No, it's closed by now."

"Oh, I saw the lights and—"

"Mr. Ahmed leaves them on for security and advertisement."

"The night of Nora's disappearance," I say, "can you remember who else came in later—after Jerry Melvin left?"

"I'm not sure I had any other customers that night," she says. "Mr. Ahmed may have. I can ask him tomorrow if you like."

"He was there after you?"

"Yeah. He always comes in to close and run the receipts and everything—covers the last few hours of the night shift while he does that."

"Where does he live?" I ask.

"He's got a place out behind the store," she says. "It's an old trailer. There's a path through the woods to it. Why?"

"Just curious," I say. "Don't mention anything to him and don't ask him about the other customers that night. I know how he is about this case. And it doesn't matter anyway."

"Okay," she says.

"Thanks for all your help. And sorry again for calling so late."

"No problem," she says. "'Night."

SIXTY-SIX

I walk toward the light, following its pale glow as it dapples the dew-damp ground.

When I reach the fence, I look around for a way Nora might have gotten over it.

I find a long spot where the barbed wire is missing and a small section that can be crawled through.

I climb over instead of going through the opening in case her prints can be lifted from it.

When I'm on the ground on the other side of the fence, I look around, scanning the parking lot, the pumps, the convenience store, and the restrooms on this side. Both restroom doors are open, revealing the small, dingy restrooms beyond.

There is no movement, no sign that anyone is around.

Giving the store a wide berth, I walk around the side to the back and look around.

Seeing the path to Ahmed Farooqi's place in the back that Sharon had described, I take it.

The path is small and overgrown and unwelcoming.

Several times I step into small branches growing over it. Some of them hit me in the face, which, though better, is still sore and bruised from the wreck.

Eventually, the path ends in a small lot with an old single-wide mobile home on it.

The trailer is so old and dilapidated, the lot around it so overgrown, that it has obviously been here for a long time—perhaps from when the store was first built. The store and the trailer probably came together and Ahmed purchased them both at some point.

There are no exterior lights on the lot or the trailer, and only a little illumination comes from within.

Carefully and quietly, I approach the trailer and try to find a window or a door that I might look through.

Most of the windows have blinds or curtains but a few have gaps in them or spaces at the bottom.

Making my way over to the one with a gap at the bottom nearest to me, I look inside.

I can make out a cluttered living room with a ripped and torn couch and chair and a television sitting on a stand that is too small for it. And though no one is in the room, the TV is on—tuned to a channel that runs infomercials overnight.

I walk along the trailer to the other windows on the front, but either none of the other windows have blinds with gaps or they are in rooms that are dark.

There are no windows on the end, but the first one in the back has a small gap in the blinds.

My heart starts pounding and I start shaking when I look through the dirty pane of thin glass.

Nora is naked, tied spread-eagle to a bed that fills most of the small room.

She is so still that I can't tell if she's dead or just sleeping.

There is no sign of Ahmed.

And when the barrel of the gun presses into the back of my head, I know why.

SIXTY-SEVEN

"Move," he says. "Walk. No. That way."

I glance back at him and notice again that his lips are roughly the same color as his skin.

I begin to walk slowly, moving toward the middle of the small yard and the center of the back of the trailer, stepping around the trash and debris in the yard.

"Yard man's day off?" I say.

"Who are you? Why you here?"

"Census taker," I say. "Just have a few quick questions for you. Won't take long. Is it just you and your prisoner residing here?"

Images of Nora tied to the bed and thoughts of the horror she has endured flash in my mind, and I can feel the rage rising inside me.

I think about Blade and the sexual trauma she has endured. I think about Kaylee and wonder where she is and if she has been in a similar situation all these years—a thought that is as unbearable as any I've ever had.

"Is she still alive?" I ask.

"Why? You wanna go at her?"

I actually begin to see red spots at that—red blobs, floating, elongating, expanding and contracting, as if my head is a lava lamp.

I start to shake all over, my hands clenching into tight fists.

Hold it together. Don't do anything stupid. If he kills you she has no chance.

"Who know you here?" he asks.

I take a deep breath and let it out slowly. "My partner and an investigator with the Bay County Sheriff's Office."

"You lie. Why you here alone then?"

"They're checking out other leads. They'll be here soon. Oh, and Sharon Rolland knows I'm here. I just spoke to her. Call and ask her."

"She turn me in?"

"No. And she doesn't know why I'm here, just that I am. You have no play except to turn yourself in. Don't go down for murder. Turn yourself in and all you'll get is a little kidnapping charge. You'll be out in no time."

"Ha ha. You funny. You don't know how many people I kill."

We reach the back door and the four wooden steps that lead up to it and he says, "Go inside."

I climb the stairs slowly as he watches from the ground below.

"Open the door," he says.

I do. The room holds a washer and dryer and stacks of filthy clothes.

The trailer smells so bad I gag. "Maid's day off?"

"Quiet. Get inside."

Gagging and choking, I bend over and cough, turning slightly as I do.

He relaxes slightly and I jump inside and close the door.

I get on the floor as low as I can and hold my hand on the handle.

He fires a round.

It goes through the narrow window in the door and hits the wall in the laundry room.

He begins to climb the few steps.

When he reaches the landing, I slam the door into him.

He falls back.

I then lunge toward him, tackling him, knocking him down the steps and onto the ground, grabbing the wrist of his gun hand with my left while punching him in the face with my right.

I hit him several times with the front of my fist, then begin to pound down on him with the bottom of it.

I feel his nose break.

He lets out a cry.

I keep punching.

He drops the gun and uses both his hands to defend himself.

I keep punching. With both fists now.

He begs me to stop. Pleading. Bargaining.

I keep punching. Keep hitting him over and over.

Eventually, I knock him unconscious and his hands fall to the ground beside him.

I keep punching.

Later, when I become aware again, my hands are even more bruised, bloodied, and swollen than before.

I rush into the house and to the back bedroom.

Nora is alive.

"Nora," I say. "You're okay now. I'm a private investigator. You're safe. I'm going to untie you and call an ambulance."

She shakes her head. "Emma. I want to see Emma."

"Okay, I'll get her here."

I untie her and call Candace and ask her to bring Emma to the hospital. I then call Blade. An ambulance. And Jack Bullock.

I look around for something to cover Nora with.

When I find a raincoat in a pile of clothes in the corner and try to cover her with it, she shakes her head and holds up her hands. "Nothing from here," she says.

I nod. "Okay. Here."

I take off my shirt and start to put it on her but see it's splattered with blood.

"Sorry," I say.

"Is it his?" she asks.

I nod. "It is."

"I'll wear it," she says. "Is he dead?"

"I'm not sure," I say. "Do you want me to make sure he is?"

She shakes her head. "No. I want to do it."

SIXTY-EIGHT

"So let me get this straight," the investigator is saying to Blade. "You're the one who fought with the victim even though it's his hands that look like he's some kind of bare knuckles boxer?"

"That's right, Officer," she says. "I was struggling with the — I'm not going to call that piece of shit what you did. He had a gun and was threatening our lives. I managed to hit him hard enough to get him to drop it."

"You hit him hard enough and long enough to smash his face in and give him brain damage."

"Luckily, Nora was able to pick it up and shot him."

"And what were you doing while all this was going on?" he asks me. "And what the hell happened to your hands?"

"I was trying not to get shot and to protect the victim, Ms. Henri. When I saw what he had done to her I just lost it and started pounding on the headboard of the bed."

"There's no blood on the headboard," he says. "What y'all are saying doesn't—"

Bullock walks up. "It happened just like they say it did," he says. "Understand?"

"Yes, sir."

"Good work, you two," he says. "You saved that young woman's life and kept her from more rape, torture, and suffering—something we should've done a couple of months ago. Y'all won't have any problems from us. Hell, y'all did our damn job. I'm glad the sick fuck is dead. And I'm glad he got to suffer having his face beat in first. I don't care who did what."

SIXTY-NINE

"All I did was think about her," Nora is saying, looking at Emma asleep in her arms. "No matter what was happening, no matter what he was doing to me, I was with her—in my mind. Trying to survive to get back to her."

It's two days later and Blade, Candace, and I are in Nora's hospital room.

"And you did," I say.

She nods very slowly. "I did."

We don't know exactly what she endured at Ahmed Farooqi's demented hands, but we have an idea. And we know she wasn't the first. So far FDLE has discovered the remains of at least two unidentified females buried in his backyard and two more at his previous place on a farm in Central Florida.

Evidently, he had hidden cameras set up in the women's restroom of the convenience store with both a live feed and a recorder. When certain women showed up alone late at night, especially walking or hitchhiking, and he was the only one on duty, he'd let himself in the bathroom with the duplicate key he had for that purpose and overpower them while they were in a vulnerable position. Of course, in Nora's case he didn't even have to do that.

"I can't thank you two enough," Candace says. "You saved my girl and her girl from . . . You saved them."

"It was our honor," I say. "And a lot of people helped make it happen. Especially an investigator in the Bay County Sheriff's Office named Pete Anderson."

"Please thank him for me," she says. "And I'll try to do it properly later when I can."

"I can't thank you enough either," Nora says.

"We're just happy to see you two back together," I say. "More than you know. It's not how these things usually go."

"It's true a lot of people contributed," Blade says, "but y'all sittin' here today because of Burke."

"Thank you, Mr. Burke," Candace says, beginning to cry again. "Thank you so much."

"Yes," Nora says, shedding a few quiet tears of her own. "I still can't believe that Dad is dead and Shanice is in jail."

"It's a lot to take in," I say. "Especially after what you've been through."

"We gonna get up outta here and leave y'all alone," Blade says, "but before we do . . . I want to tell you something. I been through some shit like you just went through. And I want you to know . . . really know . . . you're gonna be okay. It gonna take some time, no question. And you gonna need to talk to some people—family, friends, and a professional. You gonna have to let go of everything, especially blamin' yourself for anything—including puttin' that rabid dog down. But you gonna be okay. And if you ever need anything at all . . . you call us."

I nod. "Don't hesitate to," I say. "We feel responsible for you two now and will be here for you for the rest of our lives."

SEVENTY

"Savor this one," Pete is saying. "Not many like it."

He holds up his glass and Blade and I clink it with ours.

We are at the back bar on the upper deck of Uncle Ernie's, the sun setting over St. Andrews Bay behind us.

"To the good guys getting one," Pete says.

"You really are one of the good guys," Blade says to him.

"Nah," he says, "fuck the po-lice."

She laughs.

As the sun begins to sink into the horizon, the darkening waters of the bay are bathed in a deep orange as the calm, airy, quiet of the end of magic hour descends on all things.

I turn sideways on my barstool so I can watch the sunset while still seeing the others.

Pete follows my gaze. "Wouldn't think what happened to Nora and Emma could in a world this beautiful."

The condos lining the far side of the bay are backlit by the shimmering orange orb declining behind them, their rooftops burnished a dark gold.

"Far more ugly in this world than beautiful," Blade says.

Though I disagree, I don't say anything. I know why she holds the opinion she does, and who am I to contradict it?

"Y'all think she's gonna be okay?" Pete asks.

I nod.

"As okay as someone can be after all she been through," Blade says. "Any of us okay?"

"We're okay," I say.

"Okay, Mr. Beat A Man To Death," she says. "Then let the victim shoot him."

"Seemed like a good idea at the time," I say.

"Lettin' her slay the dragon may have given her her best chance of recovery," Pete says.

"Or may have fucked her up for life," Blade says. "But you prob'ly right."

"So what was all that stuff she was saying on the 911 call?" Pete asks.

I shrug. "She doesn't remember. Probably drug-induced paranoia and some hallucinations. Saw things that may or may not have been there that scared her. She was lost and alone and . . ."

"Trippin' her damn balls off," Blade says.

"But it's possible someone was chasing her," I say. "With as much date rape drug as she had in her, she's never going to remember."

"Too bad she can't not remember all the other shit that happened to her," Blade says.

We are quiet a moment, each taking another sip of our drinks, each glancing out at the sunset.

"Forgot to tell y'all . . ." Pete says. "Ahmed's vehicle isn't the one that ran y'all off the road, so it wasn't him."

I nod. "Probably one of the misguided Sons of Liberty," I say.

"Or some random hit-and-run," Blade says. "Probably never know."

"Unknown enemies are the worst," Pete says.

"I don't know," I say. "Known ones are no picnic either."

"Heard anything out of Logan yet?" he asks.

I shake my head. "Not yet, but it's coming."

"I'm keeping my eye on him and have others doing it too. Let me know when he reaches out to you and we'll see what we can do about it."

"Thanks."

Our food arrives and we each dig in.

Across the way, Lexi enters with a group of girlfriends. She flashes me a small smile when she sees me.

A few moments after they're seated, I see her pull out her phone. A few moments after that I receive a text.

Meet me in the park when we finish up here?

Would love to, but I'll have Alana.

Cool for me to come by?

Of course.

Maybe we can go get some ice cream together.

Rainbow. With all the sprinkles.

"Y'all gonna do the documentary on Kaylee?" Pete asks.

"Burke is," Blade says. "I'm undecided. You?"

He shakes his head. "I don't think I am. I asked the sheriff and he didn't seem too hip to the idea."

Later, as we're taking care of the check, Blade asks Pete, "Got plans in the morning?"

"Not yet, why?"

"Might have a new case we're gonna need to talk to you about."

"Payin' client?"

"You'll be able to tell by where we ask you to meet us."

"Interesting case?"

She nods.

"Missing persons?"

"You know it."

"A truly baffling one," I say. "Unlike anything we've ever worked before."

"Then I look forward to discussing it with you over a big breakfast."

PLEASE POST A REVIEW

Please take a moment and post a review of this and other books by Michael Lister. It really helps and is greatly appreciated.

JOIN MY VIP READERS' GROUP

Join my VIP Readers' Group Today by going to http://www.michaellister.com/contact and receive free books, news and updates, and great mystery and crime recommendations.

HUGE BOX SET SALE!

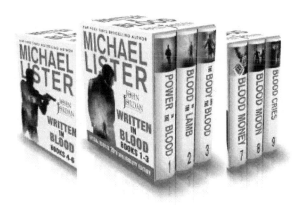

ALL of the thrilling John Jordan Mystery series Box Sets are ON SALE right now. Save big today only!

CLICK HERE to get the special limited-time deal.

ALSO BY MICHAEL LISTER

Books by Michael Lister

(John Jordan Novels)

Power in the Blood

Blood of the Lamb

Flesh and Blood

(Special Introduction by Margaret Coel)

The Body and the Blood

Double Exposure

Blood Sacrifice

Rivers to Blood

Burnt Offerings

Innocent Blood

(Special Introduction by Michael Connelly)

Separation Anxiety

Blood Money

Blood Moon

Thunder Beach

Blood Cries

A Certain Retribution

Blood Oath

Blood Work

Cold Blood

Blood Betrayal

Blood Shot

Blood Ties

Blood Stone

Blood Trail

Bloodshed

Blue Blood

And the Sea Became Blood

The Blood-Dimmed Tide

Blood and Sand

A John Jordan Christmas

Blood Lure

Blood Pathogen

Beneath a Blood-Red Sky

Out for Blood

What Child is This?

(Jimmy Riley Novels)

The Big Goodbye

The Big Beyond

The Big Hello

The Big Bout

The Big Blast

(Merrick McKnight / Reggie Summers Novels)

Thunder Beach

A Certain Retribution

Blood Oath

Blood Shot

(Remington James Novels)

Double Exposure

(includes intro by Michael Connelly)

Separation Anxiety

Blood Shot

(Sam Michaels / Daniel Davis Novels)

Burnt Offerings

Blood Oath

Cold Blood

Blood Shot

(Love Stories)

Carrie's Gift

(Short Story Collections)

North Florida Noir

Florida Heat Wave

Delta Blues

Another Quiet Night in Desperation

(The Meaning Series)

Meaning Every Moment

The Meaning of Life in Movies

MORE: Do More of What Matters Most and Discover the Life of
Your Dreams

Made in the USA
Monee, IL
08 May 2023

33317342R00180